# Other Books by Kevin Stokker

## Fiction

*White to Move and Lose*

*Black to Move and Draw*

## Nonfiction

*Public & Private Space: A Short Treatise on Knowledge and Well-being*

# Kevin Stokker

# Writing in Circles

and other short stories and poems

**Butch Press**

# Butch Press

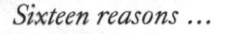

*Sixteen reasons …*

# contents

# preface

The great Scottish empiricist David Hume, while writing a book on philosophy in 1729, suffered a nervous breakdown from the effort. Me, I got lucky. I found a writers group instead.

Not intentionally, mind you. I'd thought I'd signed up for a class—the kind that would remind me how to write a three-point paragraph and summarize my conclusions. The continuing adult education brochure that showed up in my mailbox one day had simply listed it as "Writers Circle." The class was being offered at a local high school on Thursday evenings. I'd been vigorously studying philosophy for the past four years, and I had a tottering stack of index cards on my desk filled with notes that needed to be arranged into a book. So I signed up.

But the Writers Circle was no traditional class. I thought I'd be taking notes and writing practice essays, but instead found myself in the midst of people in various stages of writing novels, memoirs, plays, and poems. The emphasis was on critique, with classwork consisting of people volunteering to read portions of their work out loud (or have them read silently) and then listening to any feedback others wished to provide. The class was led by a fellow named Bill Kent, whose role consisted mostly of enforcing his four rules:

1.  *Compassion*. Be kind to each other, for the world is hard. Be kind to yourself, for writing is harder.
2.  *Focus*. The words on the page are what matters.
3.  *Primacy*. Whatever the author wants to write, provided it isn't hateful toward someone, is valid. The author gets first and last say on their work.
4.  *Autonomy*. No one is ever required to bring work or comment on work.

And here I'd always thought that novels were written by English majors!

I did write (and publish) my philosophical treatise, *Public & Private Space*. But a whole world had been opened to me. I bought a copy of *On Writing Well* by William Zinsser and discovered that writing was something that can be good … or bad. Previously, if I called some author a good writer, I'd have been referring to their storytelling. Writing, I was learning, is different than storytelling.

From there, Stephen King's *On Writing: A Memoir of the Craft* taught me that *real* writing is *fiction* writing. (I don't think he ever wrote those words, but this was nevertheless my conclusion.) Fiction—creation *ex nihilo*—is the ultimate in writing. I had to try it.

After a number of false starts, I wrote *White to Move and Lose*. More technically a novella than a novel (it clocks in at around 35,000 words), it proved to me that I could do this thing. I could write.

Having no additional mentor (not to be confused with muse) beyond Mr. King, I took most of what he said about writing as gospel. In particular, I took to heart his advice to put aside your first draft, once finished, for at least six weeks before looking at it again in preparation for a rewrite. (The idea is to distance yourself from your creation as much as possible before taking a scalpel to it. It'll hurt less that way, and you'll be able to cut deeper. Kill yer darlings, baby. Kill yer darlings.)

I needed something to write while I waited for *White* to ferment, so I started in on some short stories. Some years later, while *Black to Move and Draw* was similarly in isolation, I added to my short story collection. Then I wrote a few more, just to come up with a good number. I've put all of them together for you here.

When I first read that Hume suffered a nervous breakdown while writing a book on philosophy, I assumed that the cause was the reality-shaking implications of his philosophical investigations. Only later did another possibility present itself to me: It was the act of trying to write. I like to believe that my writers circle, along with my wife Laura and daughter Mallory, who always have an ear to listen, saved me from Hume's fate.

Over the years, many people have come and gone through the circle. I'm dedicating each of these stories to a current member of the circle or a past member who particularly contributed to its nature and evolution.

# Writing in Circles

# to the victor, the spoils

She rides with her head down, one hand digging into the horse's mane, the other still clutching the katana strapped improperly at her back, and the wind that chases her across the dark and frozen Mongolian steppe plays hell on her face. Against the field of snow stretched out before her, the scattered camps of nomads are constellations of glowing orange dots. One such nomad, all of them nameless to her, she has slaughtered more than a half hour ago in a camp that now lies many miles behind her. One such orange dot, still several miles ahead, marks the location of her contact.

The woman steals a glance behind her, checking for pursuit, the darkness revealing no more than it did the last dozen times. Still, she knows what she knows, and it's time to make a move. The horses are rented, the katana stolen, and the girl who rides just behind her is still a bit green—although she is coming along nicely. No matter, the woman will take care of things.

She looks over her shoulder at the girl, whose breathing outpaces the wind. The kid is terrified. Could have used another week of riding practice. Catching the girl's eye, she makes the hand signal for *attention*, then for *right*. The girl gives her a sharp nod.

The steppe that lies across the breadth of Mongolia is largely barren, but the woman calculates that a rare copse of birches will soon appear ahead of them. The parchment map that had shown up at her New York City address last month had been carefully hand drawn and was very detailed. Since then, the woman has made this trip a dozen times in her mind.

They cut to the right. Downslope from them, the woman spots the anticipated cluster of trees.

She once again makes the hand signal for *attention*. Then she adds *go* and uses the blade of her hand first to point to the trees and then to cut to the left. She adds *go* once again.

The woman knows that the girl will get it. The kid is sharp. She is, after all, the woman's niece, and she is learning what it takes to get things done.

As the kid breaks to the left of the trees, the woman slows her horse and enters the copse. To anyone following at a distance, she hopes the horses and trees will all appear as a single, indistinguishable smudge. The trees are sparse—the woman doesn't need to slow very much—and as she reaches the other side she can already see the girl riding on ahead. By the time their pursuers realize they are only following one horse, it will be too late. That won't be long now, the woman figures. She pulls the hood of her wool parka close around her face, and she waits.

The hit had been as opaque to her as they always are. Up in the good old USSR (the woman involuntarily glances north) everything seems well in hand, although this Gorbachev fellow coming along seems like the kind with ideas. Maybe the hit had been political; maybe it had to do with a yak's asshole. She doesn't know. It makes no difference to her. What matters is that the shadowy overlords in Shanghai have been kept happy and that her worth has been proven. Again. The woman has an operation to set up in Manhattan (she already has her front—a Harlem kung fu studio in sudden need of a manager), and she is showing the right people that she knows what it takes to get things done.

The hit had been opaque, but the sword—*that* was a nice bonus. Beautiful Japanese steel. What the poor fool she'd killed was doing with a katana, she doesn't know. But as she had muttered to her apt pupil as she'd grabbed the sword and the two of them had run for their horses, to the victor go the spoils.

The woman reaches behind her to tighten the strap on the sheathed katana. The damn thing had been slapping her back the whole ride. As she does this, two pursuers go by. The woman springs from her blind, draws a pistol, fires two shots—and two horsemen hit the frozen ground.

The black land speeds by. Behind her, Xiang hears two faint cracks—gunshots—over the howling wind. Her aunt's, Xiang figures, as she rides on.

Not that *rides* would necessarily be the word Xiang herself would pick to best describe the action. She feels *being taken for a ride* might be one good way of putting things. The beast she clings to with legs and hands and everything she's got is galloping at god only knows how many miles per hour. At this speed, steering feels like an unsure proposition; looking behind her, suicidal. And being able to look behind her would be nice, given that men intent on her death may still be pursuing her. She and her aunt had landed in Ulaanbaatar a week ago to give her time to learn the ways of the horse. A *week*. To learn everything she needed to know for this ride-along. She smiles grimly. Her first *literal* ride-along.

Then comes another thought, this one all too familiar, and the smile disappears: it is even possible that she has killed someone, once. That business last summer in Hamilton Heights with the fire alarm and shutting the power to the lights and the tripwire in the stairwell had never fully clarified itself to her. Xiang is *pretty* sure that she is the only kid in Marcus Garvey Junior High to have ever been both the captain of the chess team *and* suspended (twice!) for beating the shit out of some deserving twerp. But she would lay very long odds indeed that she is also the school's only practicing assassin.

And the hits themselves? They're never something clean and easy. Not like she would do. (*Wait*, she thinks. *What am I saying?*) They're never something clean and distant and impersonal. Like a gun.

Take this present case. If a gun would have been too loud, why not a bow and arrow? Nope. Never. Her aunt—the sister of her recently dead mother—doesn't mind getting her hands dirty. She *likes* getting her hands dirty. And just about an hour ago, Xiang had had the privilege of being there for the dagger's crimson spray.

Out of exhaustion more than any sense of safety, the girl's body eases, and her horse slows down in response.

The woman emerges from the shallow valley. Ahead, she sees the girl's pace slacken. The woman slows down a bit herself and for a while is content to watch her niece canter along as they approach the camp. A rim of gentle hills lies to the right. Across these, in the morning, will be their final trek north, into Siberia. Two more days on the horse, two more contacts, and then the series of flights home. Depending on how quickly the corpses that lie behind her in the snow are found and how important the two fools had been, the ride will be either exciting or quite boring. She expects boring. The steppe, which the woman is developing an admiration for, is vast and empty, and the anonymity it provides is of a completely opposite flavor than that of the city. Still, she prefers the city. So much easier to get lost among the many than among none.

They come to the camp: a scattering of gers like giant cheese wheels under the moon's white rind. The woman detects the growl of a hidden generator; she smells the smoke of the wood-burning stoves that sit at the heart of each ger, warming them, sending an orange glow through the chimney holes at the centers of their roofs. She nudges her horse forward and catches up to her niece.

"This is the hard part, coming up."

"What now?" says the girl. Her eyes in the moonlight are white and round, like the gers.

The woman lifts an admonishing finger. "You must know when to fight and when to flee," she quotes from Sun Tzu. "We've done both. It's just the afters, now."

The woman cares nothing for afters. Over the course of her life, she has allowed four men to have her, three to go home afterward. Those were the ones who didn't want afters. The woman cares nothing for afters—only nexts.

Her niece sends a stream of white breath into the wind as she looks toward the camp. "Which ger is ours?" the exhausted girl asks.

"You see the cutting through the middle?"

"Yes."

"Second to the right."

The girl gives a little laugh. "Second star to the right and straight on 'til morning?"

"What do you mean?"

"Forget about it."

The kid often says strange things like that, and when she does, the woman thinks maybe she's quoting whatever book she's just finished reading, or the Beatles, or maybe even Jesus. The woman herself knows none of Jesus or John Lennon. Sun Tzu is her Jesus, and she attends a church of one. Two, now, with her acolyte. Three, when she remembers to count the boy, her nephew. Older and stronger he is, but less pliable than the girl. Less ... *hers*. The job they are on right now, the woman thinks, would not have been as enjoyable with him along. No, the girl is better. She gives cover. Besides, her brother would just want to hit everything. One must know when to fight and when to flee.

The woman and the girl find the paddock. They walk their horses out, untack them, brush them down, check the water and the food troughs. They walk to their ger.

A door opens and a man steps out toward them. He speaks in English and says his name. They don't always say their names, the contacts, but this fellow has a wide grin, and when he welcomes them inside, it turns out he has a wife. The wife also speaks English, when she speaks at all, and maybe her name is Elke. The wife's silence strikes the woman as smart. What is there to say?

But this man with the grin, whose bed the woman will be sleeping on that night and whose food she will soon be eating, seems very insistent on being present. After stew and beer on a hastily set-up card table, he offers television, and when the woman declines that, he suggests cards. This, too, she declines, but the man just keeps on smiling, his wife the whole while sitting silent and huddled on their bed, and when the next idea enters the man's head, he snaps his fingers and says, "I know just what."

He goes to a table where the woman guesses the man and his wife eat their meals. It has a white linen tablecloth embroidered in red latticework and holds plates, mugs, a pair of lighted candles. There are a few framed photos as well. All of this the man removes to the top of a cabinet, placing the candles on either end and everything else in the middle, folding the linen into thirds and then in half the other way and then in half again, gently laying it atop the photos.

The table beneath is a rough-hewn chest from which the man produces a polished wooden box the size of a small briefcase, inlaid with black and white tile squares. He undoes a clasp, removes two felt bags from within, and unfolds the box into a chessboard. Loosening the drawstrings on the felt bags, he pours a jumble of exquisitely carved chessmen onto the board.

"It's the Mongols versus the Russians," her contact explains, setting up the pieces. "You play?"

The woman feels she has no choice. Annoyed, she decides that the Russians are White and the Mongols Black, and with no discussion or ceremony she sits down and turns the board so that she has White. She makes the first move. Her contact, oblivious to this display of presumption, or perhaps immune to it, ponders his response.

In size and shape, the structure of this ger is identical to the one Xiang and her aunt had left behind to death and disarray. Here, however, in this ger, there is no man doubled over a chair, his butt weirdly higher than the rest of him, with blood gushing out of his slit throat, and Xiang thinks to herself that this fact alone gives the place a certain charm over the other. She wonders if anyone has moved the body yet, and she wonders how much of a body's blood will come out of a body before it stops coming, and how much blood that is.

The man in this ger, very much alive, has introduced himself as Xan. There is also a woman, and Xiang is unsure who she might be. She has spoken her name, but too quietly. She looks not much older than some of Xiang's friends at school. But she had acted the good wife just now, offering her guests bowls of hot stew and mugs of beer poured from cans taken in from the snow outside. Xiang didn't recognize the brand from the design on the can, but as this was her first beer, and given how repulsive and bitter she found it and how unlikely it is that she will ever have another, she feels that the brand is a matter of indifference. She finishes her stew, forces down her beer, and wonders what will come of the rest of the night. She's exhausted, and she's not sure how her stomach is going to handle the beer. She wants to be home.

The man, Xan, had quite remarkably gotten out a chess set, of all things, and he is still playing chess with her aunt now. Normally, Xiang would want to watch and call to play winner, but she feels no inclination. She looks around the ger and sees the wife—if that is who she is—sitting on a bed. The wife waves timidly, and Xiang goes over and sits next to her.

"I'm Rilke," the wife says, probably figuring no one heard her the first time. "I know enough to not ask your name."

"It's okay."

There is an awkward pause. Xiang becomes aware of the horse stink on her city body and that she is sitting on this person's bed. "I smell like a horse," she says.

"It's okay," Rilke says. "This whole country is horse."

Her English is broken but still pretty good. Xiang wonders if everyone in Mongolia knows English, and then a bunch of little questions like that occur to her. Are there schools out here? And what about television? She knows about generators, so that explains the electricity, but what do they *watch*? Maybe even out here they have VHS? She imagines taped copies of *M\*A\*S\*H*. That had been a good show. It sucks that they ended it. She needs to say something.

"What do you do?"

The question is weak, and Rilke shrugs. Xiang tries again.

"You and your husband." She points to Xan. "What do you do? How do you—"

Rilke laughs quietly. "This is my father," she says.

Xiang is mortified.

"It's okay," says Rilke. "You are American, yes? The world must be so strange to you."

Xiang's mortification deepens: This stranger has hit upon a personal fact. They are supposed to be incognito, nameless. Still, Xiang figures, her accent is a giveaway.

Rilke apparently sees Xiang's fear. "It's okay," she says once more.

Xiang notices that this is a favorite phrase of Rilke's and then reflects that maybe she's simply latched on to the first thing Xiang herself said to her. Then she thinks how strange it is that it should be strange to be an American. She thinks that, if she moved out here, to Mongolia, she wouldn't bother with television. She'd get rid of it. Not have even one. She imagines life on the steppe: no streets, no noise, everything grass and horses, no people. Well, okay, there are people. The camp she is in right now has maybe twenty gers.

"Do you move around a lot?" she asks. She wants to ask everything but is afraid to look stupid.

"Sometimes."

Xiang goes the other way. She imagines Rilke as a teacher at Marcus Garvey Junior High. She'd be the kind whom everyone loves and some kids take advantage of. She'd be a history teacher, maybe. Start an after-school horseback-riding club. In New York City? Well, maybe she'd move to White Plains. But of course Rilke will stay here, in Mongolia, where there's nothing to have and she has all of it.

Xiang returns from her thoughts. She sees that her aunt and their host are still playing chess.

Rilke asks, "You play chess, too?"

"Yes," says Xiang.

"Are you as good as—?" Rilke points to Xiang's aunt. She does not know how to call her.

"Better."

Rilke smiles.

"I'm going to see what's going on," Xiang says. She gets up and stands near the table to watch the chess.

It's the endgame. Her aunt, playing White, is down to just two pawns, both halfway down the field and, more importantly, separated by a lot of space. If either pawn reaches the other side, it will promote to a queen, and that will be that. Xan, playing Black, has only a knight with which to stop them, and he is shaking his head.

The woman has never studied chess, but she knows what she knows. She knows that if she takes care of her pawns, they can one day become queens.

Nevertheless, she had played in a manner that tends to make for very short games. She had castled her king the opposite way from her opponent. These are the kinds of games she likes: bloody. The first to flinch loses.

But then there had come a series of trades, and the energy had left both sides' attacks. There would be no quick checkmate. The woman couldn't remember how many pawns a knight was supposed to be worth, but she remembered that pawns promote and knights don't. So she had traded a knight for a couple of pawns and soon picked up a third, although one of her own pawns fell to her opponent's king, which had to walk all the way across the board to get it.

The fog of war clears, and the woman is smiling. Her two remaining pawns are well on their way to the other side of the board, where one or both will become a queen—and she doesn't see a way for Black to stop them both.

Her opponent looks up at her, then back at the board. He is shaking his head. The fool is trying to find the impossible. His game is lost. And yet, fool that he is, he can't come to terms with the fact.

And this is when her niece, goddammit, steps forward and says, "I can do it. I can stop both pawns."

Immediately, her contact beams. "Ah!" he says, rubbing his hands together in delight, "I smell a bet!"

The woman has heard this about these nomads, that they love wagers and betting. She is not motivated to cater to this man's pleasures, but neither does she wish to appear weak. She checks the board again, thoroughly considering the various routes the black knight could take to stop her pawns. No matter which paths she tries, it doesn't work. With one pawn or the other, she will get her queen.

She looks up at her niece, expecting to see her also studying the board carefully. Instead, the kid is paying attention to practically anything else. It's almost as if she's intentionally not looking at the board.

*It's a trick*, the woman thinks. The impertinent child *wants* her to think she's being overconfident and that she has spoken foolishly, when in fact there *is* a way to stop both pawns after all. The woman studies the board again but finds nothing.

She looks up at her niece again, ready to accept a bet, and is surprised to see that this time the kid is staring intently at the board with eyes that are shifting back and forth over the squares. *Dammit!*, the woman thinks. The girl has discovered the truth of the matter and realizes her folly. There will be no bet.

Unless … unless this, too, is a trick! The silly girl is now giving her head a final nod, as if to say that her doubts are put to rest and her calculations complete. The woman is not fooled. The girl is like a clumsy poker player too obviously bluffing a weak hand.

The woman almost goes back to studying the board again, then decides she will not be played with. There exists only this one, unassailable fact: *The black knight cannot be in two places at once.* It is time to end this foolishness.

"What will you give me, girl, when you lose?" the woman demands.

The kid pretends to be taken aback. "Oh, I dunno," she says. "How about I promise to read Sun Tzu every morning before breakfast for a year?"

"We already do that!" the woman says. "What else?"

"I'll go with you on every job?"

Such impertinence! The woman decides she is going to have to have a conversation with this child at the first opportunity. For now, she contents herself to say, "You're already doing that, too."

"Fine." Her niece pauses, seeming to think. She says, "The age of emancipation in N— … the place we live" (had her niece almost said "New York"?) "is sixteen. If I sit down to play Black right now and you promote either pawn, I solemnly pledge that at the age of sixteen, I will quit school and devote my life to your service. Sufficient?"

The woman doesn't need to think; the offer is too damn good. "Yes," she says. More than anything, she wants lieutenants. "Now sit."

Her contact interrupts. "And what will you offer her if she wins the bet?"

The woman is taken off guard, annoyed. She had forgotten about her contact and nearly forgotten about the other half of the bet. Not that it matters, because she will win.

The kid speaks up. "I want the sword."

"Done," the woman says. "Now sit."

The contact speaks again. "You have to shake."

"What?" the woman says.

"You have to shake her hand."

The woman and her niece shake hands. The contact gets up from his chair to allow the girl to sit down and play.

Xiang sits down. It is White's turn. Her aunt pushes a pawn forward—but she has forgotten a central tenet of Sun Tzu.

One must know when to fight and when to flee.

Xiang looks across the board at her aunt, and with the pinky of her right hand, while holding her aunt in her gaze, she topples her king. Xiang has resigned her game. In so doing, she has stopped both of White's pawns from promoting.

There is a moment of silence as the simplicity of the girl's swindle becomes clear. Then Xan laughs—a loud guffaw in a tight space. It is a bad move. A very, very bad move.

"Unfair!" cries the aunt. "The sword is mine!"

"No, it's mine! I won it!" In parody of her aunt, Xiang holds up a finger, but not the teacherly one. "One must know when to fight and when to flee, right Aunt Fan? As you so recently told me, to the victor, the spoils!"

In a fit of adolescent petulance, while giving the middle finger, Xiang has spoken her aunt's name. And although the outburst came out entirely in Mandarin, the girl in the very next moment knows herself to be responsible for two more deaths.

She pleads with her aunt. She pleads for the life of Xan and Rilke. She offers even to relinquish her right to the sword. But when the sun spills into the ger after a night of fitful dreams, she wakes to find the man and his daughter still lying dead in a pool of their mingled blood.

The woman packs up the chess set, and the two of them walk out of the ger into a blazing white morning. As they tack up their horses to flee, the girl reaches out to the vast anonymity of the steppe and clutches it, along with the sword, to her body.

# thinking of John

Those who've read *Black to Move and Draw* know that the story involves a sword and that enigmatic woman who belongs to it, Xiang. In the book's climactic fight scene, one of the protagonists, Butch, whose sense of *nous* never quite matches his skills in kung fu and chess, offers, in the middle of battle, to tell his fellow combatants the backstory of the katana: how it came to be in Xiang's possession and how it had created the bad blood that exists between her and her aunt, Mi Fan. Butch's friends assure him that the middle of a fight is not the right time and place for storytelling.

As soon as I wrote that scene, I knew that at some point I simply had to find the right time and place for the story of a sword and its girl. I hope you enjoyed it.

Coming up with the story, one of the first things that became clear to me about it was the place: Whatever was about to happen, it was going to go down in outer Mongolia. As so often happens, I drew inspiration from the movies. In *Raiders of the Lost Ark*, Marion, tough as the night is cold, is closing up her bar. She might be calmly polishing glasses now, sure—but she's also going to need to wipe down that counter where she recently drank her customers under the table, and she also might want to tend to her hand after having a few moments ago belted her former lover, Indy, across the jaw. Marion's general badassery is reflected in the bar itself, which seems carved out of rock. The fire crackling in the background barely holds off the bitter air that blew in just now along with a surly, mouse-like villain, who had been fool enough to open the door in the first place and who is about to wish he'd stayed in for the night.

This was the kind of joint where I initially imagined Xiang would acquire her sword. Even more perfect was that the bar would be situated in some far-off location, the kind of place Hollywood routinely asks us to believe is lawless and exotic, the kind of place where a storyteller can really get away with shit, because *who knows* what goes on in the remote corners of planet Earth?

Problem was, the country where Marion ran her bar was, I think, Nepal. Now, I want you to read the following sentence, and if you don't mind, I'd like you to read it out loud.

*She rides with her head down, one hand digging into the horse's mane, the other still clutching the katana strapped improperly at her back, and the wind that chases her across Nepal plays hell on her face.*

Did that sound right to you? *Not bad,* maybe you'd say. Perhaps you'd even be generous enough to call it good. But it's not perfect. At least, it didn't sound perfect to me. I'd spent about twenty minutes on my opening sentence, and it still wasn't reading right.

Now let's replace *Nepal* with *the dark and frozen Mongolian steppe.* Read it again, and see if you hear what I heard.

*She rides with her head down, one hand digging into the horse's mane, the other still clutching the katana strapped improperly at her back, and the wind that chases her across the dark and frozen Mongolian steppe plays hell on her face.*

Prose, like poetry, should have meter. It needs to *sound* right when read out loud. I believe this to such a degree that I often don't know what's going on in my stories until I like how the words sound. *Then* I know what happens.

As an added benefit, it turned out that Mongolia was the right place for horses, as well as for isolated collections of gers, where you can easily imagine all kinds of lawless shit going down. Sometimes in writing you get lucky. But you also need to be ready to do some research. I have no idea how anybody wrote before Google.

I'm dedicating this story to John Bohane, who, in my early days of writing, eventually lost patience with me and insisted that I goddamn finish something. That something turned into *White to Move and Lose,* without which the world wouldn't have Xiang, Butch, Martin, Monika, and all the rest. John was also the first person in our circle to utter the words "I hate this!" about *someone else's* writing (mine, as it so happens), thus turning a corner for our little group, freeing us to truly speak our minds.

Thanks, John.

# entertainment for men

We enter the office together, I take the sofa, Jane takes the easy chair with the big floral print on it.

There was plenty of room on the sofa.

The doc is standing in front of her desk. She calls herself Dr. Nan. Turns out this woman, Dr. Nan, is just about the worst marriage counselor in Sacramento. But we find that out later. For now, she's asking a few questions, going over things. I barely listen. I'm looking around her office.

It's a home office, and we're on the ground floor. Outside the window, someone is mowing the lawn. The place smells of clipped roses and cut grass. Dr. Nan's got this aquarium up on a bookstand. There's a plastic oyster sitting on the turquoise rocks at the bottom, sending up bubbles. A few fake plants wave in the water, and the backdrop shows a couple sipping drinks under a palm tree. The picture doesn't belong. But it figures there had to be a fish tank. I know Jane sees it, because at the very least there's the bubbles. How do you overlook a thing like that?

Dr. Nan's a tiny little number. She looks like you could just put her in your pocket and take her home. She's got this face like she stopped to help a homeless man, but then the guy told her to go to hell and walked away, and now she's standing there alone on the sidewalk. She looks like you could put her in your pocket and go home.

"Ed?" Jane goes. She's looking at me.

I look at Dr. Nan. She says, "Ed, was there something?"

I look at Jane. I go, "Already?"

Jane goes, "This was your idea."

Now, this last bit was entirely untrue, unless maybe she meant telling about what happened at the mall. I'm sure that's where all this started, that fish tank at the goddamned mall. But this whole idea of seeing the doc in the first place? That was Jane's. Me, I was fine.

I look at Dr. Nan. I imagine her having a degree in English literature or something like that. Something hoity. Not a real doctor. These days everyone's calling themselves a doctor. So I go, "I just wish you would just calm down, Jane," but Jane goes, "Ed," and so it's up to me.

I go, "Where do you want me to start?" Jane shrugs her shoulders. This was her idea! I don't know what to do. "I'll start at the mall," I go.

"No," Jane goes, "start with picking up Sue on the way. You just had to pick up Sue, *didn't* you."

She emphasizes the *didn't* like she's gunning for something. I go, "I don't see why we need to bring Susan into this." Susan's a real looker.

"Start wherever you want," goes Jane, and she shrugs her shoulders again. Jane has this blond hair that comes just down to her shoulders, where it makes a little turn so that it's always catching the light when she shrugs. I go, "I'll start with the book reviews," and I tell what there is to tell.


I wanted to go to the mall and Jane didn't. It was a Saturday, our usual day for that. My father was visiting, again. I figured Jane would've *wanted* to go to the mall, if for nothing else than to get out of the house. What I mean is that Dad is always telling these embarrassing stories from when I was a kid. Jane and I have been married for three years—*three years*—and my father still acts like it's been two months. My whole life he's been waiting to tell these stories. He would say, "Just you wait, Eddy, my boy!" Like when I was five, and I sat on Santa's lap at Macy's and sneezed a big wet one into Santa's beard, he would say, "Just you wait and see, Eddy, my boy. Someday you'll have a wife. Then we'll all get a big kick out of this. Just you wait!" These are the kinds of stories I mean.

Dad and Mom split up a while ago. It was a relief to everyone. Now he goes around with this girl Jill. Jill is seven years older than me. Seven years. She'll go around my house barefoot and braless and smelling like watermelon, wearing these big gold hoop earrings and a Led Zeppelin concert T-shirt over a black leather miniskirt. That kind of look. She touches herself a lot, by which I mean she'll be fiddling with her hair one minute, wrapping it around a finger, and the next she's got her chin resting in her hand, a long, painted fingernail stroking at her cheek.

Dad lives with Jill in the house I grew up in. I wake up sometimes with nightmares about the two of them doing it in my old bedroom. My father in these dreams will sometimes be wearing my old Superman pajamas. Imagine, a thing like that.

Anyway, it was Saturday, Dad and Jill were visiting, and they were in our living room watching TV. I was in the kitchen reading out loud from Jane's book reviews on Amazon. Jane publishes these books online. She can't stand to see for herself the reader comments, but she needs to know what people are saying just the same, so she has me do it. I do it every Saturday. Every Saturday, I am to read the comments out loud, sorted from worst to best. Jane usually has a bottle of Teacher's in front of her on the kitchen table while I'm doing this.

So that's what I'm doing, I'm reading strangers' comments out loud to the kitchen while Jane is drinking Teacher's from a glass. But what I wanted to be doing was getting the hell out of there and going to the mall, see? But Jane didn't want this.

Now, I'm not the sort who asks their wife to do something she doesn't want. So I simply made the *suggestion* that we pick Dave and Susan up along the way. That's all it was. Dave and I are friends, and Susan and Jane get along. I thought it would even things out. More people to spread Dad's attention around.

But Dave was sick. So when Susan came out her front door, she was by herself. I was driving; Jane was in the passenger seat. Susan came around my side of the car. I rolled down the window. "Dave's sick," she said. Then she reached in. She said, "Here, you've got a little cowlick." Using her fingers, she then smoothed out some of my hair. It's possible she had wet her fingers from her mouth first, I don't know. Either way, I can see how things were probably already off to a bad start from Jane's point of view.

Then Susan got in the back, behind Jane, and she sat on Jill's lap. We have a Tercel. That's not a lot of room. So it only stands to reason she'd have to sit on Jill. The whole trip to the mall, I'd look from time to time into the rearview mirror and see things. At one point, just to give an example, Jill brought up a cigarette from somewhere. She'd hold the cigarette lightly in her fingers and smoke from it, then hold it in front of Susan's lips and let her drag on it as well. When these things would happen, I'd look across to Jane in the passenger's seat and know that of this, too, she was aware. I really don't know what we were thinking, inviting Dave and Susan along.

We're still in the car when Dad said he wants to go to the Jade Garden for dinner. That Chinese place, there at the mall, you know? We've eaten there a few times. Homemade noodles. Dad said, "Maybe Chung will be working today. How would that be for kicks, Ed?" he said. "Chung?" he said.

"Ching, Chang, Chung," said Jill. That's the kind of thing this girl is in the habit of saying. There's no end to things like that that she'll say. What does one do with a girl like that?

"What's all this about Chung?" Susan asked.

"She waits tables at the Jade," said Dad. "Ed here thinks she's got a nice can." He leaned forward and pushed at the back of my seat. "Isn't that right, Eddy?" he said, pushing. "Nice can?" But I never said a goddamn word about Chung's can. Dad's the one who keeps saying that.

Jill said, "You can look at the menus all you want, boys, as long as you eat at home. Isn't that right, Paul? Isn't that what I always say?"

There was nothing Dad needed to say in that direction, so he just sat back and smiled. And that was the last of the conversation as we pulled into the mall parking lot.

Now, the Jade Garden's not like the takeout joints we have near our house. At the Jade they sit you down. They give you plastic chopsticks and cloth napkins. There's Chinese music on the speakers, and they've got a few different rooms. There's framed pictures on the walls, too; mostly of the Eiffel Tower or maybe Central Park. If you look, you can see they're the pictures that came with the frames.

The restaurant was busy, so we put in for a table. They said about thirty minutes. Dad said he wanted to go to B. Dalton's while we waited. Jill talked like she wanted to go everywhere. We walked along for a bit, Jill looking in through all the windows. Then we were outside Victoria's Secret. Vicky's is always having a sale, and they were having one that day, too.

"It's buy three get the fourth free!" Jill said to Dad. Then she said to Jane and Susan, "I'm going in," and they all went in together.

My father called after Jill. "Get something good!" he said.

I said something to Jane, too. Something like, "Don't buy the whole store!" But I knew. She wasn't going to buy a goddamned thing.

I was left in a position of standing there with my father, needing to kill time. There were two posters outside Vicky's of supermodels in their underwear.

Then there was the mall directory in the middle of the hallway. Next to that was an advertisement framed in glass and lit up from inside. It was two ads, actually. The first said: SISTERS OF MERCY HOSPITAL. FIRST RATE HEART CARE FROM THE HEART. You'd read that for a time, then it would scroll up and disappear while a second poster came up from the bottom. The second ad said: A-PLUS CARPET CLEANING. RATED #1 IN SACRAMENTO COUNTY. Then you'd be back to the first ad. Then the second ad.

First ad. Second ad. First.

Second.

"Doing well, Ed?" my father said.

"Sure, Dad," I said.

We moved out of the way of some high school kids who were laughing to each other as they passed by. I read some more from the moving advertisements. Dad read the directory.

"Let's go to Dalton's," he said. "The girls will find us."

We got to the bookstore and split up. Dad said he'd be at the magazine rack and to get him when everyone was ready to eat.

I started with the travel section, where I thumbed through a street guide for Bruges. Then in self-help I read from the covers of some books without bothering to pick any of them up. On the clearance table, I found a hardbound collector's copy of the life of Marilyn Monroe. There was really nothing in the store I needed.

I wandered over to the mag rack. Dad was leafing through a skin rag. I was standing behind him as he tilted the magazine sideways. The centerfold unfurled and dangled there in space. He looked at it and took in a breath or two. Without turning, he said to me, "You know, Ed, I just don't feel a thing?"

Jill came up. "Tummy staples!" she said, seeing the centerfold. Then she said, "Can we go? Our table should be ready." I looked around for Jane and spotted her out in the hallway with Susan. We all headed back to the Jade Garden, and this is when Jane finally is about to get upset over the fish tank, or rather what happened as a result. But it wasn't me, it was my father. I only wish Jane could see that, you know?

Our restaurant hostess looked sixteen, tops. She led us through a beaded curtain into a back room. The room would be about right for a private party, if there wasn't much to it. It's just the one circular table. I remembered we had eaten in that room once or twice before, but it had been some time.

Our hostess said, "Chung will be your server tonight," then she left us. I remember thinking the dinner crowd must've already been simmering down. The table was big enough for twelve, and here we were, just five. I sat next to Jane, and Dad sat next to me. Jill went to sit next to Dad. Then she complained she couldn't see anybody, and she took a seat clear across the table.

Susan was the fifth wheel. She didn't know what to do. She took a seat next to Jill. Then she's up again, checking out the room. She went to look at some of the framed pictures. Then she moved on to a statue of a horse on a pedestal, then a potted plant in a corner, then a shaded floor lamp. There was a framed Certificate of Occupancy on the wall next to a picture of the Eiffel Tower. She looked even at these.

Finally she spotted a big aquarium, sunk into the wall. The way it works, there's a room behind, to access the tank. I didn't remember the tank from before, so it must've been new. Susan got right up and placed her hands on the glass, peering into the water.

Jill was watching Susan from across the room and running her fingers through her hair. "Paul!" she said all at once. "Tell the story."

"Story?"

She said, "You know." Then she looked at Susan again, there at the tank. Then at me, then back to Dad.

My father's face brightened. "Sure," he said. "Eddy was about three or four. Mona—that's Eddy's mom—and I had just put in a fish tank. It was like this one here, but smaller. Cut into the wall, you know? This is our living room I'm talking about. The tank was a real beaut. I thought it pulled the whole room together, and Mona agreed. This was back when Mona could still agree to things. You remember, Ed? You remember your mom and me cutting that tank into the wall? What a project it was. You probably can't even remember a time before that fish tank."

"No," I agreed.

Dad went on. He was really into it now. "But you can at least remember where we'd go to get the fish? You can remember Mel's?"

"I don't remember that part," I said.

Right around now is when Chung showed up, and Dad's story was interrupted. Susan came back to the table and sat next to Jill. Chung started in with the napkins, putting them in front of everyone, then the chopsticks. She was smiling as she gave out the chopsticks. Quite the looker, Chung. Not quite at Susan's level, but still.

Dad carried on with his story. "We'd go on Saturdays. Saturdays was our day to go pick up a new fish or two at Mel's. You remember, Ed? The tiny little number working the cash register?"

He was talking about Lisa. Mona is my mom; this woman's name was Lisa. Mona, Lisa. I don't know exactly when it was Dad started sleeping with Lisa. I was too young to see anything like that. It was later that I had to hear about it all.

"Remember her name?" Dad pressed. "Lisa?"

"Maybe," I said.

"Oh, yeah. Lisa was a tiny little number. She was the kind you could just put in your pocket and take home with you." My father picked up his chopsticks from off his napkin, then carefully arranged the napkin on his lap. "So we've got this beautiful new fish tank in our wall. Mona and me. You were fascinated with it, Ed. You'd go right up to it, like you were trying to get in through the glass. Swim with all the little fishies. But do you remember what your mother would always say to you? Do you at least remember that part?"

I just sat there and let him go on.

"She'd say, 'Just look! Don't touch!' She'd say it over and over again to you. 'Just look! Don't touch!' You remember, now? You remember what part comes next?"

Chung had just finished pouring everyone's ice water, and now she started in on the orders. Susan took the Twice-Cooked Pork. Jill got the Happy Family. Chung came up to Jane next, but Jane told her she didn't know what she wanted. That put it on me, and Chung walked up close. Her pink waitress frock made her look like she belonged in a diner, but then there were the heels—purple leather straps and shiny gold clasps—which to my mind placed her in a club. She would have a drink or two at the bar; maybe she'd start with a cosmo, then chase it with a watermelon martini. Her date would take her out onto the floor. He would hold her by the waist, and she would do a turn or two for him.

The scent of perfume lifted off her arm as she held her pad, waiting.

When Chung had started with the orders, Dad had just kept going with the story. Now he was saying, "… so there we were in bed, Mona and me, finished with everything for the night. I was just drifting off when we heard something downstairs. It was you, of course, Ed. You were talking to somebody, but damn if either of us could figure out who you thought you were talking to, or what you were saying. Mona said she'd go and see, but I got up, too, and followed her down.

"It was you, Ed. You were talking to the fish, or maybe to yourself. You had gotten into the storeroom behind the tank. You were in your Superman pajamas. You remember those Superman pajamas, Ed? They were your favorite. I figured you'd take them with you to college. Anyway, you remember what you were saying? You were up on a stepstool. You had slid the top of the tank aside, and you had the pajama sleeve on your right arm rolled up almost to your shoulder. And there you were, your hand down in that tank, chasing all the fish in great big circles. And you were saying, 'Just look, don't touch. Just look, don't touch. Just look, don't touch.' Jesus, Ed, it was the cutest thing."

And that's all there is to the whole fish tank thing, really, because that's when Chung said something like, "That's so cute," and she placed her hand on my shoulder, and Jane threw up all over her. Come to think of it, I had kind of thought she'd been looking pale.

I'm done talking. I look to Jane to see if she's got anything to add, but she just sits there. She uses a fingernail to outline the floral print on her chair.

"Jane?" I go.

She goes, "Ed."

"Well," says Dr. Nan, as if something has been accomplished. Then she comes over to where I'm sitting on the couch. And after everything, after *all of that*, and everything I had just said, when she gets up close to me, she puts her hand on my shoulder.

It is in this regard that I consider her to be the worst marriage counselor in Sacramento.

Later that night, Jane and I are home, watching a rerun of *Taxi*, eating hazelnuts and drinking port, smoking a little grass. By the time we had gotten halfway home from Dr. Nan's that afternoon, we were laughing. After TV we go to bed, and maybe it wasn't the best, but there we were anyhow.

All of that had been in Sacramento, in the '80s. We left Sacramento for Jersey, but it turns out Jersey isn't great for do-overs, and so we tried Maine. We're still here. And still, sometimes, when the tide comes in, I can feel that hand on my shoulder, and it's like a million tiny bubbles all coming to the surface.

# for Dawn

The 2014 movie *Birdman* employs the common trope of a story within a story; in this case, a play within a movie. As good as the movie itself was, I was equally intrigued by its internal play. On a careful rewatch, I noted that its name, as briefly displayed on a marquee, was "What We Talk about When We Talk about Love." Half expecting the thing to be a fabrication, I looked it up, and that's how I discovered the late, great short story artist Raymond Carver.

Carver amazed me with his bald yet beautiful writing style. He said exactly what he meant to say and no more, and it was up to me to make what sense I could of what little was on the page. He wasn't there to help me but to tell me about the world as seen through his eyes and related through his typewriter. (Carver *did* live long enough to have encountered a word processor, but I simply cannot imagine the man using one. What would've been the point? Everything sounds like it came out exactly as it was meant to be, with no need for correction or editing.[1]) His stories are populated by drunks, polyamorists, murderers, and delinquents, all of whom relate to one another by what they don't bother saying. The poverty of their environment is depicted by physical description that Carver doesn't bother to write. Like Charles M. Schulz with his *Peanuts*, he draws with a minimum of strokes. And yet, the stories live, and it is certain that whatever Carver was trying to say, he said it.

I simply had to try my hand at this, and the story you just read was that attempt. Hope you liked it. And if you said to yourself, "Aw, c'mon. This guy's trying to imitate Raymond Carver," go ahead and take a bow.

In writing this story, my morale was boosted by Stephen King, who, in a number of his books, gives his blessing to beginning writers who want to emu-

---

[1] It turns out that this was the exact opposite of the truth. When I discovered the editorial brilliance of Gordon Lish and learned that what I had read in *What We Talk About* was actually edited—sometimes very, very heavily—I immediately got a copy of Beginners—Carver's unedited stories—and assiduously studied the deep cuts and brutal alterations Lish had made. The discoveries I made here felt like divine revelation.

late their favorite authors. King himself does so in his own story "Premium Harmony." Quite coincidentally—and to my amusement—the author King emulates in that story is ... Raymond Carver. Now how 'bout that? Myself, I think I did a better job at emulating Carver than King did, but who knows, maybe he'd disagree.

As for the content of "Entertainment," I imagined a couple of Raymond Carver's characters going to marriage counseling. I'm dedicating this story to Dawn Miller, who showed great courage at our circle by discussing her own experiences in this vein.

# eight feet dangling

"What do I see? I see a towel wrapped around my head, of course. What do you expect me to see when you go and wrap a towel around my head and then ask me 'What do you see?' I see a towel. Wrapped around my head. That's what."

And they *should* be happy, the three of them, to even have a beach towel with them at all. And the picnic basket, and the sunblock. The radio. It's not that Henry's let's-all-go-to-the-island suggestion was bad. It's just that going to the beach is such *work*. Not for the children, of course, nor even for Henry. Wasn't it just like Henry to wake her up at seven, suggest going to the beach, and then spend the next two hours running his model trains in the cellar?

It had been over two years since the family had last ferried out of Hyannis for a day in Nantucket. Ashley was nine now and could be trusted not to go into the water on her own; and of course Bobby was Bobby. There he was—Marlene had instinctively lifted the bottom fold of the coarse, gray towel Henry had placed over her eyes just now, asking her what she saw, to search for Bobby's tousled brown shock of hair—*there* he was, standing like a statue of St. Francis, holding court over a few sandpipers that pecked at the firm, wet sand around his feet.

Bobby would never be different. Marlene had accepted this. No, Bobby would never be different from the boy he was on that day six months ago (right after Christmas it was, too) when Mrs. Policastro had called Marlene in for a parent-teacher conference. Mrs. P wanted to talk about Bobby, and about not making friends well, and taking everything literally, and only answering Mrs. P when he seemed to feel it was worth his time, and how kindergarten was all about finding out these sorts of things.

"In many ways, Mrs. Lutz," Mrs. P had said, "in many ways, Bobby is simply *miles* above his peers." She mentioned again Bobby's aptitude scores and his wide-ranging vocabulary. "And there are *infinitely* more resources available to help him—I am talking socially, now—than there were even a few years ago."

There had been no Mrs. Cody to sit for Bobby that day—something about a doctor's appointment—and so she had had no choice but to bring Bobby in with her for the conference ("You just sit there, now, and color and be a good boy while I talk with your teacher"), and of course he had heard everything, and Bobby would spend the next week telling his sister how many miles ahead of her he was and describing to her his "infinite reinsourcements."

Marlene felt a stab of anxiety. "Where is Ashley?" she asked Henry from under the towel. "I didn't see Ashley just now."

"She's fine," Henry assured. "She's playing in the sand."

"And that fat man with the big red belly? Has he moved on?"

"Yes, Marl. Everything is fine. Everything is fine."

"Well what did a man like that want with us, anyway, selling—What was it he wanted to sell us? Parasailing? Send us all up, miles into the air?"

Henry made no reply. Marlene sneaked another peek from under the towel to see him squinting his eyes after the pear-shaped man with the sunburnt belly who toddled his way briskly down the beach, roaring his advertisement in competition with the din of the surf's crash.

"Paaaarasailing! Paaaarasailing!" The man's baritone bellow attenuated with distance; Marlene listened to it, quieter and quieter, until it pulled itself once and for all under the waves of music emanating from the radio and the infinite churn of water.

Now Henry turned to Marlene and pulled the towel back down over her eyes, resuming his ridiculous experiment. He said, "Bobby says he saw the ocean when he wore this towel folded in pleats over his eyes. I tried it, and I think I saw what he meant. What do you see?"

"Oh, for heaven's sakes, I don't see a thing. Are you sure Ashley is playing in the sand?"

To Ashley, the announcement that morning that they were all to go to the beach had provoked romantic visions mostly gleaned from the insides of YA novels and the outsides of other books she was told she was not quite old enough to read. Immediately, she had asked to wear the beautiful white dress that she wore whenever she attended church with her best friend, Maddie. Mother had insisted that she wear her swimsuit. This was sensible, of course. Now, as Ashley sat in the sand halfway between the surf and the small stake of beach claimed by the family's rainbow-striped parasol, her fingers slicing ever-expanding circles around a pink seashell, the peevish straps of yellow polyester dug red ridges into her skin. She rubbed her shoulders and wished again for her dress.

"If you really wish to," Mother had opined over the pages of her day planner, forever ago, when Ashley had asked permission to accompany Madison Speece and her family to church on Sunday mornings, "if you *really* wish to, I suppose you are old enough to walk as far as St. Mark's." After a few seconds' hesitation, Mother had added, "But you'll have to set your own alarm." To which was further added, "And you'll have to make your own breakfast."

This concession to friendship was more easily gained than Ashley had expected. Getting Mother to buy the dress that had floated like a cloud in the bulging window of Janice's Boutique on Duke Street was a more difficult thing. Even with Daddy's help, the Sunday dress came only at the expense of a precious birthday present request.

It had been worth it. Maddie Speece was so much fun! She lived just around the corner at North Maple and up two blocks, right above the store where Mr. Miller sold blue raspberry slushes and Topps bubble gum. School was out, and most days Mrs. Speece would let them walk Rex to the park to play fetch. Mrs. Speece had made it clear, though, that if Ashley wanted to play with Maddie on Sundays, that she must go to church with them and that they always left bright and early and that there wouldn't be any time for standing around at her front door, waiting and waiting. She knew Mrs. Speece was just trying to be scary again. But it didn't work, and St. Mark's wasn't going to scare her either. Something in the contented way Father Tolbert, with no urgency at all, would jangle the bells ahead of the host. And in the muted angles of his face as he recited the creed to the Apostles. There they were, those Apostles—silently shining their musky light down from where they stood, frozen forever in the red and blue glass that hung high over the altar. These comforts communicated to Ashley a secret. A secret that only she knew and which was simply this: that Father Tolbert wasn't bothered by anything that hovered infinitely above cold rafters or that writhed in fiery pits miles beneath creaky floorboards.

Here came Bobby, and he walked right through her circles, completely ruining them. He was once again doing that thing where he stared around at nothing, and then he wandered off. With the side of her hand Ashley wiped the sand flat and clean and began again, carving her circles.

Back where Daddy was trying hard to tell something to Mother, Ashley heard the radio blare a favorite tune. She was singing to the ocean when Bobby showed up in the middle of her circles again, right smack on top of her pink seashell.

"Mother has a towel over her face," he said.

Bobby missed his towel. The towel had felt good on his face. Father had taken it, and he shouldn't have, and now the sun hurt his eyes. It hurt even when he looked at the sand. The wet sand was better than the sunny sand. It was better because the wet sand wasn't as bright as the sunny sand and because, when you looked at it, you could see birds. Mother couldn't see the birds in the sand (he had already asked twice), and he believed that she wouldn't see the ocean in the towel, either. Mother never saw oceans in towels or black marbles in faraway houselights at night when you take off your eyeglasses or the pink bubble wrap that shows up on the insides of your eyelids when you squeeze them shut very, very tight. All of this seemed like a thing Father ought to know about Mother.

Father ought to give him back his towel.

A man with a round belly and no hair and who looked like a lobster was walking around. He was yelling a big word that sounded like *sailing*. It was hard to tell. The radio was making lots of noise. The red-belly man was walking away. Even as he walked away he looked like a lobster. Ashley was saying something. Whatever she was talking about, it wasn't the lobster man, because she wasn't looking up at him.

The lobster man was saying, "Laaaaaahbster sailing! Laaaaaahbster saaaailing!"

Soon, the lobster man would be gone.

Bobby came up to Ashley and stood very close to her so that she could hear what he had to say. He stood so close that his skin—its sensitivity increased by salt, sand, water, and light—prickled, as the tiny hairs that covered both their skins, as they do the skins of all mammals, touched.

"Mother has a towel over her face," he said. Without waiting for a reply, he walked over to Father and Mother. Ashley followed him. His parents were talking about him. Mother said something that made no sense:

"Oh, forever snakes, I don't see anything."

"Your eyes are squeezed too hard," Bobby said. "You're not doing it right."

Marlene looked down from behind the towel to see her son and daughter, and Henry reached for her hand. She relaxed her eyes, stared straight ahead, neither above nor below, and there it was: a line, made by the folds in the towel, that stretched across her field of vision. The horizon line of the sea.

And she perceived this to be the same line that, forever ago, first separated sea from sky, and that, ten million years (infinitely) from now, would remain, unaltered from that day—any day now—when the Earth would be given over, suddenly, to the creeping tyranny of insects and the churning of molten rock hundreds of feet (miles) beneath its desolate and uninhabitable surface.

An hour later, eight feet dangled halfway between the heavens and the earth. Ashley was singing into the wind, Bobby was pointing out patterns made by the whitecaps far below, and as Marlene reached out for Henry's hand—Henry, who was thinking god alone knew what—she looked down through whipped and unruly hair to spot the distant red belly of the jolly man who drove the powerboat that was parasailing her family high above the glassy waters of the Nantucket Sound.

# for Janet

As "Eight Feet Dangling" was the first short story I ever completed—after at least a half dozen false starts on other stories—it's fitting that I should dedicate it to Janet Hicks. Outside of myself and Bill Kent, who founded our circle, Janet is our longest standing member. I think she's read literally every story I've ever written—or even attempted. Furthermore, when I told her that I planned on dedicating each of the stories in this collection to a different member of our group, she specifically asked for this one. I asked her why, and her answer was immediate: "You nailed those characters." So let's talk about them.

Like many of the stories I've written here, "Dangling" began as self-assignment. I had just read *To the Lighthouse* by Virginia Woolf, and I wanted to try my hand at stream of consciousness. I was assigning myself all kinds of work at that time, actually, as I kept falling in love with different authors and then trying to mimic their styles and voices. The moment I'd think of a character or a situation, I'd just start writing whatever occurred to me, most likely in the voice of whoever I'd just finished reading.

I'm not sure if this is a good way to start writing or not. It certainly generated a lot of wasted paper and time. (I can never tell if what I've written is any good until I print it out.) But maybe this was the only way that I, personally, *could* have started. I'd had no idea that I even *wanted* to write until I accidentally fell into it one day (let's put a pin in that). I'd had no formal education in creative writing beyond a single introduction to poetry class in college. People tell me that I have now developed a voice of my own, and if that's so, I'm happy about it.

As I said, I'd just finished reading Woolf's brilliant *To the Lighthouse*, and so my mind was naturally still wandering the dunes and wading in and out of the surf at some mystical, imaginary beach. It wasn't hard to imagine a family vacationing in Nantucket, where Laura and I had once vacationed and which echoes the feel of New England, where I lived from 1988 to 1990. (For reasons that were probably lyrical, I later moved the setting of the story from Nantucket to Martha's Vineyard.) As I started bringing in pieces of the story to our circle, Bill Kent explained how stream of consciousness worked. He said you had to imagine the characters on a stage with a spotlight moving from one person to the next. Whoever had the spot had the mic, which they would think out loud into. Or something like that. Whatever he said, I thought I understood it enough to keep going.

I quickly homed in on Bobby as my main star. Bobby, whoever he'd turn out to be, would always be Bobby. This simple idea intrigued me. I thought maybe I could write a series of stories, each featuring an episode from a different year of Bobby's life, beginning in this story with him in kindergarten. Perhaps I'd write up through Bobby's graduation from high school: thirteen stories. In this way, I needn't ever tell too much in any one story. Heck, I wouldn't even have to "spot" every family member in every story. For example, I could leave Henry, the father, as a blank to be filled in later. I felt this could be done to good effect, as we observe the mother, Marlene, there at the end, wondering to herself what on Earth her husband is thinking. That would be a character point all by itself.

And so I wrote. I just put myself in the mindset of each person as the story kept winding itself back around to a specific point in time, namely, the placing of the towel over Marlene's eyes.

# the adoration

Looking back over the day, Henry figures he could have played it differently. Everybody could've gone to the picnic after all, instead of to the bowling alley. Or, that morning in the narthex after Mass, he could've kept his comments about Father Tolbert's waistline to himself.

Always with the cheek. You must think of the children. That was Marlene. Bobby is watching everything you say, she's liable to remind for the umpteenth time in a day. Only recently has Henry realized—Marlene, too—that neither of them has much to say anymore about Ashley. Ashley, who, he surmises, has already been raised to the point where the rest will come on her own turning: a fresh needle set down with love on old vinyl, seeming to wind its way round and round in circles when in fact mostly standing still, slowly nudging along a straight line toward a small black hole in the center, where there is no music, and the whole while the hits keep coming, one after another. Today, felt letter boards and sticker books; tomorrow, white lace and registries.

So, he thinks again (he watches Bobby send another into the gutter—Ashley triumphant, Marlene pragmatic as she sips coffee from a Styrofoam cup and jots another dash onto the scoresheet with one of those little yellow eraserless travesties of a pencil), he could have taken them to the picnic instead of bowling. It was what they had set out to do, after all—touching home just long enough to get out of their Sunday best and (this had been Bobby's contrivance) to fetch Maggie. Dogs, Bobby had declared, belong at picnics. Never mind that the picnic would be indoors (A Holiday Inn? This was the best the Picnic Committee could come up with?) and that the dog would of course need to be kept in the car, where it would get cold. It was January. To be specific, it was the 6th— Epiphany. Not that anyone cared—or should care, particularly—about such a peculiar day on the church calendar.

But about the dog, Bobby had prevailed.

Against the protestations of Marlene, then, Henry had unceremoniously tossed Maggie into the back seat of the Buick between Bobby and Ashley, where the dachshund received a quick pat on the head before a pair of headphones temporarily removed his daughter from the world.

The detour, too, was not of Henry's doing.

"Animals, Dad! Animals!"

Through the car window and across the road, in a field behind a brown fence, the animals, most of them, were just standing there—rather stupidly, Ashley had thought. The sheep, actually, had been lying down in the grass. There were three of those, as well as some goats and a camel with a big hump and a handsome gray donkey and something she hadn't ever seen before, tall and white and beautiful with a giraffe neck and big black eyes. Then all of a sudden she knew—remembered from a long-ago picture book that had been outgrown even by Bobby. It was a llama.

"Animals!" Ashley exclaimed again, pushing a bent finger into the chilly window, pointing.

To her surprise, her father pulled over.

"Huh!" Dad said, craning his neck around so he could see everything. "Manger animals. They must belong to that Baptist church right there. They probably put on a live nativity scene."

"There's no llamas in a nativity scene," informed Mom.

"It's manger animals," Dad repeated.

"Llamas are from South America."

"It's manger animals."

They all got out of the car to look. It was cold, and the day had been weird to begin with, and then it got weirder when Dad decided, after they'd all looked at the animals for a while, to take them bowling instead of to the picnic. Dad had said something earlier that morning to Father Tolbert at church that made Mom mumble and curl her fingers in the way that meant all of them would march straight into the living room when they get home. Then she and Bobby would be asked to sit outside in the hall, where, snooping from behind the blue and white floor vase with all the umbrellas, they would listen to Mom talk about "using filters" and "impressionability," with Dad agreeing to everything and yet still, somehow, keeping the argument going.

Ashley supposedly didn't hear what it was Dad had said at church, but of course it had been about Father Tolbert getting fat (which, anyway, he was). It was funny to think how she had once believed that it was fat old Father Tolbert who was God, destined to ascend first into the frosty stained glass windows, then up through the wood-slatted roof, disappearing forever into the sky. It was funny to think that God could even *be* something fat, like Father Tolbert or Santa Claus.

Bobby, she realizes, as she now watches him gleefully throw another ball into the gutter on purpose, might still believe. That's okay, she thinks, Bobby still talks to the dog. And anyway, it was he who had first made the discovery about Maggie that morning, in front of the manger animals.

"Over here! Over here!" Bobby urged.

He understood now about the rituals of grownups (these days, even Ashley) getting from one place to another, how time is needed for *everything*: seatbelts and questions, shirttails and wristwatches, words and *more* words, purses. But he liked to encourage it along anyhow. "Over here!"

Father had parked the car in some grass kind of far from the animals, so Mother was still in her purse when Bobby got to the fence. He was holding Maggie like a baby. The animals had all come over to see her. The white llama led the way. He was taller even than the camel. He was the animals' leader. The sheep got up from their nap to see what was going on, and they came behind everyone else. The llama's long neck was way out over the fence, and he was talking to Maggie.

"Bobby, hold that dog!" Mother was trying to walk without letting her shoes touch any of the dirt. Her arms flapped like a turkey that hadn't been told it couldn't fly. "Henry, tell Bobby to keep hold of Maggie. That dog is flyable to run under the fence." Mother was very smart about dealing with important people like Mrs. Smithers at school, but there were some things she didn't know very much about at all, and dogs were one of them. Maggie would never jump out of his arms, and she certainly couldn't fly. Sometimes she would get heavy, and then he would put her down, and right away she would want to jump back up. Maggie didn't need to go under the fence to talk to the animals.

Finally, everybody came. "Look, everybody!" Bobby said. "The animals all came to see Maggie!"

"Nonsense," said Father. "They want food." He must've thought nobody heard him, because he said it again. "They just want us to feed them." Then, as Mother liked to say, he really rubbed it in. "They're just animals."

Bobby scowled. Father had been saying bad things all day. If things were the way they should be, he would send Father to his room. But grownups didn't have the kind of rooms people go to.

Father tousled Bobby's hair, trying to erase the thoughts. "I tell you what," he said, "we'll do a spearmint. You see those stables over there?" Father pointed to a long spot in the fence with a roof and piles of hay and two windows in the shapes of diamonds. "I'm going to take Maggie and walk on the far side of that stable, where nobody can see. Then I'm going to come out the other end, and we're going to stand right over there, Maggie and I, on the opposite side of the fence." Father pointed way across the pen, like Christopher Columbus discovering America. "Then we'll see what the animals do."

Bobby said that Maggie wouldn't like going with Father. Father said she would be just fine. Mother reminded everyone that the outdoors was cold.

Father took Maggie, who—he was right—didn't complain. Holding Maggie, he turned his back to the animals. Right away, the white llama stopped looking at anything and sat down. The rest of the animals stood around. Father walked like that, with his back to the animals, hiding Maggie. He walked right around the corner of the fence and all the way to the stable. Bobby waited for Father to appear with Maggie on the other end. While he waited, he counted to ten, and then to nine, and then to eight. It was a trick he taught himself to help get to sleep, although it never worked, and then he would have to start at ten again. Or think of names for stars. Or imagine people who didn't exist yet.

Father and Maggie appeared on the other side of the stable. At first the animals didn't do anything, even though some of the sheep were staring right at Maggie. Then the llama turned his neck and saw her. He got up and ran all the way to the other end of the pen, with all the animals running behind him.

Father came back. "Well, I'll be damned," he said.

Marlene watches her son toss another into the gutter, and she smiles. Bobby. He'll never change. Then Henry gets up. He does his little butt wiggle and his little foot shuffle. He's trying to convert a seven-ten split. Good luck with that.

While her husband prepares to bowl, she chuckles softly to herself, remembering what he had mumbled to her at the manger scene.

"The Adoration of the Maggie," indeed.

But she understands. Henry is trying to convert something much harder than a seven-ten split. *Un*convert would be the word for it. He wants to prove that he's over it but that he still can look its forms in the eye, coexist with them, without holding any of the corresponding beliefs. Good luck with that, too.

For herself, she stopped believing years ago.

She watches him wind up, left-right-left with the feet, hook the ball ... this, too, ending in the gutter. She takes another sip of coffee and records another dash on the scoresheet.

# thinking of Tammy

Some stories come along seemingly apropos of nothing, while others are inspired by a specific, true-to-life event. "The Adoration" is one of these.

We had a dog, a Japanese Chin named Cherry Blossom by our daughter, Mallory. When Mallory was about seven, we visited relatives "down the shore" (as they like to say in Jersey) around Christmastime. We were returning home, the four of us—Laura, Mallory, CB, and me—via Rt. 9. Along the side of the road, one of us (the dog?) spotted a fenced lawn in the middle of which a bunch of barnyard animals were lazing. I don't know if Mallory asked or if I acted impulsively, but I pulled the car over to the shoulder so we could all get a better look. I think it was Laura who stated out loud what was silently being suggested by the adjoining church: that these animals had recently been part of a live nativity.

We got out of the car, at which point the gist of what you just read in "The Adoration" happened in real life. All the animals, with the llama in the lead, came over to see Cherry Blossom. Whenever I, carrying CB in my arms, turned around, hiding the dog from the animals, they would lose all interest. Whenever CB re-appeared, even if it was on the opposite side of the fenced-in lawn, they'd perk up and run over to see her.

Immediately, I thought of Bobby. He'd go nuts over this. (As a writer, I have these invisible friends: the characters who have thus far shown up on my pages or who are still lurking around the dark recesses of my mind, begging for the opportunity.) So I shelved the idea (notepads on phones are great for this), and maybe a year later I wrote it.

Whatever character traits had revealed themselves to me while writing "Eight Feet Dangling," it was now time to decide (discover, if you prefer) which of those were important and defining enough to carry over into this second installment and expand upon. Clearly, the whole family was at one stage or another in figuring out what their religion meant to them. I began with Henry, who had been left out of "Dangling." The setting of the live nativity, in conjunction with the Christian observation of Epiphany, would dovetail nicely into the theme of religious discovery (even if that epiphany, or discovery, was the *rejec-*

40

*tion* of religion) that seemed to now be a defining characteristic of this series—if that is what it truly was turning into.

I'm dedicating this story to Tammy Davidson. A year or two into the life of our writers group, the circle began to degenerate into polygons of increasing desperation and decreasing sides: a pentagon; a square; finally, a triangle. We were just three: Janet, Tammy, and me. Tammy didn't last too much longer, either, but she stuck around long enough to keep us on life support while we built our numbers again.

Tammy, if you're out there, the circle is indeed unbroken (by and by, Lord, by and by)—and we've got you to thank for it.

*They're all part of sixteen reasons ...*

# prime directive

"Slow down, Bobby dear. Eating's not a race. There is much to do today."

This last sentence, to anyone else a non sequitur or even a contradiction, was to Marlene's mind neither of these. For it was precisely the abundance of things that needed doing and the arranging of time and resources around those things ("Let each task be paid in full," she was known to sometimes firmly recite in the context of being asked to speed up something she was doing) that produced in Marlene the state of harmony she looked forward to creating each morning—Henry already off to work, Ashley safely on her school bus, her number-two child (if she were being honest with herself, wouldn't that be her number-*one* child, really? Would she ever let Bobby grow up? Would she someday run from the church, sack lunch in hand, after the limousine as it pulled away, the words JUST MARRIED scrawled in white shaving cream on its rear window, silver cans clanging and gold streamers fluttering in tow?), her number-*two* child, Marlene had been saying to herself before the future had so rudely broken in with this business of the streamers and cans, her number-*two* child quietly munching on a bowl of his favorite breakfast cereal—as, amid the God beams made possible through a combination of airborne dust and the angle of the sun flooding in through the kitchen window and mingling with the smoke coils of her cigarette and the steam off her coffee, she mentally processed the day ahead of her.

So much to do today. Mrs. Cody would be coming in for the weekly housecleaning that afternoon. She would need her check, and there were still a few things that needed putting away. Somewhere, Henry had a Hechinger list. She rifled through a short stack of unopened mail on the kitchen table and found the list tucked between a NYNEX bill and a letter from Food for the Hungry. She added a few items of her own. Then there was Mrs. Holloway to deal with. Brenda Holloway had been requesting yet another parent-teacher conference for days now, and the two of them had been playing phone tag. So that needed

43

tending. The agenda for tomorrow's PTA meeting needed to be assembled and last month's minutes edited and filed. Too, there was Mr. Kinsley, the new neighbor, to deal with. He owned a dog, and *something* had to be done about that barking. Several checks needed to be deposited at the bank....

"Slow down, Bobby dear. Eating's not ..."

To her son, these words did not convey a statement, let alone a command, but were instead a necessary part of the room, taking their rightful position in time and place: after the pouring of the milk over the breakfast cereal and before the final putting away of the orange juice, hovering in the sacred space over the kitchen table, where meatloaf and family decisions were made. As for the firm tone with which Mother spoke, this too was understood as nothing requiring action but merely a necessity to ensure her words were lifted above the angry groans coming from the black and menacing furnace lurking in the basement—a spider in a dark corner, all legs and eyes—as it strove against October's windy bite upon the windowpanes outside.

Comfort. Comfort was Mother's prime directive (Bobby had learned these words from that wonderful TV show *Star Trek*). And there was indeed a great deal of comfort to be found in the strong and soft and predictable motions Mother made in the execution of her many secondary tasks. He watched now, for example, calmly spooning Fruity Pebbles into his mouth, as Mother worked her way mechanically through the stash of envelopes tucked on their sides between the pepper grinder and the napkin holder, the four red dashes that were the fingernails of her left hand marking her progress. He noted the ease and quiet of those motions—her fingers cradling each letter as she read, as if the paper were fragile and apt to tear apart at the slightest touch—completing and somehow perfecting the clatter she was creating with her right hand, continually clicking and tapping along the trail that led from her coffee mug to the glass ashtray to the wooden tabletop and then back to the coffee.

Mother was a fast reader and could often finish a letter with a blink of her eyes and a single swipe of her hand. In fact, Bobby marveled at how Mother could use her X-ray vision (Was another explanation possible?) to read letters *without ever taking them out of their envelopes*, allowing her to send some letters (and the envelopes they were still in) straight to what Mother called her circular file. By this strange name, Mother clearly meant the trash, although the name made little sense. The trash can in the kitchen was rectangular.

One such letter seemed on the verge of being thrown out when Mother interrupted herself mid-toss, handing the narrowly salvaged envelope to Bobby.

"Open this one, Bobby," she said. "See what it is."

Bobby read the envelope: Food for the Hungry. He had seen letters from that place before, and he thought he knew what to expect when he opened it …

… and he was right. Inside was a photograph of a grinning, colorfully dressed dark-skinned boy standing on a dirt path. Bobby held the picture for a moment, returning the boy's grin, trying to curl his fingers around the picture, just like Mother. To have a shirt like that! The colors! Then he set the picture down and returned to the envelope. Inside were two pages, each folded in thirds.

The first said, A LETTER FROM YOUR CHILD. The top half was written in pencil, and here was something worth investigating! A foreign language! Bobby spent several minutes poring over the many strange words scrawled here by this boy, the boy in this picture lying next to him, who grinned at Bobby over a distance so unimaginable that the letter may as well have come from a different world.

The bottom half of the letter was more understandable but less interesting. TRANSLATION, it said. What followed was typed in English. Skipping this, Bobby flipped the paper over to see the drawings the boy had made there. They were done in a colored pencil. A ship, an airplane, a suitcase. Each object was labeled twice: once in the foreign language, written in the boy's hand; once typed in English. There were two verses from the Bible: "I can do all things through Christ who strengthens me" (Philippians 4:13) and "Ask whatever you wish in my name and I will do it" (John 14:13).

And that was all. Bobby sighed and set down the letter.

There was the second page to look at. It said, WISH DIEUDONNÉ A HAPPY BIRTHDAY! After that, it was mostly just blank lines.

Bobby handed all of it to Mother and went back to his Fruity Pebbles.

But Mother could write as quickly as she could read, and before Bobby could get to the buildup of sugar that Mother allowed him to spoon over his cereal and that refused to dissolve in the milk but instead invariably accumulated into a soggy, dense, delicious mass at the bottom of his bowl, she was handing the pages back to him along with a pencil.

"Here, Bobby," she said. "I've started a letter to Dieudonné. Why don't you write a few words, like last time? I'm sure it will make him very happy. Don't forget to ask questions."

Bobby took the letter Mother had written. It said:

Dear Dieudonne,

We are so very happy to have received your wonderful letter and picture in the mail. You are ten! We are so very proud of you, and we are pleased to be your sponsors. You are growing into a fine boy.

Speaking of boys, mine would like to share a few words with you. I am turning the letter over to him.

The rest of the lines were still blank. In the time it took Bobby to finish off the sugar at the bottom of his bowl, he decided what to say. He took the pencil and started writing.

Greetings, Human! (That was supposed to sound like Spock.)

I see Mother said all her usual stuff. Dont feel bad. She says the same things to me all the time. Fathers are easy. They dont say much. I'm eating Fruity Pebbles and getting ready for school. At school Mrs. McCaskey taught us about injustice. I thought of you. But you are 10 so you are in 5th grade and you must already know all about injustice. Probably a whole lot more too. 2nd grade is easy. I cant wait for 5th grade. Jared says they get Miker scopes in science class. Sometimes he says they even mix chemicals. Jared is very smart. Mrs. McCaskey is my teacher. Mother says I go to a private school now but I don't get it because the teachers see EVERYTHING just like the old school. I saw how much money Mother wrote on your check last month. If your surprised I know about checks its because Mother taught me. Not Mrs. McCaskey. I'm still not as smart as Jared though. Most people arent. Ashley DEFINATELY is not. She is in the 5th grade too and still goes to the SAME SCHOOL! Ashley is my sister. You probably remember that from the last letter. But for a girl she is pretty smart. Anyway you got more than my WHOLE ALLOWINCE! By a lot! But dont worry I'm not mad. I have a house so I guess it comes out even. Jared says you dont need a house because in Africa it never gets cold. Mother says you probably DO have a house but not a very nice one, and theres a lot of other stuff you dont have. She likes your drawings. They go on the frigerator. For a while anyhow. I like your drawings too. But you dont need to send the Bible verses anymore. I'm in 2nd grade and thats old enough to know better. I know all about Santa Claus too. I'm the youngest, so now all of us here are done with church. We still do presents though. You dont think THAT will ever stop do you? I hope not. That reminds me, Mother said to ask questions.

Do they mix chemicals in 5th grade in Africa? What do you do when it rains? Does your Mother always repeat herself?

Live long and prosper! Follow the prime directive!

(This was Bobby by the way. Not Spock.)

This was the letter as Ashley found it that evening, placed in the exact center of the kitchen table with a pen on top of it, moments after dinner had been cleared and directly before that final putting away of the house, heralding the onset of bedtime. It was a letter to that kid in Africa. D-something, Ashley thought, trying to recall the name. Mom had asked her to add a few lines, further instructing her to remember to ask questions. As if she didn't already know that?

Ashley couldn't *imagine* what questions to ask that wouldn't sound *every* bit as canned as the ones she had asked the *previous* month, when she had done this the *first* time. She couldn't imagine what to say. She read what Bobby and Mom had written. Then she shook her head and smiled a little. Bobby. She loved him. He would never change.

But *Mom's* letter? Awful. Canned! Absolutely 15,000 percent canned. All at once, Ashley felt sorry for this kid … *Dieu*-something. … Ah! There it was, printed on the letter. *Dieudonné*. Ashley saw what Mom was doing to poor Dieudonné. Getting rid of the boy. Handing over the letter—handing over *everything*—to Bobby.

Bobby. Bobby got all of Mom!

At the same time—Ashley sensed the contradiction only faintly, like a whisper that goes silent before you can stop talking to hear what was said—what *was* it with Mom these days? She acted like *everybody's* business was *her* business. Did Mom think that she, Ashley, didn't see her come into school that afternoon during lunch? Another conference with Mrs. Holloway?

And Mom wasn't the only one. *Lots* of moms were coming in for conferences with the teachers these days. Her friends reported snippets of what was said: "intervention," "proactive" something-or-other, and—Ashley's personal favorite—"positive behavior modeling." Every time Ashley saw one of *those* posters taped on the walls at school (always some cute animal—a panda or a tiger or something like that—telling the children to be good) she just wanted to rip the stupid thing down and throw it on the floor and stomp on it. Finally find out what detention was like.

Just like that, Ashley found the words she wanted. She grabbed the pen and wrote to Dieudonné what little she thought was worth saying.

Hey Dieudonne,

It's Ashley. You remember me, of course. How is school going for you? Do you have bullies in your school? What do you do about them?

Love, your foster sister,

Ashley

Ashley glanced over her letter. Satisfied with it, she went to bed.

Just before one o'clock in the morning, Henry came down to the kitchen for a little ice cream. Sex, he told himself (and not for the first time), was like ice cream. Even when it's bad, it's pretty damn good. And tonight's had been particularly good, despite the neighbor's dog barking several times in the middle of everything. "Let each task be paid in full," Marlene had somehow managed to mumble when he asked her to speed up the pace just a touch. And boy did she ever. Henry giggled. The ice cream from the freezer was good, too. Häagen-Dazs Vanilla Bean? Impossible to beat.

He saw something on the kitchen table. It was a letter to that kid Marlene had wanted to sponsor. Lived somewhere in Africa, Henry was pretty sure. He read what his wife and kids had written. He smiled, nodded, wrote "Happy Birthday, Kid!" at the bottom, and went back upstairs to bed.

Henry was asleep; Marlene was not.

Before they'd started, Henry had put the TV on. This was standard procedure, drowning out any noises the kids might hear. The TV had been playing that show Bobby liked, *Star Trek*, the one with that handsome William Shatner in his gold and black captain's suit and (in Marlene's secret opinion) the even handsomer Leonard Nimoy—Mr. Spock—so dark and tall and cool in his compelling logic. The last thing Marlene had been aware of, before Henry's hand had started circling her like the USS Enterprise orbiting an alien planet, was a troop of red shirts beaming down to certain doom.

A reasonable amount of time later, the show, too, had reached a climax, and Marlene's awareness of the TV returned in time to hear Mr. Spock say, "… but does our involvement here also constitute a violation of the prime directive?"

Marlene turned to Henry to ask him what that meant, the prime directive. But he'd already left. For the kitchen, no doubt, and his ritual after-the-fact ice cream.

She turned off the TV; the show was over. Henry returned and crawled into bed.

"Henry?" Marlene asked. "What's the prime directive?"

"Why do you ask?"

"Spock said something about it." She paused and added, "Bobby, too."

Henry's eyes were already closed. He yawned, then mumbled, "It's a guiding principle of Starfleet that prohibits its members from interfering with the natural development of alien civilizations."

Through the window, everything looked small in the moonlight. Marlene put on her slippers and went downstairs. She put on her coat. Stepping outside, she looked up to see the stars, so bright. Somewhere—out there, thataway, the Final Frontier—Captain Kirk had saved the galaxy from another calamity.

A noise from behind startled her. Mr. Kinsley, the new neighbor with the dog, was pulling his trash can down his driveway to the curb. He stopped when he saw Marlene, the echo of his trash can dissipating into the cold air.

Cautiously, Mr. Kinsley walked up. He stared into space, and Marlene did as well.

"Quite a night," he said.

"Yes. Very quiet," she said. "Very peaceful."

"I know."

A few moments passed.

"Listen," Mr. Kinsley said. "About the dog. I'll make sure she's quiet."

"That will be fine, Mr. Kinsley," said Marlene. "Good night."

"Good night."

Marlene went inside. In the kitchen, she warmed some milk for herself and read the letter to Dieudonné while she drank. Then she set the letter down, washed up, put the glass and pan away, and went upstairs to bed.

In the morning, over breakfast, she had Bobby seal Dieudonné's letter along with the monthly check into the self-addressed stamped envelope provided by Food for the Hungry. She had him put the envelope in the pile of outgoing letters intended for the mailbox. Then she drove Bobby to school.

After dropping off her son, Marlene returned home. She opened the envelope and ripped up the check inside. Then she wrote out a new envelope to Food for the Hungry and placed the letter into it. She then sealed it, stamped it, and set it back in the outgoing pile. Then she opened this envelope as well, removed the letter, and, with a souvenir magnet from Martha's Vineyard, secured it to the refrigerator door. Finally, she ripped up the letter and tossed all of it into the kitchen trash.

There was much to do today. To the list, Marlene mentally added two phone calls.

# for Erin

Re-reading a well-written story can often be fruitful for anyone, especially if their life has somehow changed since the last reading. Fiction is non-fiction, re-organized—and a story, like a painting, is completed in the mind of the audience. A story's value will therefore change between people, and even with the same person between one time in their life and the next. (Which is why I hold things like a Best Picture Oscar in a state, not of contempt, but shall we say of healthy skepticism.)

But in the case of a writer, this phenomenon of reading a story and getting something new out of it is modified into something akin to professional interest. For me, it's so bad that I just can't read anymore. Not like I used to. It's an occupational hazard. When I read now—including things I'm reading for the first time and ought to be just enjoying—my mind isn't on the plot. It's on the author's choices: the narrative voice, the diction, the physical descriptions, the dialog. Hell, even the punctuation doesn't escape scrutiny.

Then, sometimes, I can get a whole story from a re-visit—especially if it comes at the hand of some other story element idea. (This is different than writing in the voice of another author.)

It happened like this. I was writing a letter to our sponsored child one day, when it occurred to me that many orgs that help impoverished children trying to live in desperate nations are religious in nature. This made me think of the Lutzes, who all seem to be in the midst of religious transition, and I in turn recalled "Dear Alexandros" by John Updike, in which an out-of-touch man who lives in New York City writes a letter to his sponsored child living in Greece. (What a scene.) The Lutz family, I thought, could very plausibly have a sponsored child of their own. What would a letter to such a child look like, if written by Bobby? Marlene? Henry? Ashley? Heck, this story was practically going to write itself!

So after a quick revisit of "Alexandros," I started writing. I soon discovered that I didn't really have a story. Not yet. What was to tie these letters together into something larger than themselves? I was stuck, in need of inspiration. Usually I have to wait for lightning to strike before I can begin a story. This can take a long time. But if I'm in the middle of a story, actively looking for lightning, then it usually doesn't take so long. I just listen extra carefully to everything around me.

With my antennae up, I stumbled upon the so-called Prime Directive from *Star Trek*. Right away, I realized this was the missing piece. Marlene was interfering in alien civilizations—or so it would appear to her. And it wasn't just the poor kid's civilization she was interfering in, either. There was also Ashley's environment. Her school. So Marlene decides she has a couple phone calls to make.

Not many in our group write about children, but Erin Price-Jones does. Her voice keeps everything youthful. Channeling this perspective was helpful to me in getting Bobby's and Ashley's voices right when they wrote their letters. I think that Ashley, especially, would fit well into an Erin Price-Jones creation.

# situation on pier 38

Something about the way Buzzy says it. "Shipment." It isn't sitting right with me. Hell, this whole job isn't sitting right with me. I reach into my jacket pocket and rub between thumb and fingers the paper of the letter concealed there, feeling its linen texture and finding the corner that got bent at some point before it was given to me. The letter is handwritten. Prettiest handwriting I've ever seen. I've read it maybe half a dozen times, and I'm getting ready to take it out and read it once more when he says it again: "Wanna go to Lacey's after this shipment?"

*Shipment.* As if we're fuckin' Amazon or something.

I try to get this point across to him. "Buzzy," I say, probably a little louder than I needed to. Buzzy is deaf in his right ear and blind in his left eye. Or maybe it's the reverse. I can never remember. I just talk loudly in his general direction and hope for the best. "Buzzy," I say again. "A shipment is something that's fuckin' *normal*. What we're doing right now? This is *not* normal. You understand? This here situation is fuckin' very far from normal."

"Fog," he says, summing up that situation quite aptly, poking a stumpy finger at the white mist that's been sinking down on us for the last ten minutes.

Very good, genius. Very astute of you. Fog.

But it's hot. The fog is *hot*. Yet my skin is cold. I feel like a fish that just got pulled out of the river and slapped onto the pier, and it knows right through its cold skin and into its bones that it's food.

Cold skin and bones, indeed. I cringe. And this sudden mist—it's just one piece of whatever it is that's going on around here. And it's not the weirdest piece, either. No, sir. Not by a long walk on a short pier. Things are missing. Things like ships. And people.

The mist started coming down as Buzzy and me were making our way down to the river from the street. Like I said, this was about ten minutes ago.

That's fifteen minutes ahead of schedule. I'm not taking any chances with this fuckin' job. But even before we got down to this deserted pier, the emptiness of the place was already something you could feel. Palpable, like. I mean, sure, it's late. But this is the city. People are around. I mean, people are *usually* around. Tonight, nobody is around.

And it's not just people that are missing. There's also the lights. Upriver and across the bay, you can still see the lights reflecting off the ripples in the water. But look inside a block or two of Pier 38, where we are, and the river is utterly black. As we were walking to the dock just now, the windows of the buildings were going black one by one as we passed, like the darkness was marking our progress.

Sounds, too, have gone missing. I can still hear the lapping of the water. And when he's got something to say, I can hear Buzzy. Everything else is muted. It's all muted, actually. When I scolded Buzzy just now, I heard myself like I was talking into a pillow. The earth has been silenced by whatever it was that did away with the lights and the people.

And then there's the sky. Just as the letter in my pocket had predicted, the moon is rising. But with all this fog, I shouldn't be able to see the moon. Yet there it is. And I know it's just a trick of the moisture in the air—but the moon is splitting. It's splitting in two. The moon is now a pair of pallid yellow eyes, and unless I've completely lost my fuckin' mind, those eyes are watching me. I ain't lookin' at 'em. No, sir.

Buzzy is standing at the edge of the pier. He's saying something. I go over to him.

"Lacey's," he whines. "I wanna go to Lacey's. I wanna—"

Dammit, he's still talking about the fuckin' bar. "Jesus, Buzzy," I say, "when we get to the bar, I'll fuckin' buy you your bottle of Keystone Light tonight. Just—"

Then he turns, and I see his face. The man is scared. He's scared spitless. He was blabbing just now for no other reason than he's got no fuckin' idea what to do with his fear. I can't blame him; I sure as hell don't know what to do with mine. Fifteen minutes ago, I was looking forward to ordering the biggest steak that Lacey's has got on the menu. Now scared is all I've got room for.

My hand is still in my jacket pocket, fumbling around with the letter. The fog is thick and getting thicker, but there's a halogen lamp overhead, and its grainy orange glow cuts through just enough that I can probably still read.

I pull out the letter. It's addressed to the dock station, put to the attention of my boss, Herbert Kessler. Mr. Kessler is the loading and unloading foreman. The paper the letter is written on is thick, almost leathery, like some kind of old-fashioned parchment. Maybe it was cut from the same stock they wrote the Declaration of Independence on. From the handwriting, the theory fits. The penmanship is elegant, almost ... calligraphic. If that's a word. Pretty. Nobody writes like that anymore.

By this point I've got the thing practically memorized, but I squint my eyes and read it again.

23 August

My dear Sir—

I trust that this missive finds you well, and that all your dealings with my barrister, Mr. Porter, have been to your satisfaction. The shipment he has discussed with you shall presently be arriving at your facility. Whatever details exist regarding time and place, I am certain Mr. Porter has advised you accurately. I wish now to emphasize the importance of following to the letter any guidance my humble servant has given you, no matter how unusual said instructions might appear. Should you yourself, due to status, be inappropriately suited to the carrying out of such menial tasks, and should you prefer to delegate these to a subordinate, I will not presume to question you in your professional capacity. Be certain, however, that all instructions are fully and precisely conveyed to any such deputies. In closing, I ask that you trust me when I say that the faithful execution of your duties, as laid out by Mr. Porter, will result in your generous and appropriate compensation. Follow these exhortations well, Mr. Kessler, and do not fail. For my pain is sweet, the dark is young, and there is much to do beneath a swift and rising moon.

Believe you me,

Yours affectionately,

Nickolas von Neumann

I gently fold the letter and return it to my inside jacket pocket. *No matter how unusual said instructions might appear.* Who talks like this? Why, that chummiest of chums, Nickolas von Fuckin Believe You Me Neumann! That's who! An affectionate fellow of the gilded tier genteel.

Sure. I'll fuckin' believe him that.

For maybe the tenth time since sitting in Mr. Kessler's shithole of an office that afternoon, watching his pasty white face bead with sweat as he went over Mr. Porter's "said instructions" again and again with me, I mentally review the first of them: *Immediately board the ship without hesitation upon the first opportunity, for there shall not be a second.* Mr. Kessler had made me recite that one verbatim three times before going on to the next. What on God's dirtball of a planet have Buzzy and I gotten ourselves into?

The two of us are standing at the edge of the pier. We're looking south, downriver—the direction whence come all good ships, laden with the prize possessions of the Earth: food, spices, books, furniture, car parts, electronics, dildos. Someday (believe you me!), a lock in the Panama Canal is going to bust, or there's going to be a fuck-up in the Suez Canal of biblical proportions, and then what will happen to the world when all those dildos can't get through? It is indeed a most very important fuckin' position that Buzzy and I hold in the world order.

And so here we stand at the water's edge, awaiting a shipment that, given the hoopla, I can only assume in all fuckin' probability must be greater in value than even a boatload of dildos. We're staring into the night at a dark river that ripples along industrial shores, and although the preordained hour of arrival is rapidly approaching, one thing is clear, even through the mist: We are staring at a river that is 100 percent devoid of ships.

Buzzy is holding his pocket watch out in front of him. Now he's brought it comically close to his face. Now he's holding it out again at arm's length. He squints. Then he nudges me with an elbow. "Three minutes," he says, and hands the watch to me.

The time is 11:57.

This is the first I've been allowed to hold Buzzy's watch. It's heavier than I would've thought. It's gold, at least in color. I mean, I doubt it's real gold. But I like to imagine that Buzzy's watch is his one great treasure on earth, handed down through generations of half-blind, half-deaf grandfathers. To tell the truth, I feel kind of honored that he's letting me hold it. Or maybe Buzzy is just so scared out of his mind, he doesn't know what the fuck he's doing. I hand him back the watch, and we continue staring downriver at nothing.

Or ... almost nothing. Buzzy points. I see it, too. About one thousand yards off, on the river, there's a blacker patch on top of the black. The water out there has become smooth, but deeply indented. It's a streak of calm, a huge depression in the water, about a hundred and fifty feet in length, and it's moving toward us at maybe ten knots. I'm thinking, *This is what water underneath ships must look like all the time.* We just never see it, because the ship's in the way. Then I'm thinking, *But if there were an invisible ship, this is exactly what the water would look like.*

What a fuckin' stupid idea. Invisible ship. I look over to get Buzzy's reaction to things. But he's not there. My heart skips a beat, and I look around wildly. Then I spot him standing about fifteen feet behind me, still pointing out at the water. The little shit-stain had backed away.

I look where he's pointing. The black patch is getting closer. I look at it coming toward us, and I decide maybe I better back up, too.

Together, we watch the black patch as it slides along the water, closer and closer, until it finally slips in along the edge of the pier. I don't need a watch to know the hour of its arrival. The hour is precisely midnight.

I look over the side of the pier. There it is: a stretch of smooth, lifeless water that stands in place without a single ripple to mar its glasslike surface. Behind me, Buzzy is whimpering. I'm pretty sure he's just talking to himself, and I'm pretty sure the subject matter is the bar. I let it go.

*Immediately board the ship without hesitation upon the first opportunity, for there shall not be a second.*

Ship? Yes, ship. The ship might be invisible, but imaginary it is not. The ship is real; the ship is there. I know it. I know it for a stone-cold fact. Partially, I know because I can hear it. A gentle, rhythmic creaking is coming from the empty space in front of me. Like all other sounds on this accursed night, it's muted. But it's there. What else would be the source of that sound? And how else to explain the water?

Mostly, however, I know the ship is real because the air is suddenly thick with the hoary, briny smell of old wood and wet rope.

For the moment, I let all the clues and their implications slide: the smell of wood, the creaking sounds, the aged parchment of the letter, the archaic speech patterns of that dearest of affable fellows, Mr. von Neumann. For the moment, it is enough to know that the ship is real. The ship is there. And we need to get on board. Right now.

There must be something to tell us what to do. I scan the pier but see nothing. I am desperate. I'm shocked at my desperation. I'm frightened of the prospect of this ship. At the same time, I am gripped with a compulsion to find my way onto it. Against my will, my gaze is drawn up to the hovering mist, to the twin yellow eyes that used to be the moon. The eyes are still there, looking down on me. I resolve again not to look at them, and I tear my gaze away.

For the second time tonight, Buzzy is pointing at something. I have to admit, for having only one eye, the dude is pretty good at spotting stuff. I look where he points. Down the pier, something is happening. The mist is shifting around, dancing an absurd kind of waltz. Then the movements become more localized, and the mist coagulates into definite shapes. Over the next minute, Buzzy and I watch in amazement as wet clods of air come together to form a series of white planks all held together by a network of silky, gossamer rope.

It's a bridge. A gangway to the ship. It leads about twenty feet up and over the blackness of the water and into the nothingness of space. And all I can think is, *You gotta fuckin' be kidding me.*

"You gotta fuckin be kidding me!" Buzzy says. (At bottom, dock workers are the same the world over.) "*YOU! Gotta FUCKIN'! Be KIDDING! ME!*" he repeats. "You think I'm going up there, you're fuckin' nuts! Nuts, do you hear me? Nuts!"

Exhausted from delivering a speech of such prodigious fuckin' length, Buzzy wipes a forearm across his brow and looks up and down the pier, as if hoping to see someone standing around; someone who could bear witness to this homily of unprecedented length and wit, before the moment slips away forever into the realm of legend.

"Listen, Buzzy." I point along the direction of the ghostly bridge. "There's a ship there. It's real, and I'm going to prove it to you. I'm going to walk that fuckin' bridge, and I want you to follow me. All you gotta do is follow. Can you do that? Can you just fuckin' follow me?"

"You're nuts."

"Maybe. But I'm going first. And if I fall into the water, you can laugh your ass off at me all the way to Lacey's and dance on the bar singing who's yer daddy when we get there. But if I get up to the top of that bridge, and I tell you to come, can you do that, huh? Can you do that for a pal?"

Buzzy looks over at my invisible ship. Then he looks at me. "Sure," he says. "I can do that."

The bastard is giggling. Yeah, yeah, yeah. The dipshit just wants to watch me fall into the water. But that's not going to happen, because there's a *ship* floating at the dock. There *is*. And if the ship is real, then the bridge is real, too. And it's not just any ship, either. It's …

I approach the bridge of mist. The not-so-solid steps, held together by the not-so-there ropes, lead the way into darkness for about twenty feet, then disappear.

Surely, this is our one chance to board the ship. And if it *is* our one chance, then we won't get a second. This has to work. Not only that, but the bridge has to stay solid long enough not just for *me* to make it up to the ship, but for Buzzy as well. Because I remember the rest of the instructions Mr. Kessler made me recite, and I'll be goddamned if I'm doing this fuckin' job alone.

I put my foot out. Gently, I place it down onto a cottony white plank. At first, there's nothing. Then, as I shift my weight forward, I start to feel it—a slight, springy resistance. Once, when I was a kid, I flew on an airplane. I remember looking out the window at the tops of the clouds, wondering what it would be like to get out there and climb around on them. The sensation that I imagined is exactly what I'm feeling right now.

Now that I've taken a step, the rest is no big deal. I don't look up at the moon (which is still a nasty fuckin' pair of yellow eyes), and I don't look down at the bridge of mist, either. I just look straight ahead. And before I get a chance to yell something back over my shoulder at Buzzy—something helpful and supportive like "Eat me, you little shit!"—I'm here at the end …

… where there is, of course, nothing.

I am standing high above the water of an empty dock in the middle of the night like a fuckin' maniac escaped from a loony bin. Vaguely, like he's on the other end of the universe, I hear Buzzy yelling something. I ignore him. This whole leap-of-faith thing is old hat now, and I'm all in. I suppose someone could argue that I could *see* the fuckin' bridge. Right now, my foot is hovering over nothing but air. And it's a long fuckin' way down to a hard fuckin' landing in the water if I'm wrong about this. But whoever sent the bridge sent the ship. There's just no getting around the fuckin' logic of the situation.

I set my foot down. Immediately, I'm standing on the deck of a thoroughly visible, thoroughly solid ship. Not only that, but the fog is lifted, at least up to the crow's nest. Everything beyond and above is clouded, but the ship itself is crystal clear.

And it's gorgeous. My god, it's beautiful. I'm standing on the quarterdeck of a tall ship, sailed right out of the pages of history. I used to build models of these things from kits. This here is what you call a full-rigged man-o'-war. She's a good sixty meters in length, with fore, main, and mizzenmast. There's gotta be a thousand square meters of sail on her. The freeboard is at least twenty feet. Considering the massive draft on a ship like this, she's likely to be carrying major tonnage. Unloading her could take all night. There will be substantial crew. But where—?

Behind me, a scream rends the air. I'd forgotten all about Buzzy.

I turn around. He's made it to the ship—sort of. He's half over the edge, grasping at the deck, yelling frantically, trying to scrape his way on board. That damn bridge must have given out just as he was about to embark.

I run to the side of the ship and get down close to him. He's slipping fast. Most of him is already below the plane of the deck. I grab him at the forearms. His mouth splutters as he tries to speak.

"Don't try to talk," I say. "I've got ya." I'm on my ass, pulling at his arms. I plant a foot on the siderail. "Can you swing a leg up?" His eyes are a pair of cue balls. One of them—the one on my left—is pointed slightly in toward his nose. Okay, then: it's blind on his right, deaf on the left. *Deaf on the left.* It kind of rhymes. Now maybe I'll be able to remember. I'm still pulling, still yelling at him to bring up a leg.

Finally, he gets a foot up onto the deck. It's all I need. "Push down on the foot, Buzzy," I say. "Come on. You can do this." I give a massive pull. A second leg appears, and then he's up.

He crawls onto the deck, panting; I roll over onto my back. We're lying side-by-side, staring up at a ceiling of fog that rests like a blanket over the tops of the masts. It's hard to believe that just a few minutes ago I was scared out of my mind. All I feel now is the quiet, strong calm of the sea. That and a sense that I am here for a purpose. I look for the wicked yellow eyes that used to be the moon, but they are gone.

Between heavy breaths, Buzzy squeaks out, "Holy … Mother … of God."

"Crazy, right?" I say.

Buzzy doesn't say a damn thing.

After a time, I notice he's got a finger pointing silently up toward the top of the mainmast. There's a flag up there. It's got three horizontal stripes—a blue, a red, and a yellow. In the center of the flag is the black silhouette of a bird with outstretched wings, and on top of the bird is something like a dome. Maybe it's meant to be a church. On top of the dome is a cross. Strange, though, how the cross is upside down.

I stand up and scan the length of the ship for the crew, and I still don't find a soul. I tell Buzzy to get the hell up. I stare again at that upside-down cross hanging in the sky, and I wonder where in hell those yellow eyes went.

Buzzy has gotten up. "Let's do this shipment," he says. "I wanna go. I wanna—"

"Yeah, yeah," I say, "you wanna go to Lacey's. I know. Jesus. C'mon." Fuckin' Buzzy and his fuckin' one-track mind.

I lead him aft, to the end of the quarterdeck, where a dozen stairs make a steep descent to the main deck. Buzzy starts to follow me down, but I'm too fast for him. Although the steps are only slightly deeper than the rungs of a ladder, I easily descend them, almost gliding to the deck. I guess that spooked him. He's decided to turn around and come down ass-backward, using both hands to hold on to the steps. At one point he grabs my shoulder, then hops down past the last couple of steps, landing with a little bit of a bump. Buzzy's a clumsy sort of guy, but I suppose he does all right for himself.

He's staring around with his mouth open. I understand. The deck of a sailing vessel can be a confusing place. Besides myriad wooden casks and boxes and the usual masses of rope coiled here and there and going every which way, I also notice three tall spars jutting up from the deck. They're separated from each other by about five yards. Each spar is outfitted with a rope-and-pulley system and sits on what appears to be a round wooden turntable. On each turntable is another coil of rope, fastened at one end to the pulley. The ship had come in starboard to the pier, and the spars are only a few yards inboard from that edge. Farther inboard from each spar, aligned exactly at amidships and spaced evenly with the spars, are three hatches, each about four foot square, battened down with a motley assortment of wooden bolts and latches.

Buzzy taps me on the shoulder. "What now?" he says.

I try to recall the remaining instructions that Mr. Kessler had coached me on earlier that afternoon. But it's difficult. All at once, time feels different on this ship, like everything that I did prior to getting on it happened while I was still a very young man. It's not that I feel old, exactly. An old person is near their end. No, this is more like I've simply been here forever. The ship seems to possess some tonic quality. I feel a new man—if *new* can refer to something with its entire life before it, regardless of what has come before.

Or maybe it's just the salty air. Whatever it is, the sensation passes.

With a little effort, I remember what is necessary. That most humble of servants, Mr. Porter, had imparted three further instructions.

There's: *Unfasten the hatches three and, opening, tend the ropes to their hooks.* Toss down the free ends. Now that I've seen the spars and the pulleys, this starts to make some sense.

Then we've got: *Molest not the crates, nor pay good heed to any smell or noise that issues from the depths.* Lovely.

And finally, my favorite: *Mind the gybe.*

I spell all this out to Buzzy, but he barely comprehends. It doesn't matter. Buzzy is a pair of hands. What I *don't* point out to him is that none of these instructions talk about *getting off the damned ship.* I guess we'll cross that bridge when we come to it?

I set Buzzy to the task of unfastening the latches on the hatch door farthest aft while I take the forward one. I finish first and take care of the center hatch. Then I go to remove the door itself. It looks quite heavy, but with a stout pull I easily move the square panel aside, as if it weighs nothing.

The sounds come first, but what squeezes my gut is the smell. Accosted by the rancid stench of decay, I stagger to the rail of the ship. Buzzy is already here. We puke our guts into the river.

Buzzy wipes his mouth. "Are we done?"

I wait for a moment, panting, making sure no more is coming.

More comes. I wait another minute, then I wipe my mouth. "Yeah, I think so."

"Thank God," he says. "Let's go to Lacey's."

"You lazy ass, I meant that I'm done puking! We've only opened one hatch! And there's stuff we gotta do with the ropes!"

While Buzzy whines, I stand there, leaning against the rail, dizzy from the barfing, trying to think. What's this all about? Let's say we "tend the ropes to their hooks." And then we "toss the free ends down." *Then* what? Aren't we supposed to be unloading cargo? But Mr. Kessler never said boo about cargo. None of this is making a whole lot of sense. I guess that's work for ya.

Buzzy starts in. "I'm not gonna—"

"Oh, you most definitely fuckin' are! You and I are going back to open those other hatches and take care of those ropes. And when we're all finished and the job is done, *then* we're going to Lacey's. And I'll buy you as many bottles of Keystone Light as you can fuckin' drink. Got it?"

But myself, I'm not drinking a goddamn thing tonight. I'll just be glad when this accursed night is over. And when I show up to work tomorrow morning, I'm asking Mr. Kessler for a raise.

I slide away the other two hatch doors. Each time, the sound from below gets a little louder. It's a low moaning. At first, I think the wind is stirring around down there. But there is no wind. Then I notice that at the rim of each square opening there's a loop of rope strung through a block-and-tackle gear, neatly hooked through a screw eye bolt. I glance up at the pulley at the end of the rope hanging from the spar. Then I look at the coil of rope sitting on the turntable at the base of the spar. It all fits together now.

I connect the block and tackle to the pulley and throw the free end of the coiled rope below. I repeat this for each of the three hatches. Then I make the mistake of looking a little too hard down inside one of them.

I had wondered where the hovering evil yellow eyes had gone when they'd left the sky. Now I think I know. And it turns out they've got friends. Scores of eyes that I simply know have never seen the sun peer up at me through the black murk of the ship. Like blobs of paint on a Jackson Pollock creation, they are splattered among a labyrinth of oversized crates at least six or seven feet to a side. I guess I've found the crew.

I rush to the side of the ship, ready to empty my stomach again, but of course that's already been done. Buzzy comes over. He's whining, and he wants to know if we're finally finished.

"I don't know, Buzzy," I pant. "I don't—"

A dull, slow scrape comes from deep below the deck. The sound is repeated twice more. Then all three ropes connecting the pulleys above to the ship's hold below go taut at once. The mechanisms click as they bear a load. The moaning of the crew becomes a demonic chorus. The infernal baritones take up a rhythmic chant, and with each beat the ropes are pulled and their length shortened. Something's coming up.

I watch in awed silence as three wooden crates emerge from the hold. I see now how things work. The spars and pulley are like a crane operated by the ghoulish crew below. But the mechanism by which the crates are to get onto the pier still eludes me. Mr. Kessler never said a word about us moving them. In fact, he made it quite clear that Buzzy and I were not to touch them. *Molest not the crates.*

The chant of the diabolic choir quickens, becoming wilder. With each repetition of their inarticulate yawps, I feel the ship shift. The motion is slight but growing. It seems impossible, but I believe the crew is rocking the ship. Then I remember the turntables. Too late, I fear, I also recollect Mr. Porter's final admonition. *Mind the gybe.*

I look around for Buzzy. He has wandered off again. Also, the yellow eyes have returned—this time, however, not to the sky. I see them everywhere before me, as if through a pane of smoky glass.

The ship is quite definitely rocking now, and I understand exactly what is about to happen. The cranes will spin on their turntables, bringing the cargo around in a wide arc terminating over the pier. The crew will then lower the crates with the pulleys, and this is how the demon ship will ingeniously unload itself.

I turn to watch. With a final, mighty ululation from below, the three cranes spin. I duck—and that's when I spot Buzzy. The fool is standing between two of the hatches, his idiot mouth agape at the scene.

*Mind the gybe.*

"Buzzy! Duck!"

Too late. One of the crates, the middle one, clocks Buzzy on the head. Perhaps he's got a plate in his skull he never told me about, or perhaps the ancient wood of the crates is rotting. One way or another, it is Buzzy who survives and the crate that gets its innards spilled onto the deck.

Buzzy waddles about. I yell at him to get down, but he's punch-drunk. He leans over a pile of the whatever-it-is that has spilled from the crate, and he grabs two fistfuls of it.

It's dirt. Someone has paid money to transport *dirt*. Crates and crates of everloving dirt. To my disgust, Buzzy sinks his face into his hands as if to smell the stuff. The guy must have been whacked completely off his rocker. When he re-emerges, his face is smeared in a livid green-black sludge that looks as if it had bubbled its way out of a sewer through the force of its own maculate self-repro-duction.

As he totters about the open shaft leading to the hold below, I draw in a breath intended to warn him of his peril. But the essence of the soil is in that breath, and my mind is turned from its purpose. For when the imbecile comes to the edge of the precipice and plunges through, shrieking, I immediately ap-prehend my compulsion to descend to the hold below not as an attempt at res-cue but rather as an elective yet inexorable step toward my destiny. A destiny that, ever since the moon split into a pair of yellow eyes, has been driving me forward, filling my body with preternatural strength and reinvigorating my mind with its own forgotten potency while wresting from the very fabric of the surrounding space the substance and soul of undying existence. Even my hunger is gone, replaced with an exquisite thirst the like of which I have never before felt. All that remains to me is the hidden purpose for which I have been guided to this place. I am turned—but my work is not finished. I must complete my descent.

My search leads me forward to previously unexplored regions of the ship. Beyond the foremast, I find a wheelhouse. I am about to enter when I spot the ship's figurehead jutting out below the bowsprit. The outline of the figure—I imagine a mermaid or a buxom Jenny Lind, her fair bosom stuffed into a bodice, pointing the way across the waters to the comfort and safety of a distant shore—creates a porous, gray border against the white of the lingering mist. But as I approach, I note a few sinewy tendrils that depend like thin ropes from the base of the figurehead. Arriving at the bow, I see the fragile and emaciated shape of the figure itself.

Secured to the spar with several loops of rope is a rotting corpse, cut in half at the waist. The tendrils are its entrails. A moldering layer of pallid flesh still clings to the skull, from which a single eye, lodged deep in its socket, forever scans the waters below.

I return to the wheelhouse. Entering, I find another corpse, no more than scant bones, strapped with a leathern belt to the ship's wheel. One skeletal hand still grasps at the knobby handles of the wheel; the other holds a heavy poleax. Its shaft is wooden, plated down the center with a tooled metal; the hammer opposite the axe head sports a cruel hook, while the head itself is curved and long, as if meant to hew multiple foes with a single stroke. A narrow stairway in the corner leads below, and I descend into the dark of the ship's hold.

The stairs give way to a tunnel-like corridor strewn with soil. From its far end arises again the demoniac outcry of the crew as they prepare to unload another trio of crates. I chuckle quietly to myself that not so long ago these ethereal harmonies produced in me the useless sensation of fear. I listen for a time in rapt joy, then proceed in my exploration.

The tunnel is lit by a thin blue glow that emanates from a series of chambers on either side of the corridor. An investigation of these rooms reveals the dilapidated remains of bunks on which the crew once slept. Clumps of bioluminescent mushrooms—the source of the feeble light that bleeds throughout the hold of the ship—now bunk in piles of rich earth.

I come to the end of the corridor, where an enormous wooden door blocks the way forward, filling the entire height and breadth of the passage. The chant of the chorus on the other side has grown so loud that silence is not necessary for stealth, yet it is only with the utmost caution that I push at the gate.

Slowly, the door yields. Inch by inch, I compel my head through the opening. I stand at the edge of a precipice (it is perhaps good that I did not rush forward wantonly), and I am looking down into a yellow hell. Here, the animated remains of the dead lift countless crates to an outer world they surely knew once and never will again. For although the hold opens to the night, no light from above, nor even the blue fungal glow from the corridors, is permitted to penetrate. The denizens of this nautical Tartarus are doomed to labor by whatever scraps of light seep from the luminescence of the tears that fall from their jaundiced eyes, predicating what little vision the damned possess on the contingency of their eternal suffering.

As quietly as I opened the gate, I close it again.

To my right is a bedchamber I have not yet explored. In a far corner of that room, another set of stairs leads deeper into the bowels of the vessel. As I descend, the noise from the hull diminishes, even to the point of absolute silence, as I alight on what must be the bottom-most level of the ship.

I stand in a single square chamber. The air is very close and the silence deep. The room glows a deep red. The left side of the chamber is cloaked in shadow, but along the wall to the right rests a single crate. Above it, affixed to the wall with an ornate golden sconce, is what appears to be an eternal presence candle.

I had seen one of these once, when I had occasion to attend a Roman Catholic church. The eternal burning of the candle inside the red glass container is meant to symbolize the undying presence of their god.

This candle before me, however, is no church plaything. Where I had expected the vapid fragrance of paraffin, I am instead titillated by a sharp, metallic tinge. As I draw near, I see that the container is of clear glass and that whatever burns inside casts its red pall over the room. Coming closer, I stand on tiptoe to peer inside, where a black wick burns atop a bubbling column of blood.

The crate underneath the candle stands open. Filling it almost to the rim is that same soil, so virile and fecund, that had earlier spilled onto the deck. An indentation in the surface of the soil suggests that something had recently lain here.

I may have been standing like a supplicant here before this unholy shrine for an hour or a minute; I cannot know. It is as if time has once again been adjusted, and I am held in check. A further indeterminate span of time transpires before a voice behind me—ancient, infectious, and large with malignancy—breaks my trance:

"*Inter mortem et vitam.*"

It's Latin. Somehow, I know this. *In the midst of death, we are in life.*

I turn to behold the speaker. The man before me is tall and thin, then stout and wide; he is feeble, then young and strapping; he is a she, a young maiden; then a slave, a mewling infant, a raging tyrant, a priest.

"You are Nickolas von Neumann?" I ask.

"You may call me that," he says. His form has returned to that of a tall, gaunt man of unknowable years, his colorless skin held to his frame by the thinnest of tissue. "And what manner of thing are you?"

Again time is twisted, and the memories of my life flash in my mind.

"Correct, my friend," he says, referring to this stream of recollections, though I had not given them voice. "A man is naught but the connection of his memories. This you do not yet know but only dream."

"What now?" I say. He is drawing close his face; I am at once repulsed and intoxicated.

"Now, you wake."

When the pain comes, there is no pain at all, but a sweet blackness; and in the virile dirt, I sleep.

I sleep for less than an hour.

I sleep for more than four hundred years.

I sleep for an eternity.

When I wake, I wake to the sound of a steady ticking coming from somewhere on the ship.

Before me on the floor is a pile of bones. Forgetting these, I look down at myself to behold the corpus of my new creature, stretching out, testing the strength in my limbs and digits. I have had better; I have had worse. It will do. Behold, all things are become new! Yet nothing has passed away! It is time now to feed. It is *always* time to feed.

The ticking! It originates from near the base of the foremast. I rise through the hold of the ship, barely touching the floor beneath me, drunk with heightened perception, joyful at the rediscovery of the lightness of the undead.

As I pass by the hold, I hear the soothing weeping of my crew. I apprehend the mortal hour to be 3:38 a.m. The soil will have all been transferred to the pier by now. My ground forces will presently arrive to transport the soil to a new home. I will follow soon enough. Now, there is breakfast.

In the wheelhouse, I seize the poleax from the hand of my ship's first mate. Outside on the deck, I am delighted to discover that I have left myself an easy first meal.

"Nick!" Buzzy sputters. The fool is strapped to the foremast. "Nick! Help me!"

I am a kind master. Before cleaving him in two and replacing my ship's figurehead (the other had gotten a little tatty), I first drink of his blood. Only after thus soothing him do I remove from his pocket the beautiful golden timepiece. As I place it in my pocket, I must say that I feel almost honored.

And now, to the great city. As for my ship, it will cast off to await in distant waters such time as I have need of it. I foresee that it shall remain dormant for many years. The world is ripe for the harvest. And now, come to me, all you who are burdened. For my pain is sweet, the dark is young, and there is much to do beneath a swift and rising moon.

# for Dave

Given how much I owe my passion for writing to Stephen King (If you're a writer and you still haven't read *On Writing: A Memoir of the Craft*, whatcha waiting for?), I figured I had to try my hand at horror at least once.

In Bram Stoker's *Dracula*, we see the Count coming across the ocean on a spooky old ship laden with crates of Transylvanian soil in which he'd buried himself. We see the ship coming into port with no one sailing it (awesome); then, much later, we see the soil at Dracula's lovely new home. How'd it get there?

Meanwhile, in King's *Salem's Lot*, we see crates of soil arriving at the vampire's new digs, delivered by a couple of truck drivers who would've been well advised to have taken a different job that night. But where did the crates come from? How did they get from the ship to the dock? Neither story shows us what happened between the ship and the truck. I wanted to see how huge crates of soil got offloaded from a ship with a dead crew. If you, too, ever wondered about that, then I hope "Situation on Pier 38" satisfied your curiosity.

When it comes to writing, I have a confusing relationship to music. If I'm stuck, music can cause my mind to wander or at least loosen itself from its fixed moorings. If I'm feeling unmotivated to write, music can motivate me. Different kinds of music urge me toward different voices and stories. Prior to a writing session while working on *Black to Move and Draw*, I'd often let the Bernard Herrmann score from *Taxi Driver* put me in the noir mood. But unless the words are coming particularly easily for me that day, I find that I can't listen to music *while* writing—not if the music is something I myself started playing in the context of my own home. The familiarity of the tune and of the setting gets in the way. I much prefer the background noise (including, yes, music) found in taverns and upmarket bars and like places.

Often, a musical piece previously known to me (and randomly playing at whatever establishment I'm hunkering down in) will be just the right fuel to mentally feed me while writing a scene. Other times, like with "Situation," I need to find the music first (and then write at home). For this task, Spotify is invaluable. I searched—probably for "vampire music" or some such—and quickly found "The Absurd Waltz" by Hans Zimmer. Not only was the tune perfect, but in this case I found that keeping the music going while writing was doing wonderful things for my story. I kept imagining a movie (as I often do when writing) and wondering what would be happening on the screen while the music was playing. From time to time, sure, I'd need to kill the music when the prose got complicated. But mostly I wrote "Situation on Pier 38" with Hans Zimmer playing in the background.

I'd like to dedicate this story to David Craig, who brilliantly illustrated *Black to Move and Draw*. Like music, a picture can inspire, motivate, or embody an entire book. I absolutely adore anything that looks like it belongs on the cover of a gothic romance, especially if it involves a beautiful, haunted woman running from a beautiful, haunted house. Dave captured this when I asked him to illustrate a scene I wrote in which a topless (but tastefully so) character—Shannon—brandishes a sword from the height of a Harlem fire escape. I didn't necessarily expect him to balance Shannon on top of a railing, but, hey, three cheers for artistic license.

I don't know if Dave's writing would properly be called horror by the people who decide these things, but he definitely taps spooky forces. I can't wait to see how he depicts all his ideas when his first graphic novel comes out.

# vomiting somewhere south of worcester, mass

Perhaps one day, you tell yourself, it'll be funny—a nice little story, the kind you imagine other people telling their kids, in a bid for calm, will one day be a story for them to tell their own children—the "*baaaaack* and forth and *baaaaack* and forth and *baaaaack* and forth" issuing from behind you, from the back seat of your friend's Honda, the juvenile chant—an encore performance, by the way, its initially having been enacted in celebratory anticipation of, and now again in synchronized recollection of, the car ferry's putting out earlier that morning from Martha's Vineyard on its return transit to Hyannis Port and its littoral undulations as it rocked back and forth … and back … and forth … through the choppy Nantucket Sound waters, the mere herald ("*baaaaack* and forth and *baaaaack* …") of said rocking having catalyzed your first round of vomiting, the one that led you to the side of the boat and kept you there, that act's own encore now making its way up your esophagus—punching through the heavy, greasy car air (you'd briefly considered asking your friend to switch the car's ventilation setting to Fresh, but, you know, deck chairs on the Titanic and all that) and delivered, in a sing-song treble you thought you'd heard the last of the day you left grammar school behind, from two pairs of salty lips that munch upon a shared order of last night's fries (really, Dustin, those couldn't have been polished off last evening at dinner or this morning before we all piled into the cars; or they couldn't have been tossed last night after being turned down by your kid to leave room for the funnel cake; or—how about this one—the kids could've gone with the wives in the minivan?), all while you yourself sit there, towel wrapped around your head because what else was there to do with a towel (and, for that matter, what else had there been to do, period), silently pointing out to yourself in a manner rigorous yet, you hope, should things come to it, not overly confrontational, how the entire situation had never from the first been quite in complete keeping with your designs, your having accepted—cheerfully at first, and then a second time, and then once more, that final, third, acceptance attended by an almost subconscious skepticism you'd chalked up to a reaction to the perceived embarrassment hidden within an offer immediately embraced and yet continually repeated, as if your benefactor hadn't quite expected the acceptance of his boon (ah, yes, you recollect your precise hesitations now: *What were the two of you getting into, you and Lizzy? How carefully thought out was this proffered venture?*)—an invitation to holiday with a couple of friends (married, two children—not DINKWADs, double income no kids with a dog, like yourselves—but leaving behind the teenaged daughter, who would be on her own that weekend to watch the house, and *what* could go wrong *there?*, and taking with them only the son, Joe Bob, and the boy's traveling buddy, What's-his-name, each nine years of age and now serenading you with "*baaaaack* and forth and *baaaaack* and forth" from the back seat of your friend's Civic as the four of you head south on I-95 just as quickly as is prudent, the gray industrial outline of Worcester, Massachusetts, last seen zipping past on the other side of the cool glass of the passenger-side window before, in desperation, you'd wrapped the towel around your head), said holiday promising all that might be had from a late-spring, four-day jaunt among the isles off Cape Cod: a lobster boil on a chilly beach at night; a quiet stroll among leafy, gingerbread-home-lined streets; a visit to the barnacled docks and rope-lined bulkheads that cloister the lagoons and inlets where they'd once filmed *Jaws*; a series of impromptu walking lunches and planned smart-casual, sit-down dinners, each bracketed on the front end by a disciplined bar tab of old-fashioneds (yourself), highballs (Lizzy), G&Ts (Dustin), frozen strawberry daiquiris (Tiffani), root beer floats (Joe Bob and What's-his-name), and, on the back, less disciplined, end, with unnecessary and thoroughly accepted ("Oh, I shouldn't," "Well, it *is* vacation," "Will everyone share this with me?" "Four spoons, please") confections of sugar, fat, and, depending on the identity of the evening's capitulator in chief, either chocolate or hazelnut, all surrounded by that atoning quartet of spoons, in short, an invitation to the relaxed tempo of the intentionally displaced upper middle class, self-exiled from the fetters of work and RESPONSIBILITY, i.e., family, i.e., children if you had them, i.e., shit all over the house, no sleep, fights, more to love, more to give, less you, possibly less sex, more to fear (so much more), Winnie the Pooh and Oscar the Grouch and Clifford the Big Red Dog, doctors, moving shit around, hope, joy, comparisons, tears, reunions, taking sides, more to lose, more

to watch, mistakes, more to learn, more to hurt, delays and cancellations, someone (later, so much later) to take care of you, surprises, sighs, never ever ever not
worrying, being ignored but never irrelevant, being left behind but never alone,
i.e., life, regardless of whether you actually wanted more of it (and, really,
Earth's the right place for children, that's what Robert Frost had said, or maybe
it had been love; but, you know, the one tends to follow the other, although it *is*
sometimes a question ... but is it a question of if or of when, and if if, then when
when?), and into the comforts of attainable luxury—but which holiday, upon
the conclusion of its first day, found Joe Bob with a rash and What's-his-name
with a bloody nose and a broken hand-held electronic game machine; and by
dinnertime on the second day had all the adults running scared, trying to find
said children, who had gotten lost and were then found by Lizzy after she had
temporarily given up the chase to visit the bathroom in a nearby discount news
and tobacco store, only to discover Joe Bob and What's-his-name lurking like a
couple of delinquents around the magazine rack where, apparently (Lizzy had
been very close about this when you pressed her for details), they had concealed
a *Playboy* magazine behind a copy of *Popular Mechanics*, which magazine sandwich, by Lizzy's reluctant account, they were ogling and passing back and forth
(and *baaaaack* and forth) to each other; and by lunch on the third day resulted
in what began as an argument between Joe Bob and What's-his-name over
whose turn it was to use the electronic game machine (which turned out to be
broken only insofar as the sound was disabled), but was then, through a crafty
sequence of distractions and requests from Tiffani—who turned out to be some
kind of wizard of child psychology—miraculously redirected into a story, recollected and told by Joe Bob, that featured an increasingly improbable sequence
of events that involved a blind substitute teacher, a piano on which the black
keys functioned only on odd-numbered dates and the white keys on even, a lit-
ter of eight Chartreux kittens that meowed in a French accent when given Per-
rier, and a giant PEZ dispenser in the shape of a turbaned swami that refused to
operate unless first told a riddle and that then gave out pellets of solid gold
wrapped in three-dollar bills; and on the dawn of its final day, found you (a) nauseated, then (b) looped up on Dramamine so that your thoughts had become
first fidgety, like a couple of kids in the back seat of a car during a long trip, and
then outright obstreperous, having morphed into a Maslowian hierarchy of Or-
wellian swine that needed to be herded into something like a line and from there

processed into coherency, like a passage from Virginia Woolf on a bad day or James Joyce on a good one, and then, finally, (c) nauseated all over again, as the chants of *baaaaack* and forth and *baaaaack* and forth echo the conflict of your Dramamine-fogged mind, and you ask your friend to stop the car, and, as you stand outside, bracing yourself against the cold and corrugated metal guard rail, you vomit, and you think to yourself, perhaps, and then again, perhaps not.

# for Phil

You've probably already guessed it: What you've just read was another example of self-assigned mission. Correctamundo, my friend; guilty as charged. Call the enforcers of good taste; I'll start readying my explanations. Something like:

Well, you see, officer, what had had happened was, apropos of I'm not sure what—maybe he had just finished working his way through one of my other run-on sentences—Phil Wright, to whom I'm dedicating this story (What? No, sir, he *asked* for it. Yes, sir, you heard that right. No, he's not pressing charges), mentioned to me one day that the *Guinness Book of World Records* lists the longest published sentence as belonging to this guy William Faulkner, as laid out in his novel "Absalom, Absalom" (Wow! You actually *read* the thing, officer? How was it, sir?), and consisting of something like 1,288 words. So I said to myself, "Boys, that's a mark for me." So how about it, officer? Let me off with a warning?

Yes, I do love a run-on sentence. If you've made your way through *Black to Move and Draw*, you know this about me. You've seen me attempt a few of them. The thing I realized, though, about a sentence that was going to be *this* prodigiously long, was that the content needed to warrant the form. The thing that I was trying to say needed to be served properly by a sentence of that nature. The subject matter needed to be almost obscene. It needed to *be* what it *resembled*.

*Vomit*, I realized one day. Vomit would serve nicely. Vomit shows up in a lot of my writing, actually. I don't know why.

But then, up came the problem of theme. Layers. Depth. The nonsense that allows me to daydream that one day my work will show up on the syllabus of a high school course named something like AP Seminar in Literary Analysis. Even if my writing is something, you know, for the kids to contrast with the good stuff. Some writers dream of their work finding its way to the *New York Times* bestseller list. Me, I dream of scholastic obscurity.

So, what *about* the theme? So glad you asked. It's in there, trust me. At least, I put something in there. When you read it through a second time, does anything come up?

Be sure to check out Phil's writing at VictorPenny.com. He's got a whole world in there, full of water and warriors and women! Men, too! And robots!

# this do in remembrance of me

Lake!

The whole flight up, the water, like a spirit or a naiad from mythology, has been beckoning from beyond the cabin window. Feeling this call, the lone passenger in first class fidgets in his seat and pushes himself closer, if possible, into the window, a fishbowl in the cabin wall. At $55, the purchase of the upgrade had been something of an extravagance. The flight is merely a connector from Minneapolis to Duluth, the type that his wife, were she along, would call a peashooter—take a few sips of coffee, say a few sentences, and you're there.

The man's name is Børre Lorentson, but he'll answer to either Bill or Bob. His hair is more silver and less full than the last time he came this way. Capillaries now stipple his milky and bulbous cheeks, which bracket his precise yet understated nose.

It isn't until the plane starts its descent that the lake finally begins to arrive. A mere line at first, like the leg of a coy and stockinged bride who allows her groom a glimpse from behind the dressing room door—a peep, a tease, previews of coming attractions—the lake grows into a strip, metallic blue, before emerging to become the whole world: the jutting piers peppered with tourists frozen in miniature, the thousand-footer ore boats, the city with its houses that climb the hills. Then the plane banks left, hard, pushing down and away the lake and the rest of it until all that remains is sky, blue and blank. When the plane levels, there's nothing but trees.

The lake doesn't appear again until, in a rented Buick, the man revisits Highway 61. He spots the cobalt water and veers off at the first sign for the North Shore Scenic Drive.

The facts are textbook, how ages ago, glaciers carved Lake Superior and its ten thousand inferior kin out of the waiting earth. But he feels quite the opposite, that it is the water that has been here forever, the land having merely organized itself around it to form its rocky, wooded shores. He is returning to a property he once owned himself, driving across land that he reflects was once owned by no one. He passes fish markets, bait shops, cabin resorts, campgrounds, Lutheran churches, bars, and mom-and-pop coffee shops and hardware stores. Any fool looking for a Starbucks or a Home Depot would be heading the wrong way. He feels the squandered spirit of the Native American, remembered on roadside advertisements. He crosses railroads whose hundred-car-long trains connect the Mesabi Iron Range far up in the northwest to harbor towns along the water's edge, where ore boats—those huge rust-colored floating football fields—await the taconite they will deliver to the great steel mills of America; making things, making America, making America good.

The lake disappears again behind a forest of tall pines and white birches that, pointing toward heaven, dominate the North Shore and extend far into Canada.

At last he turns off the highway. He's almost there. He frowns slightly; this next road has been paved. The hard industrial black doesn't suit the thick woods that surround him and that are just beginning to flush with autumn color. He senses exposure; feels violated, that the eye of civilization has discovered this far country and taken it into its deliberations. The road is supposed to be gravel, always has been gravel. He misses the crunch beneath his tires as he drives.

Wondering what else is in store, he arrives. Two parallel lines of dirt separated by a struggling strip of crabgrass and weeds point into the woods. He slows the Buick to a few miles per hour, then to a stop. He gazes intently at the white clapboard sign at the head of the driveway.

Lorentson's Lakeside Lodges—named after Bob's grandfather, who purchased the property in 1949—were originally built at the turn of the twentieth century by a man whose one known attribute was that he was a Finn. Given the cabins' construction, Bob, as a kid, had imagined this Finn to be a very hardy fellow—an inference that fed his already deeply engrained belief in Scandinavian self-sufficiency.

An accountant, Da had run the business as a tax write-off. This fact had come to a grown-up Bob as an epiphany when he learned of the absurdly low margins the resort had produced. But the name was a misnomer: The lodges were primitive-but-cozy one-room cabins—and only three of the seven stood near the cliff overlooking Lake Superior, the rest forming a horseshoe centered around a shower house, which provided the property its one source of running water.

The sentimental value of the place soon outstripped—and far outlasted—any economic consideration. The business perished after a mere eight years, after which the cabins served as a retreat for family seeking tranquility and temporary isolation from the world. In 1974, death played its hand, and the property passed to Bob's father. In 2001, at the centennial of the cabins' construction, they came to Bob himself. Seven years later, it was not nature but Wall Street that struck, plunging the nation into recession. Needing the money and lacking good options, Bob sold.

He had priced the property to move. Still, the first few weeks of the listing had come and gone without activity. Then, two offers on the same day. Bob learned through his realtor that the buyer with the deeper pockets was planning to raze the cabins and build a condominium on the lot. The other fellow, if Bob understood correctly, happened to be the longtime groundskeeper for a second cousin once removed to Bob's mother. Bob sold to him.

Bob undoes his seatbelt now and shifts around to get a better view out the window. He's not finding the sign he'd been looking for. A new sign—SAM'S SLEEPY SHACKS—assaults his sensibilities. Terrible name, he thinks to himself, and not for the first time. Just terrible. He had called ahead to request a cabin. He had spoken to this Sam, had thought him a reasonable fellow. But this name. Honestly. As if someone would pay to sleep in a shack? Or as if the shacks themselves (*shacks!*) were sleepy? The *sh-* in *shacks* isn't even a sibilant—disqualifying the word from the alliterative scheme. Terrible name. Just terrible.

Then he sees it: the real sign, still white and upright but buried alive among the needles and leaves. He supposes Sam must have moved it farther back into the tree line. Then he understands: The branches have simply been allowed to grow around the sign. Gobbling it up.

He is encouraged, though, looking at it—three sturdy slats having once borne the name of Da's business, one word per slat, now painted over. But the wood itself was not properly sanded, and the raised outlines of the block letters beneath the whitewash still silently peddle the past. He puts the Buick back into gear, eases the car up to three mph, and allows himself a guarded smile as the crunching gravel beneath him announces the head of the unpaved drive.

The clearing is deep and half as wide. Directly ahead, beyond the cliff at the property's limit, dusk is painting the lake a peaceful gray. During summer, the woods along the lengths of the lot might admit, at this time of day, the shimmer of a porch light being turned on by some far but still-too-close neighbor. But this is September, and most folks have left. Bob puts the car into park, kills the engine, swings open the heavy door, and steps out onto the lawn.

He breathes in the air. It's cool, like a drink, fortified with pine, cleansed by the lake. He takes visual inventory. The cabins, Numbers 1 through 7, are all there. (Where Bob's grandmother had christened the resort itself, Da had taken on the less market-sensitive task of naming the cabins. Ever the accountant and nauseated by anything so droll as Hiawatha's Hideaway or Bunyan's Bungalow, he had simply numbered them.) Bob reaches into the car for his rucksack, which holds a single overnight's-worth of supplies, and he slings it over a shoulder. He shuts the car door, goes to lock it, then checks himself: There is no need.

He walks the property, following the horseshoe path. He visits each cabin, peering through windows, skimming a hand over ancient wood, communing with ghosts. He's amazed at the restraint of a decade, how little has changed. Past here, where once he saw a bear outside the window; then here, where he and Jorgen would stay up all night playing penny ante poker; then here, where once he kissed a girl from down at Wildfire Campground. She had winked at him, her cheeks just as soft and vivid and wholesome as wild daisies, told him she was just walking through.

At the cliff he pauses to look down at the rocks. Here, finally, he receives the jolt of change and decay that he had just started to believe might pass him over. The shape of the shoreline is intact, but for as far as he can see to the right (down, southwest) and to the left (up, northeast), the *depth* of the shore has been cut in half. The water levels have increased; the lake has grown. He wonders if it's still possible to walk the rocks all the way up to John's Fish Shack or down to Wildfire. He gazes across the breadth of Lake Superior to the barely discernible haze of land that he frequently forgets is Wisconsin, and he thinks about the melting Canadian tundra, and he curses the bastards in Washington, DC.

More cabins, more ghosts. He skips over Number 6 for now—although the resort is officially closed for the season, he'll stay here tonight (there can be benefits to selling to the lower bidder)—and spends a little time outside Number 7.

He progresses to the central shower house. Despite a steadily strengthening urge from his bladder, he has saved this for the end of his tour. Here, at last, he'll be going inside something. There are two sides to the building—a men's and a women's—with a utility room between. He would love to visit all three, but he guesses that Sam will have left only the men's side unlocked, and in this he is correct.

Immediately upon setting foot indoors, he inhales deeply through his nose. If Bob had been led blindfolded into any of these cabins, he would have been able to say with certainty where he was. This, purely from smell.

He chuckles, remembering. At the age of twelve—an age when so many things are still possible—he had come home from a family vacation with ten sealed Tupperware containers. He had purchased these with his own saved allowance money at the town dime store under the patient watch of his older brother, Jorgen. (It was a patience owed largely to distraction, Jorgen having spent the entire time trying to juggle the car keys, a pack of Topps baseball cards, and an Oh Henry! candy bar.) In each container, Bob had trapped the air of a different cabin or washroom. He had truly believed that he could open them each up, put his head down into them, and announce to his family which place that container's air belonged to from its scent: from Number 1 (decorated with the trappings of hunting), the oily smell of guns; from Number 2 (what had jestingly been known as the Honeymoon Suite), the passionate *je ne sais quoi* of what Bob had for a long time assumed to be the scent of a woman; from Number 3 (closest to the cliff), the remarkably inoffensive airborne remains of freshwater fish; from the women's side of the shower house, the purifying skulk of Cashmere Bouquet soap; from the men's, the atomized balm of electric shaving. And so on.

At twelve, so many things had been possible.

Hobbled shorelines and rising water levels now reassert themselves to Bob's mind, crowding out reveries. He steps deeper into the men's, hunching himself against the low doorway, bracing against some new whip or scorn of time that surely awaits him within.

But his anxieties have again proven vain. The shower house—the feel of it, and most essentially the aroma—is unchanged. *Like everything*, Bob thinks. Like everything *so far*, he amends, wondering what he might find in Number 6.

To which he further adds, recalling the engorged lake, like everything so far *under Sam's control.*

Sam, Bob must admit, has kept the place pretty well. He reconsiders the name. Sam's Sleepy Shacks? Perhaps it isn't *so* bad.

Bob needs to pee, but not here. Instead, he walks to Number 6. He goes around back, into the woods, and relieves himself on whatever green plant he finds there, growing out of the ground. The joy of peeing outdoors fulfilled, he goes to the twin propane tanks standing against the cabin and reaches behind to where Sam had told him he'd leave the key. He finds it, unlocks the padlock on the cabin door, and enters.

With a deep breath of the room's air (woody, with the faintest trace of smoke) he surveys the rustic furnishings. At least half of what he remembers is still here. He thinks briefly about Sam—how surprised he had sounded when he, Bob, had asked to stay in Number 6. Of the seven cabins, it's neither the nicest nor the cheapest. But there was a reason for the request, and after a brief pause to simply be in the place for a moment, Bob gets down to work.

In less than a half hour, he succeeds at his task.

He sits now at a table, looking across the room through the window in the lakeside wall. Darkness has fallen; moonlight leaks through the pines. He unzips a side-pocket of his rucksack and takes out a lighter that he had purchased only a few hours ago at the airport. From a red, already-opened pack of Pall Mall cigarettes he worries one free, then with his lips he pulls it out.

He lights it; holds it awkwardly in his mouth, unsure of how much pressure to exert with his jaws, for he has never before smoked; inhales. The sudden injection of smoke burns his virgin lungs, and he coughs out a raft of blue-gray poison.

He continues smoking, sans inhalation, and while he smokes, he remembers.

"Jerry!" a twelve-year-old Børre yells out to Jorgen, "Jerry, wait up!"

They're walking the rocks, hugging the contour of the lake. The trip to John's Fish Shack had borne fruit: Each boy now carries a newspaper-wrapped chunk of golden smoked whitefish—the shared harvest of a dollar. With the slightest of gestures, Jorgen glances behind him, then back again to the puzzle of rocks before him. Børre watches as Jorgen selects one, hops onto it, then another and another. He's heading toward a wide shelf of purple basalt that slopes gently down into the water. He arrives, picks a spot, and sprawls out onto it. By the time he has unwrapped his fish, Børre has caught up to him and has sat down.

Working around skin and bones, the boys eat their fish. An oily perfume loaded with smoke overpowers the clean of the lake. Børre listens as gentle ripples, too small to be called waves, lap the shore, and he absorbs the almost unbearable blades of light that stab at his eyes with every fluctuation of the water's surface. The fish is salty from whatever brine it had been soaked in. He takes both of their canteens and fills them from the lake. He drinks from his until it's empty. He refills it and drinks some more before returning to his fish. Jorgen, meantime, scans the shoreline. His head moves this way and that, his Adam's apple bobbing up and down his long, teenager neck. He's looking for that first gull. Seagulls will eat anything, both boys know, and nothing draws them more mightily than a fish lunch.

In this manner, ten minutes pass, as pure and clean as the lake.

Jorgen finishes first. He says, "Come on" and spreads his newspaper flat on the purple rock and sprinkles it with toothpick-thin bones and golden fish skin. Børre gulps down the last of his lunch and does the same as Jorgen. One of the dozen gulls now congregated at a still-respectful but rapidly shrinking distance squawks, announcing the feast. The boys begin to walk home, but Børre stops.

"Hold on, Jerry," he pleads, "I want to see this."

Jorgen stops and turns around to watch with his younger brother as scores of gulls descend seemingly from nowhere onto the abandoned dregs of their meal.

"Like this, Bill," Børre hears Jorgen say. He looks at Jorgen: They hadn't walked far enough to be out of range of the gulls, and his hands are up over his head, his fingers laced together into a protective shield. "Don't ever get bird shit in your hair," Jorgen advises.

Børre absorbs this wisdom and mirrors Jorgen's posture. They watch until the skin and bones are gone. The gulls, the boys know, will remain standing there for a long time. Without further speech, Jorgen turns away, and the boys walk the rocks back home.

They climb the wooden staircase that scales the side of the cliff and that, at the end of the season and with considerable effort, will be taken up and stored under several layers of tarp. Børre starts toward the shower house to pee, planning to then proceed to Number 4, where a half-finished jigsaw puzzle awaits him.

Jorgen, however, has another idea. "Bill," he says conspiratorially, "come with me."

"Sure," says Børre. They walk past Number 5, leap over a shallow gully, walk past Number 6. They're heading to Number 7. With a single furtive glance behind him and a flip of a wrist—*follow me, Børre*—Jorgen slips behind the cabin.

"What are we doing back here, Jerry?" Børre has been in these woods countless times, but he looks around as if for the first.

Jorgen sits down on a thick mat of pine needles. He settles his back up against the cabin. Sunlight dapples his face through the trees. He motions to Børre to come over next to him, which Børre does.

"What are we doing back here?" Børre asks again, sitting down next to his brother.

From his pocket, Jorgen takes a red pack of cigarettes and a book of matches.

Børre's mouth makes a perfect O. "Where'd you *get* that?"

"Dime store vending machine. You were at the counter buying all that Tupperware shit. Whatcha planning to *do* with that shit, anyhow?"

Børre shrugs his shoulders and lets his brother keep talking. It's the most Jorgen has said all day.

"Want one? I'll betcha cigarettes would go great with the fish. Smoky!"

Børre takes the cigarettes. He flips the pack around in his hands, examining it like so much treasure. Pall Malls. He is aware of the brand. "WHEREVER PARTICULAR PEOPLE CONGREGATE" says the tagline below what looks like a trio of lions wearing medieval armor. There's also a phrase—Latin, he thinks—but he can't read it.

"*In hoc signo vinces*," says Jorgen. "It means 'In this sign, conquer.' It's from the Roman Empire. You'll get it in history."

Børre begins to rip the paper off the top of the pack. He has just exposed a cluster of cigarettes when both boys are brought to their feet by a query barked in a harsh Norwegian accent.

*"Børre Lorentson, what has you there!?"*

The boy's instinct is to hide the contraband behind his back, which he begins to do. But of course there's no point. So he holds the cigarettes out to his grandmother—an unholy offering fit to be made at arm's length only.

She stands there, pointing at the accused. She wears heavy work gloves, her hair is tied back in a long salt-and-pepper ponytail, some three-pronged instrument dangles from her hip, and a slick of soil on her forehead looks like the mark of Cain. She glitters in sweat and indignation. Clearly she'd been working the garden up near the driveway and had seen the two of them slinking behind Number 7 like a pair of criminals. She says:

*"You will take that what you has there to your Da!"*

When Børre continues to stand there, an idiotic statue, she follows with:

*"You will show him now, ja?"*

It is not a question.

Børre loves his grandparents, as he would unto death. But Da has an old wooden paddle, used— also—for serving crackers and cheese at Wednesday night cribbage. And while events of the previous summer had definitively shown Jorgen to have crossed the age of corporal discipline, Børre's own status remains uncertain. A warm soaking fills the crotch of his pants as all the water of the lake betrays him, and he is utterly forsaken.

"Come on," says Jorgen. "Let's get it over with."

The boys turn to go. As they round the cabin, Børre looks over his shoulder at his grandmother. With an accusatory finger still outstretched and that three-pronged pointy thing dangling at her side, he figures the image to be not overly removed from the mythic angel who once had kicked a pair of errant humans out of Eden.

They're just passing Number 6 when Jorgen says to Børre, "Watch this." He grabs the pack of cigarettes and disappears into the cabin. If he's inside for more than a minute, it's not by much. When he comes back out, the Pall Malls are gone. The act didn't save Børre from trouble, but the cigarettes are never seen again.

*Lake!*

The whole trip down, the water, like a spirit or a naiad from mythology, has been beckoning from beyond the cabin window. Feeling this call, the lone occupant of Number 6 rummages in his rucksack. He takes out a picture. A black sash winds through the curls and nooks of the metal frame. The picture is of him and his brother, taken decades before the lung cancer, when the two of them had once hiked the Australian Outback together.

The man shoves aside the detritus of his recent search of the cabin to make room on the table. He sets down the picture. Then from his pack he lays out a piece of fish, purchased along the Scenic Drive, and he eats of it. In the same manner he takes out a bottle of water, and he drinks. And when he is finished, he gives thanks, and he goes outside.

From the height of the cliff he watches, still smoking, white streaks left on the water by distant ore boats, and he listens as the ripples, too small to be called waves, softly bury the rocks below.

# for Nick and Amanda

For maybe the fourth time, I was trying to read *Rabbit Redux* by John Updike. Some authors are like that: Their writing is brilliant, but the stories aren't very compelling. Other authors, guys like James Patterson, are the opposite: They can come up with a barn-buster of a tale, but the writing is about as inspiring as a Tootsie Roll on a summer sidewalk.

Anyway, I was re-re-re-reading *Rabbit Redux*, and I came upon a sentence that was so lovely that I had to stop and read it out loud several times:

> *In the twilight, we eat, still naked, salami sandwiches she makes, and drink whisky.*

For starters, there's imagery: A naked woman is sitting with some guy, also naked, in the twilight. She's making salami sandwiches for the two of them, which they're chasing down with whisky. Wow. Wow, wow, wow. So much to unpack. This definitely beats a melting stick of chocolate-flavored wax. But listen, there's so much more going on here than the bald elements of the scene. Let's imagine this same montage, but in the hands of a lesser writer (me, for example). It might go like this:

> *It's twilight, and while we're still naked, she makes salami sandwiches, which we then eat while we drink whisky.*

Every visual item from Updike's construction is preserved. But when I read *this*, all I can think is: Who prepares food while they're naked and then eats? Who pairs whisky with salami? And what's all this about twilight? Are they outside? Naked?

The jingle and rhythm of Updike's prose makes me buy what he's selling. I don't care if it's sensible; I just want to read it. (Not for nothing do advertising jingles work.) The context of what happened in the previous sentence or paragraph or chapter doesn't enter into it; the sentence stands on its own. It's poetry.

And if I *insist* on believing (again, regardless of any context), it's not that hard. They're inside, of course, where the exterior twilight, creeping in through the window, is weaving a mystical pall. They probably just had sex, and they're hungry. Not a lot of food around, but the woman manages to come up with some salami and bread. Why dress? It's just the two of them in the afterglow of carnal delight. And who doesn't like a hit of liquor afterward? If they *didn't* just have sex, it gets even better. What exactly *is* their relationship? One must be very comfortable with a person to make salami sandwiches in front of them naked.

So it's all about that construction. When I read, I care less about what the author is saying than I do how they're saying it, and when I write, it's the same. I don't want to bore my reader or myself with flat prose.

What particular stylistic elements of Updike's sentence grabbed me? I can identify three.

First, by masterfully (and yet grammatically incorrectly; this whole essay is cruelly killing my editor) employing punctuation, Updike was able to use a minimum of words. The style manuals all urge writers to omit needless words. What they mean is to shun useless qualifiers like *really* and *very* and to use strong nouns in place of adjectives paired with weak nouns and strong verbs in place of adverbs paired with weak verbs. But there are other, harder, ways of streamlining and strengthening prose. Many of these involve punctuation. Updike's sentence contains fourteen words. My own version of that sentence contains nineteen. That's a roughly 25 percent increase in word count. A 400-page book is now a 500-page book. By an economy of words and cleverly used punctuation, Updike made his writing smooth and strong. Like a good whisky.

Second, where my sentence contains two verbs that don't convey action, *is* and *are* (hidden within contractions), Updike's contains zero. Linking verbs like *was* and *were* are necessary, of course. But I'm always on the lookout for opportunities to nix them in favor of more active wording.

Third and most Updike-y of all is that masterful insertion of the descriptor *still naked* between the verb and the direct object of the sentence. Time and again I notice when Updike does this. I wanted to see what it would be like to write a sentence like this.

I gave myself another mission: to craft a sentence modeled after Updike's and then use it in a story. I had also long wanted to memorialize a place that has always been dear to me: namely, a cabin resort, located on Minnesota's north shore of Lake Superior, that my grandparents once owned and that, after decades of family retreats, was sold. So I worked at a sentence for about a half hour and came up with:

*From the height of the cliff he watches, still smoking, white streaks left on the water by distant ore boats, and he listens as the ripples, too small to be called waves, softly bury the rocks below.*

Once I liked the sentence well enough (it underwent changes as I discovered details of the ensuing story), I tasked myself with writing a short story that used it. I can't write like Updike constantly (or at all, really); probably no one can. I was going to include only one sentence like this, so it needed to be in a prominent position. This meant being either at the beginning of the story or at the end. But such a thing makes no sense at the top of a story, so it had to be the end. I didn't understand what the smoking had to do with anything, but I figured I'd find out. I wrote most of the story not knowing.

My sentence is longer than Updike's, but only because it contains more material. It had a heavy job to do, finishing a story. I like the sentence because the *height* at the beginning balances against the *below* at the end. I also like that it involves listening as well as seeing. The smoking could even count as a scent sensory detail—a recurring theme in the story. Another thing I like is the inclusion of some verbiage, *too small to be called waves*, that I hadn't originally anticipated for the final sentence but discovered in the main text during the rewrite. I felt that a reprise of that phrase would serve nicely as a reminiscence element for the protagonist as he stood there, gazing out over the water. Too, the sentence pulls in the themes of constancy and persistence vs. erosion and change found throughout the narrative arc. Centrally located is the phrase *still smoking*, slid neatly between the verb *watches* and the direct object, those beautiful ore boats (to be precise, the streaks created by them) introduced near the top of the story. Finally, I chose to have the streaks *left* on the water by the oar boats (rather than something like *shone onto* the water) as another nod to the idea of persistence: as if, somehow, the water would continue to feel the passage of the oar boats long after they had gone.

Nickolas and Amanda, you were the last folks to join our circle, and you always come eager to pick up pointers and ideas as well as to share your thoughts. As measured by impact, though, I don't think anything will ever beat your engagement announcement, right in the middle of the group's deciding which piece of work to read first. That was classic, you two. I'm dedicating this story to you.

*That's just half of sixteen reasons ...*

# the bringer of jollity

His full name, as I was soon to learn, was Harold Jovis Grimes, and by an unforeseen turn of events he was on his way to our house. He was coming for dinner. I was concerned: The last time I'd seen him, prior to three weeks ago, I had thrown a stick at his head. This had been on the school playground, I a mere second grader, he an infinitely older and wiser fifth grader. I couldn't tell you why I'd thrown the stick. Now, a quarter century later, Milly and I having entered that stage wherein it is possible and thereby fashionable to appraise life in terms of fractions of large quantities—a half decade of marriage; a quarter million dollar townhome; a third of a century each of patinated memories, lovingly coated—this man, a doctor now, Dr. Grimes, was due to arrive at our home in ten minutes. A sixth of an hour.

He was our on-call obstetrician; Milly's regular, Dr. Sutton, having been unavailable. Three weeks prior, on January 1, 2001, Dr. Grimes had delivered our baby—our son—into a world that had itself just been birthed into a fresh millennium, each of them, the world and tiny Daniel, the smallest of fractions along their ways into another thousand years, a human life. Where images of life prior to Daniel had, despite recency, already begun to take on the muted sepia tones usually reserved for shrunken antiquity, the elements of Daniel's birth had received, perhaps as an equalizing gift from insensate time, an illumination akin to that of hagiography (another phenomenon, like patination or the discoloration of photographs that comes with age, usually reserved for the arbitration of many years), now brightening and expanding those memories: the sudden blessedness of Milly's face, an epidural now loaded firmly into the base of her spine as she lay on her bed like an apparition of Our Lady of Fatima, Sedated; the pair of wide Scandinavian nurses with their twin admonitions of "Push!" and "Breathe!" scourging life into existence; the wallop of ammonia and last night's kale as Milly vomited into a rubber dish; the radio, Philadelphia's own WPHT, delivering without consideration or prejudice its philosophy to seemingly the entirety of the hospital, the quick and the dying alike.

And Dr. Grimes himself, flitting like a blue-eyed Caucasian shaman in and out of our semi-private room. During those intervals that he was with us, his whole world was Milly's anatomy, his handiwork the prying into of her physiology. With his scrub sleeves coiled up around the meat of his ample forearms and his round doctor's cap bobbing up and down like a turquoise beach ball between Milly's knees, neither of us yet realizing that I had at one time thrown a stick at this man, he delivered our boy. Later, after washing up and with a hearty "Enjoy your new life!," he shook our hands. He then headed for the door.

I imagine that he stopped there, perhaps consulting his charts one more time before mentally preparing to push the three of us—huddled on the bed, a family now—into the oubliette of finished business. Perhaps he'd heard Milly speak my name as we held our child in our arms, still deciding what to call him.

At the touch of a hand on my shoulder, I turned around.

"George?" Dr. Grimes said, suddenly there. "It *is* you, isn't it! George Boighan? I never pay attention to the fellows."

Now, as I stood suspended in the savory smoke of outdoor grilling, watching from the elevated position of my balcony the shimmering flecks of light that painted the frozen chunks of the Susquehanna orange beneath me while, indoors, Milly clinked the dishes in preparation for this man's arrival for dinner, I recollected this comment from Dr. Grimes and found amusement in the mutual irrelevancy that it implied between us. He, more as a priest than as a supplicant or worshipper, had spent time in the inner sanctum of my wife's body, whereas I hadn't known even the man's first name. What were either of us to the other?

I must've confirmed my identity to him, at which point, comprehending his state of temporary non-existence, he had simply stated: "Shady Elm Elementary School." Just enough to establish a genuine connection before making his exit. He'd shaken my hand once more, then Milly's, who managed this without removing any other part of herself from our son, crying and unnamed and squirming in her arms. "You two have important things on your minds," Dr. Grimes had said, and he left us. I touched my boy's face and returned to Milly.

Later that same evening I again sat by Milly on the hospital bed, again held her hand. Our son, fed and sleeping and still nameless, had been taken to the newborn ward by one of the shift nurses. Hospital visiting hours were nearly over; I would be going home soon. Milly was reminding me that it was Thursday (Earth, this whole while, had apparently continued spinning on its axis) and that the recycles needed to be put out.

There came a gentle knock at our door, which opened just enough to admit first the head of Dr. Grimes, then his entire body. The doorway had given birth to our obstetrician.

"Do we have a name yet?" he wanted to know.

Milly and I traded glances and a shrug.

Dr. Grimes smiled. "This is very common, folks. See it all the time. Would you like some help?"

"Please," said Milly.

"Umm?" I agreed.

"Okey-dokey," said the doctor, pulling a chair over to the bed and sitting down. He tossed his right leg over his left and with two sharp snaps pulled off his rubber gloves and stuffed them into the pocket of his doctor's coat. He then removed his face mask while keeping his turquoise cap in place. Thus transformed into a human being, he positively beamed. He then shocked me, a little, by pulling out from the breast pocket of his scrub top something I at first took to be a pack of cigarettes. He tilted the box a smidge and gave it a tap. A thin stick like a piece of chalk slid out, and he placed it between his lips, instantly smudging his mouth with white.

It was candy. I tried to recall the last time I had seen candy cigarettes.

He leaned forward and, planting his elbows on his knees and holding out the box of candy cigarettes toward me, sighed. "I'd offer you a cigar," he said with a roll of his eyes, "but I'm afraid Admin wouldn't approve."

I declined the faux cigarette, and Dr. Grimes then made the same gesture of offering to Milly, who surprised me by taking one. Probably my most enduring memory of that day, which years hence I will play over in my mind as I lay dying, will be of Milly, lounging on that hospital bed, smiling like the hosts of heaven, rolling a candy cigarette back and forth on her white-flecked lips and looking expectantly at Dr. Grimes, her wide eyes soaking up the teal of his scrubs.

"Now," our new friend said, rubbing his hands together, "who likes what?"

"Oh, it's not like that," said Milly. "We each like the name Daniel, and we also like Timothy."

"We just can't decide between them," I finished.

Dr. Grimes steepled his fingers together. "Ah, yes. Tell me more. These names—do they have history in either of your family trees?"

"No," I said.

"We like them is all," said Milly.

"It is the very best way," said the man. "Well." He leaned back in his chair to cast a judicious gaze at the drop ceiling. "Deciding between things is often a matter of deciding how to decide. As it happens, I have on my person a tool ideally suited to our purpose." He reached into the pocket of his scrub pants and produced a quarter. "Like any tool, in order to use it properly, you must understand its function." He held the quarter aloft and with a squinted eye appraised it exactly like I would imagine he had examined countless ultrasounds. "It's not the quarter that's doing the deciding," he said. "You do that. The coin merely helps to reveal. Milly, give me a name for heads."

"Daniel," she said.

"Very good," said Dr. Grimes. "Heads will be Daniel; tails, Timothy. Now, when the coin lands and I announce heads or tails, what you both must do is check the immediate reaction of your hearts. You are looking for regret. Follow?"

Milly and I had barely indicated our understanding when Dr. Grimes flipped the coin into the air. He caught it in the palm of his right hand and flipped it onto the back of his left. Peeking at the coin, he announced, "Tails. Timothy."

Milly and I glanced at each other. The man raised an eyebrow. "Well?"

"I— I'm—" Milly said. "I don't know."

Dr. Grimes looked at me in turn.

"I'm not sure either," I said.

"Perfectly normal," he said. "Now prepare to take inventory of your hearts, and we'll do it again. George? I need a name for heads."

"Why not Daniel again," I said.

Without hesitation, Dr. Grimes launched the coin into the air. Catching it as before, he announced, "Heads. Daniel." The immediacy with which the doctor then cast his gaze at us, as if he were afraid of missing some visual clue, some symptom he needed to see before making a diagnosis, made me almost laugh.

"I don't know," I said. "Milly? Is this helping?"

"It's ... interesting," she said.

Dr. Grimes shifted his attention back and forth between us. "Anything?"
I shrugged.

"All very fine," he said. "I propose a final toss. Best of three. Heads will be Daniel; tails, Timothy. However it lands, it lands. Objections?"

This time he *did* wait, but when he saw that neither of us had anything to say, he tossed the coin into the air. By accident, I think, he failed to catch it, and the coin bounced off his hand. It landed on its edge and rolled into the narrow space between the door, which was opened into the room, and the wall. He crouched down, reached behind the door, and, pulling the coin out and glancing at it before placing it back in his pocket, announced: "His name is Daniel."

Milly and I looked at each other. She was beaming. "Daniel," she said. I have heard priests utter the name of the Mother of our Lord in that same tone.

"It's a great name," I offered.

"Thank you, Dr. Grimes," said Milly. She was utterly radiant.

"Yes, thank you, doctor," I said.

Dr. Grimes once more shook our hands. He then removed his turquoise cap and with a swipe of a forearm across his brow said to me, "You really don't remember me, do you?"

The doorbell rang. I scooped up the brisket and fava beans I'd been cooking and went inside. (Absent heavy precipitation, barbecuing in the cold is a simple matter of a decent-sized balcony and generous amounts of lighter fluid.) Across the counter that separated our kitchen from our dining room, Milly smiled behind a smorgasbord of wedding presents, many out of their boxes for only the second time in five years: a Waterford crystal bowl that gleamed around a sticky pyramid of A&P macaroni salad; a teakwood platter overlaid with whole-wheat crackers, gouda, and red grapes; a trio of long-stem wine glasses; a second trio of tumblers for water, each half-filled with miniature, pineapple-shaped ice cubes; a chip & dip set with three bowls for salsa, queso, and sour cream mixed with a packet of French onion soup mix; a tidy heap of flatware, Lenox plates, and napkins. Vanity Fairs—extra large, extra nice. On the CD player, Milly had queued up some background music; the chords of *Tristan und Isolde* gently began stretching the air to maximum tautness. The choice of music wouldn't have been my pick, but there was the doorbell to tend to, so I shoveled the brisket into a casserole beside an unopened bottle of Bordeaux, saturating the room with vinegar and honey, health and good cheer, and I asked Milly if we were ready.

She was already halfway down the hall toward the front door. I followed after.

"Dr. Grimes," we both said, opening the door.

On the porch stood our friendly neighborhood obstetrician. His black greatcoat lent him the illusion of height, and a grin lit his face. A pair of Bloomingdale's shopping bags, quite large, dangled from his hands. On his forehead, slightly to the left of center, was that same red oval-shaped mark that I'd remembered from a quarter century ago and then had seen once more, three weeks previous, on the day of our son's birth, when Dr. Grimes had finally taken off his doctor's cap to ask me if, really, I didn't remember him.

Holding aloft the shopping bags, he paraded inside behind them. "Good evening!" he said.

"Aw, you didn't need to go and do that," I said, pointing to the bags.

"Nonsense," he said. "Open 'em up."

"Let's at least get you out of that coat first," said Milly, holding out a hand. She hung his coat in the hall closet while I got his bags. One of them felt heavy and solid, the other nearly empty in comparison.

"Good Lord!" exclaimed Grimes, gazing around the place. "You sure I have the right house? A newborn lives here?"

"It didn't exactly look like this a couple hours ago," I confided.

Grimes lowered his voice to match mine. "And the little fellow? Where is he?"

Milly held up two pairs of crossed fingers. "He went down for a nap about an hour ago."

"Want to see your handiwork?" I asked.

"My medical opinion? Let sleeping babies lie."

Milly laughed quietly. "I'll take that advice."

I said, "We might only have a few minutes of peace."

"Then let's enjoy them," said Grimes. "Now, has anyone seen a pair of runaway shopping bags—Good heavens, what *have* the two of you been cooking up besides babies? The smell from your kitchen is dee-*vine*!"

"Brisket and fava beans," I said.

"Shall we?" said Milly, indicating the dining room.

Grimes had only just sat down—Milly and I were still ferrying the elements of dinner from counter to table—when my wife came out with, "What do you make of this Marc Rich guy?" The question seemed directed at a spot of air a few inches above Dr. Grimes's forehead.

"Aw, Mill, what the hell?" I said.

"I want a conversation about something other than naps and poop."

She had a fair point.

"It's okay," said Grimes, organizing the silverware around his plate, "I don't live in a cave. All subjects are fair game. You're talking about this fellow whom Bill awarded one Get Out Of Jail Free card to on his last day in office?"

We were all seated now, passing the dishes around. Milly was in her usual chair, Grimes across from her in my normal place, I at the end of the table, tucked in-between, in the spot Milly and I were planning to soon put a high-chair. Across from me, a solid red LED on the baby monitor represented a fourth presence, Daniel. Our heads were soon down over our meals.

"Just yesterday, in other words," I said around a mouthful of macaroni salad, "and already the news is calling it Pardongate."

"It's this Rich fellow," Milly said, "and something like a hundred more pardons."

Grimes said, "Well, I liked Clinton, I won't lie. But you're right, Milly, this doesn't smell good."

"It's the president's right to pardon people," I said.

"It's not a question of rights," said Milly. "It's a question of, like, the biggest tax evasion crime in history, which this guy is guilty of. What kind of note is that to end a presidency on?"

I started in on the brisket. It was delicious, yet incomplete. "All I can say is, if we want to keep this little party of ours from becoming Dinnergate, we better get that bottle of Bordeaux over here."

Grimes had been busily eating. At the mention of wine, he snapped to attention, a doctor once more.

"Breastfeeding?" He pitched the question at Milly like a tennis coach sending a rocket across the net to a student.

"Similac," she returned.

He relaxed. "Good choice. I also recommend Enfamil."

I brought the wine over myself. "All right, you two, enough shop talk."

I uncorked the bottle and poured out for everyone. Grimes made a show of swirling the wine in his glass, which he held by the base using his thumb and the side of his curled-up pointer finger, then deeply inhaling the bouquet before indulging in what at first began as a sip, then grew into a hearty swig, and finally resulted in the draining of the entire glass.

"Pairs excellently with the meat, you two," he said. He went to wipe his mouth with the back of his hand, then stopped himself and used the napkin. "Nicely done."

I refilled his glass. For a few minutes, everyone ate.

Milly said, "Anyway, what *does* give him the right?"

Like Paul Masson, who sells no wine before its time, Milly will not let a topic go before it has aged to completion. Knowing this about her, I had spent the last minute or so preparing for this exact question.

"The Constitution," I answered.

"That's not what I mean at all!" She looked across the table to Grimes as if for help, then quickly shifted her gaze to the side. This was the second time she'd done something like this, and this time I finally understood: She was embarrassed by the red oval on Grimes's forehead. She continued, "I mean, what gives him the *moral* right? People violate people, they go to church, expect God to forgive them. But what gives even God the right to forgive anyone? You violate somebody, who gets to forgive that? The victim, that's who. Nobody else. People lose sight of that."

Grimes said, "Well, maybe it's sort of like, as president, Clinton represents the people. Tax evasion is a crime against the people."

"Maybe that's the way it is with God, too," I said.

"How do you mean?" asked Grimes.

"I don't know. God represents the will of the people?"

Milly said, "Oh, that's definitely true, but maybe not in the way you mean it."

"Politics and now religion, too?" Grimes was thrilled. "I had no idea what I was getting into when I accepted your dinner invitation."

"I'm sorry," said Milly.

"Not at all!" he said. "I have a degree in philosophy. All this is right in my wheelhouse."

"Philosophy?" I said. "Don't you have to take pre-med to get into med school?"

"A common misconception. Fact is, your undergrad major can be just about anything. They really just want to see excellent grades in challenging classes. I decided on philosophy."

"Why that?" asked Milly.

"It's something that always interested me."

"What interests you about that?" Milly asked, re-molding her original question without missing a beat.

Grimes, chewing a mouthful of fava beans, thought for a moment. "I guess the paradoxes are what first attracted me."

"Example," my wife said.

"Here's one," he said, swallowing his beans. "Ever heard of Zeno's Dichotomy paradox?" He gave Milly and me time to share a shrug, then continued. "Let's say you want to get from here to the kitchen. To do that, you're first going to have to get halfway, right?"

"Sure," I said.

"But to get to the halfway point, you would first need to get halfway to *that*. And to get to *that* halfway point, you would need to get halfway, and so on." He let this sink in for a moment, while he polished off his second glass of Bordeaux. "See?"

Milly said, "You're saying, what, that you could do this forever? Keep going halfway to a place?"

"I'm saying there's an infinite number of halfway points. To get to the kitchen, then, you must first accomplish an infinite number of tasks."

"That's how I feel about it some mornings," I said.

"So ... what?" Milly pressed. "You're saying it's impossible? You can never get to the kitchen?"

"Only if you can perform an infinite number of tasks in a finite amount of time."

"That would be true over any distance at all, no matter how small!"

"That's true."

"But it's *not* true. We've been to the kitchen, like, a million times."

"Of course."

"So how about it, Doc," I said. "What's the answer?"

But Milly jumped in first. "Hold on. This isn't even about distance. Not really. I mean, how do you get from one *minute* to the next? Aren't there going to be an infinite number of halfway points in *time*, too? Thirty seconds, fifteen seconds, and so on?"

"You're doing well," said Grimes.

"Or let's say I want to lose ten pounds of pregnancy fat. First I have to lose five pounds? But before that, two and a half? One and a quarter? I guess Mr. Zeno figures I'll never do it? Nothing ever *resolves*?" In the background, softly, the strains of *Tristan und Isolde* teased a climax.

"A story tries to come to a point, but never *gets* there?" I offered.

Milly contemplated the emptiness of her wine glass, then—deliberately?—filled the glass about halfway. I suppose that in doing so, she accomplished an infinite number of tasks. She said, plopping the wine bottle back onto the table with what might have been a smidge more force than was necessary, "Okay, then. Like George said, what's the answer?"

"Me, personally?" Grimes turned up his hands. "To me it's a matter of naming things. Identification. You can label something an infinite number of ways, slice it up first if you want to, but it's still just a finite entity. What we're dealing with is a classic example of indirection and verbal obfuscation. Philosophers can be dishonest; you gotta watch them. Two things seem to equate, or to at least commute with one another, when in fact they're different subjects altogether. In the case of getting to the kitchen, the question of identifying the infinite number of ways that that trip can be measured and mathematically described is quite separate from the finite amount of time that it takes to get there."

"That's smart," said Milly. "That's really smart."

"Jesus," she added after a finite amount of time.

"Frankly, most philosophy comes down to language: what we call things, what we mean by those things."

"Philosophers treat questions like doctors treat diseases," I put in.

"Wittgenstein!" said the delighted man. "I didn't realize I was in the presence of a fan!"

"Just a little something I remember from I don't know where."

"A particularly sophisticated fortune cookie, perhaps," jested the doctor, "or—"

"And how about *your* name?" broke in Milly. "You realize neither of us knows it?"

This time it was quite obvious, her embarrassment, as her gaze shifted away from Grimes's face and onto a barbecue sauce stain in front of her on the tablecloth.

If Grimes noticed or was offended, it didn't show. He sat back in his chair and flexed his arms behind his head, stretching. He leaned forward and steepled his fingers together. Finally, addressing me, he said, "You know, I realized the other day, far from expecting you to remember my name, it's a minor miracle I ever remembered yours. I mean, there was the incident...." He paused and looked at Milly. "Your husband *did* tell you about the playground?" Upon her affirmation, rather diluted, he continued. "Apart from that, George, we never knew one another. Probably the only time either of us heard the other's name was in the principal's office that day. You were so humiliated and fearful, I doubt you registered it."

Milly came to my defense. "We *are* talking a quarter century ago."

Grimes looked at my wife apologetically. "Of course. But to answer your question: Harold. Harold Jovis Grimes." Seemingly unsure of what to say next, he added, "At your service."

"Jovis," repeated Milly, testing it like it was a hypothesis. "And what does that mean?"

"Aw, what the *hell*, Mill?" I said. "It's his name."

"No, it's a fine question," said Harold. "Neither of my folks ever said, but I've always assumed it's this mark." He pointed to his forehead. I shot a glance at Milly. If she'd had that oval on her own forehead at that moment, it would've blended right in, she had gone that red. Harold paused a moment to make sure we understood what he was trying to say. Then, "You know? Jupiter? It's got—"

I said, "Yeah yeah, I know. The big red spot. I just—"

Milly took over. "Are you saying that that mark on your forehead has always been there? It's ... a birthmark?"

"Yes?" said Harold, confused at the confusion. Then, "By the gods, George! Did you think that *you* ... ?"

"I ... guess so?"

Now it was Harold's turn to ruddle. "All this time? It would've healed a long time ago—"

"Yeah, I know that, I just—"

"You know," said Milly, "I'd really just like to hear this whole goddam story, once and for all?"

So Harold Jovis Grimes, with Richard Wagner the whole time pressing quietly on in the background, told the story of us. All the parts that were new to Milly—that was most of them—were new to me as well.

"I was in fifth grade. Shady Elm Elementary, you know, was K through five, so my friends and I would go around like we owned the place. Trading insults, discovering girls, walking on water. Day in question, it was lunch time. They did lunch in two shifts, so that meant half the school's in the cafeteria. Everybody was just winding up, getting ready to go outside for recess.

"Trouble was, little Harvey Fiddlesticks—nobody ever used his real name; I think even he forgot it—well, he'd lost his lunch money. Only, he didn't really lose it, right? He'd been relieved of it by somebody. *Somebody*, of course, was the Right Honorable Misters Potsy Kopple, Pup Barbarossa, and Kim Klein. For the second year in a row, the three biggest fifth-graders in the school. Big, and just getting bigger. Pup's still around, did you know that, George? Runs his dad's furniture store, Country Wicker, up on City Line Avenue. Yeah, that's Pup's now. I lost track of Potsy. Probably in jail. Kim actually ended up with a law degree, I think. Got some corporate gig up in a New England state, maybe Connecticut.

"You didn't know these kids like I did, George; you were in the second grade. Anyway, Little Bo Peep had lost his sheep, right? Couldn't tell where to find them. But Miss Marge, she knew *just* where to find them. Now, you absolutely *must* remember Miss Marge, right? Combination cafeteria aide, recess monitor, school bus driver? Big square head that came up from a big rectangular body, no neck. When she turned her head to talk to you, her whole body would come along for the ride. I swear, her cheeks would sweat. You could hear her huffing as she came toward you, like God brought a school bus to life."

I gave a little laugh, remembering. Harold went on:

"Now, Miss Marge knew those kids had taken Harvey's money. But she couldn't prove it, and she'd spent all twenty-three minutes of lunch trying to squeeze a confession out of anyone she could corner. It was like watching Robocop trying to round up the Little Rascals. Nobody was saying a thing, and Miss Marge had done everything short of sitting on the whole damn fifth grade, and I suppose she was getting ready to do just that when the bell rang. You better believe she was worked up, and so she resorted to her one remaining weapon. *'Fifth grade! You're gonna stand for recess!'*

"So, terrific. The entire fifth grade marched out to recess just so we could stand for a quarter hour in three straight lines under a cloudless sky. Everyone knew that the charter members of the Future Criminals of America, Shady Elm chapter, had taken Harvey's lunch money. The perps knew it, Harvey knew it, Miss Marge knew it, and I and all my friends knew it; probably the guy who ran the Texaco station down the street knew it. But the trouble was, Pup 'n' Pals *knew* that I knew it. I had *seen* Pup lift it out of Harvey's bookbag, and *Potsy had seen me notice him.*

"So I'm standing there, hostage, listening to these three jerkoffs tell me under their breath what they're gonna do to me if I squeal. They're gonna beat me up, bust my arm, work me over until my whole body is one big red spot, whatever. I'm trying to figure out what to do about it; I'd have to say I was beginning to feel pretty uncomfortable, when—*whoosh!*—something flies past my head. It takes a bounce, then sits there on the blacktop. It's a stick—pretty big, maybe a foot long, couple inches thick. Then, huffing and puffing, here comes Miss Marge. It must've been one fuck of a day she was having. *'Who threw that stick at you?'* she wants me to tell her.

"I truly had no idea, George, and that's exactly what I told her. So she disappeared for, like, a minute, and then she came back with *you* in tow. What the heck did you do when she asked you about it, George? Go beet red? Confess to the Lindbergh kidnapping?"

Harold paused a moment, during which time I realized I'd been asked a question, but he went on:

"And the rest of it, you already know. Miss Marge goes to retrieve the stick, then has an idea: *You* do it. She makes *you* go over and pick up the damn thing, George. I think she was so pleased to finally nail something on somebody that she wanted to make the most of it. Like, who knows, maybe *you* had taken Harvey's lunch money as well.

"So she makes you stand in front of me. She makes you hold up the stick in front of my face—I tell you, George, I felt so bad for you—and she makes you apologize to me. Then she tells you to take that stick and march straight up to the principal's office and show it to him as well. She tells me to go along. Hoping, I guess, that my being there would, what, compound your guilt?

"You and I go inside the school, we walk down the K—1 hall, up the half flight of stairs to the hall with the music room and the art room and all that. You remember? We go down that until we come to the doors with the metal-meshed windows and the breaker bars, the ones that lead to the breezeway connecting the admin offices to the rest of the school. Once we're in the breezeway—You remember, George?—I tell you to give that stick to me.

"Now, the breezeway, there's a door on the side of it, opens up to a back yard. I say, 'Watch this.' I open the door, and I toss that stick way out over the grass and into the woods. Then you and I go up to the principal's office, we tell him the truth—you tossed a stick at recess; it happened to almost hit me in the head—and, well, here we are, Mr. Principal, what do you want to do with us? I think you made off with, what, a scolding?"

It took me a moment to realize that, this time, Harold was expecting me to speak. "Yeah," I finally said. I was thinking about how little I had known about that day. "A scolding. That's about it."

"I'll bet you never threw a stick at anyone again," said Harold.

"Course not."

On the baby monitor, the LED flashed as a faint cry came across the speaker. Daniel was awake.

"I'll get him," said Milly.

"I'll come too," I said.

"That's okay, I've got it. You stay here with Harold. We'll be just a second, and then Harold can see Daniel."

Milly left. I suggested a retreat to the parlor. Harold stood and stretched, then ambled over and, with a sigh, plopped himself down onto the sofa. I sat in the loveseat.

"Golly," Harold said, "I haven't taken off my shoes. Did you want me to take off my shoes?"

"Only if you like."

"Sure you do," he said, translating from the polite to the accurate. He went over to deposit his shoes near the front door, then returned. Reclining on the sofa, he blessed the room with another sigh and stretched his arms once more above his head. Reflexively, his feet sought the stuffed ottoman in front of him. He stopped himself in mid-motion, his legs a suspended arc, and tossed me a look that I supposed was meant to emulate embarrassment.

"No, please," I said, "that's what it's for."

"Lovely meal," he said, lowering his feet onto the ottoman and crossing one argyle-socked foot over the other. He looked around. "Nice spread you've got here."

"Thanks. I—"

He inhaled sharply. "Should we get the wine? There might be enough left for two small doses. Just enough to put a polish on the meal?"

"I'll get it. We also have dessert coming—"

"Oh, lordy! I always find room for dessert."

Returning from the kitchen with the bottle—indeed, a few ounces of wine remained—I saw that Harold had found where Milly had placed the Bloomingdale's gift bags. He was holding them out to me, two large rectangles framing the circle of his face.

"Let's just give Milly a moment," I said.

"Of course." He set the bags down just as Milly entered the room. She was holding Daniel, and her face looked flushed.

"Dr. Grimes?" she said.

The doctor stood, immediately attuned to the mild strain in Milly's voice. "Yes?"

"I think Daniel might have a fever."

Grimes seemed to deflate a little, as if he were disappointed in the face of such a mild and routine predicament. "You've taken his temperature?"

"Yes."

"And?"

"Exactly 100."

Again the doctor's stature seemed to wilt as the specter of true emergency faded. He took a breath. "Rectal thermometer?"

"Yes."

"Left it in for at least a minute?"

"Yes."

"Sterilized it afterward?"

"Yes," she said. "I mean, I'll get to that."

"Be sure you do. Okay. All perfectly normal, folks. Please," he said to Milly as he indicated the couch.

Milly sat down, cradling Daniel, who was mewling quietly, in her arms.

Dr. Grimes laid a hand on Daniel's head and inspected him closely. Seemingly satisfied with what he saw, he said, "There are three primary causes for a low-grade fever: dehydration, overheating, and infection. I know better than to ask if Daniel has been properly nourished. I see that you have him bundled up pretty well, Milly. May I ask what temperature you have the room set to in there?"

"Same as the rest of the house: 73, I think."

"We could lower it," I offered.

"Only if that's comfortable for you," said the doctor. "Just clothe him the way you would yourselves; babies can easily overheat. Now, as to infection, most of us are equipped with a sophisticated immune system. But a baby's is still developing. This makes them prone to infections that are not dangerous, necessarily, but that our fully developed bodies would easily fend off.

"Daniel doesn't appear overly stressed. I recommend we take his temperature again in half an hour. Meanwhile, I can sterilize that thermometer for you, if someone can point me to a bottle of rubbing alcohol and give me use of your kitchen. In fact, if one of you could give me a hand, I can help clean ..."

I gave a little jolt. I was sitting on the couch, holding Daniel. I realized that I had dozed off, just for a moment. I looked toward the kitchen. Milly and Harold were cleaning up, Harold still lecturing on the subject of illness and thermometers. The child, too, had fallen asleep, his tiny head a warm and breathing orb on my chest.

Leaned against the frame of the couch were the two gift bags, slightly open. I considered peeking inside, then decided to wait for Milly, to wonder together what more things yesterday might bring. Holding Daniel, I went outside onto the balcony. The air was chill, the river lucent with the ambient light of the city. Within the metal bowl of the grill, the coals burned a bright orange, still alive. Indoors, barely audible, Wagner forgave the dissonant past. I lifted my face to the luminous night, to the stars and the planets, those jovial wanderers of immensity: fractions, named into existence only as, silently and over an infinite number of paths, their light reveals themselves to us in parts. Absolved, I accepted the unopened gifts of the past and the future, and I held in my arms the present joy; in my heart, the fullness of a complete moment.

# for Roopa

While I can sometimes hear the voices of authors past (or present) graciously encouraging me to write  (Hemingway: "Write the truest sentence that you know." Gaiman: "Do only what you do best. Make good art."), the specters of Raymond Carver and John Updike give me nothing. Carver reclines drunk upon a celestial couch, reminding me that I'm not, never have been, and never will be an alcoholic and exhorting me to leave the writing to the professionals, while John Updike, in the twilight, ignores, still writing, struggling scribblers he confounds, and drinks whisky.

Nevertheless.

If I'm going to channel an author, it's important for me to not write too soon after having read their work. I want to feel their rhythms, not plagiarize their words. Bill Kent, when he still regularly came to the group he created, assured us all that we needn't worry too much about mimicking authors, because if we work at something authentically, then anything we eventually write will indelibly be our own. Stephen King likens this phenomenon of personal voice to a fingerprint. I'm still not sure *how* this works—there are only so many words in the English language, and there are only so many ways those words can be connected together in keeping with the rules of grammar. But it really does seem to be the case. Partly out of limitation and partly out of possessing my own mix of ideas and experiences, I have found that, yes, my work has settled into something people assure me could have been written only by me.

But I still really enjoy channeling Updike, as I did with this story, knowing from the start that I'll fail in the narrow sense but will, with luck, end up with something better, i.e., my own story with my own fingerprints all over it, regardless of my muses.

I sat down to write. I'd recently watched the movie *Melancholia*, in which an errant planet crashing into Earth causes (spoiler!) the end of the world. The whole thing was deliciously dreary. Permeating the movie like the A-flat that drip-drip-drips throughout Chopin's "Raindrop" was Richard Wagner's prelude to *Tristan und Isolde*. The piece was unfamiliar to me, but it soon became clear (at least to me) that the movie owed its existence to *it*, rather than, as is more often the case, the other way around. Imagine if John Williams's iconic *Jaws* music had preexisted the eponymous movie, and that one day Steven Spielberg, listening to it, had said "Shark!!" In a similar fashion, I imagined Lars von Trier (also previously unfamiliar to me) listening one day to *Tristan und Isolde*, when suddenly visions of a wandering planet and a critically depressed woman strayed through his head.

If *Melancholia* is the moving picture offspring of Wagner's opera, then "The Bringer of Jollity" is perhaps its literary sibling.

Siblings often have opposite personalities. Nobody in "Jollity" is depressed (although George is anxious), and my story involves the beginning of new life, not the world's ending. In the movie, the approaching planet, despite being a herald of destruction, brings temporary contentment and peace to an otherwise troubled and depressed woman; in "Jollity," a doctor named after a planet brings temporary anxiety and concern to an otherwise untroubled and happy man, George. By the simple act of coming to dinner, Dr. Grimes brings to the present an anxiety rooted in George's past, so George finds himself being drawn into the past and worried about what he will find there, even though the birth of his son would normally inspire him to look toward the future. There's a lot to unpack here, and I fear that I've already said too much. I'd rather you decide for yourself what it's all about.

But in connection with the music, what *Melancholia* and "Jollity" have in common, besides the elusive yet inevitable resolutions both by Wagner, inside, and George, outside, looking up at the planets, newborn son in his arms, is a continual, purposeful, almost (but hopefully not quite) painful crescendo, seeming to forever, like this sentence, escalate, without ever getting to its destination. I researched this and discovered that the musical device behind this never-arriving is the Tristan Chord, named after this very piece by Wagner (although Wagner apparently didn't invent the chord itself).

I'm dedicating this story to Roopa Culas, whose writing never fails to delight with its brilliant and compelling imagery. Roopa, I was thinking of you when I wrote about the fractured Susquehanna and the live coals in the grill and the sticky pyramid of store-bought macaroni salad resting in a crystal bowl. I hope you enjoyed the visuals.

# he would have told her everything

The boy stands halfway down a hill, calculating the geometry of the midnight campus. Below him, Folger Hall, a long and low rectangle of turquoise and glass, makes an acute angle with Hurley Street. Behind him and above, Carlsen House, his own dorm, stands sentry, holding the perimeter against the encroaching woods beyond. A single tree, apart from the rest, leans into the breeze, its unfurled leaves partially obscuring the lighted window that marks the boy's room. Beneath the tree, a forgotten grocery cart.

The boy taps out a cigarette from a pack of American Spirit Ultra-Mellows, lights up, and stuffs the pack into the front pocket of his jeans. His gaze moves beyond Folger and across the empty athletic fields to the tennis courts and the dark student union building, and finally to the neon glaze that spills up into the night from the parties on distant frat row.

He thinks as he smokes. Whatever path he's going to take, it shouldn't be the straightest one. Nor the most obvious. Schlitz Hall, home to the electrical engineering department, situated on the far end of the academic quad, is his intended destination. Third floor, one of the double-E labs: This is all the information he's been given.

The academic quad lies off to the left, down Hurley. At this hour the quad should be empty; maybe a couple kids heading back from a cram session for finals, here at the end of term. Not many people to interfere. Once he's in among the gently sloping buildings that trace the Quad's parallel lengths, most of the remaining trek can be gained under cover. But how to get to the Quad? Aye, there's the rub. The direct way will be watched.

He reconsiders Folger, where but a single room advertises life—purple light pulsing from inside a window. Someone having sex? Yes, he could go that way, through Folger. Exit by the food service dumpsters, then it's a scramble up and around the hedges to the entrance of Mary Mattson. Once inside, Double-M is mostly one long corridor with classrooms hanging off it. Wouldn't want to get caught in there, though. But the building has two levels, and he could peer around corners, check that it's clear.

He begins down the steep driveway. Once off the hill, he's fair game—that's the rule. He picks a car parallel parked along the near side of Hurley and crouches behind it. He checks left and right, then left again. He crosses Hurley like a WWI soldier up from the trenches. Screw Folger, he decides. He goes right, jogging around the length of the dorm to its backside; then, weaving around the cars, he navigates the parking lot.

He makes it across. Before him, atop a small slope, stands the length of Double-M, defining a binary decision. Outside, the tennis courts are ominous— all cages, like a trap. Inside would be better. That had been the initial plan, after all. Scrambling upslope, he slips a little, gets some mud on the knee of his pants, drops the butt of his smoke, stamps it out like he was done with it anyway.

Double-M is one of the music halls. Someone at freshman orientation, four years ago, said it had been the setting for *Creepshow*, but no one knew if that was true. He opens the door a crack, slips in, and is immediately overtaken by the smell of floor wax.

The vestibule is cavernous and, like all the buildings that belong to the fine arts school, beautiful in a Neoclassical kind of way. Or so everyone had been told. Latin inscriptions are carved into white stone walls; statues stare down through aloof and lidless eyes.

The upper hall is the way to go. Get an overview of the outside before leaving the shelter of the building. That, and the upstairs just feels more hidden. Secret.

He climbs the stairs and peers around a corner into the main corridor. The way looks clear, so he jogs along quietly, not quite able to keep his sneakers from releasing the occasional squeak as they rub against the hardwood planks. Last year he'd done a solfege class in this hall. He finds that exact room, tries the cut-glass doorknob, and enters. He flicks a switch; the room hums with light.

The classroom organizes itself around a Cristofori upright piano. Damn. It had been a good class, solfege. Turned out he had better pitch than he'd been led to believe in high school. Plus, there had been Jennifer Wallace. God. He never did ask her out to a movie. Would've had a shot, too. College really had done away with all that out-of-your-league high school bullshit. Well, most of it, anyhow.

Outside the window is Franz Hall and the outskirts of the Quad. Behind that, carpeted over in lights, is the rest of the world. The *world*. Which is more like the real world: college or high school? Maybe neither. Is everything going to revert, once he's graduated?

He spots the Hunter running around on the ground below him. He pulls back, out of the window frame. Crouches on the floor, slowly raises his head above the sill to peer back outside. The Hunter has hair so brown it's almost black. Looks like it's been scrawled onto his scalp with a charcoal pencil. Also, the dude is thin. He was thin when the boy had first met him, and four years of greasy cheeseburgers, large fries, refillable Cokes, a second Reagan administration, and $3 late-night pizzas had done nothing to the goddam fact. The guy must just shit like a champ, is all. He's running now, the Hunter, moving around between (for him) *hiding* spots: a tree, a lamp post, a goddam stake in the ground. When you're that thin, what isn't a hiding spot? The rules of life just don't apply, that's all. The dude'll end up a Republican. Hell, if he's not careful, a Baptist.

The boy considers fooling around on the piano and decides against it. He looks out the window again. The Hunter is gone. Probably went to stake out around Miller, the building opposite Franz where they try to teach humanities to computer science majors. If so, the quickest course would be to double back the way he'd come and take the straight shot to Franz. The above-ground floors of that building are meant for general math and science classes, with large auditoriums. But underneath, it's one sub-basement after another. Architecture students are rumored to have gone down there their freshman year, never to be seen or heard from again. But if he's wrong … if the Hunter has not retreated, but is hiding in his blind somewhere, hanging out down there …

One way or another, it's time to get out of this place. Best to stick to plan and continue down the length of MM—opposite from Porter, but also farther away from Franz Hall. The more time that elapses, the wider the area the Hunter will feel he needs to cover. At bottom what's at play here is a variation of the uncertainty principle that old Dr. Seneff used to lecture about in physics.

The boy comes out of MM, close to the student union. There in the dark, on a bench, a couple of kids sit holding hands. Near the door to the place that serves salads and other vegetarian excuses for food, a group of shadows are hanging out. They're theatre students, no question about it—dressed in black and doubtless reeking of body odor. No loners here; no one slowly breaking off from a group. The boy had been tricked that way once before.

The path to Franz is a concrete sidewalk maybe eighty yards long. Fully in the open now, the boy starts to walk. Running only draws attention. He scans the lawns, the tree line along the Cut, the benches, the distant Wren Library and its perimeter of benign boxwoods. He notes the Fence, where, underneath decades of paint advertising parties, religious functions, and concerts, the existence of wood is a mere assumption, and where four years ago his parents had finally left him alone to himself, after which they had presumably driven themselves back home—east, down the Pennsylvania Turnpike, the way they had all come.

He's halfway to Franz when a shadow emerges from behind the hedges in front of Wren. Haltingly, the shadow begins in the boy's direction. Involuntarily and ever so slightly the boy quickens his gait in response. The shadow moves to keep pace. A voice begins to drone in the boy's head: "Let $x$ be the distance between Ship A and Port B. We shall give the ship velocity $v_1$. At an angle that we shall label *theta*, a torpedo is launched from a submarine at point C...." The boy shakes his head, shutting out the voice of his old calculus professor. He again quickens his pace. The shadow lurches itself forward to match, then breaks into an all-out sprint. The boy flies for the archway around the front door of Franz Hall and hurls himself inside.

The building was designed to be a steel mill. A backup plan, should the whole school thing not work out. The main corridor is wide and sloped downward at a fourteen-degree angle, with concrete stairways in the wings that lead up to the second floor. Twin rows of sconces line the brick walls along the bottom edges of an arched ceiling, lighting students the way to dusty auditoriums. The only way to get lost—and the boy absolutely wants to get lost, and the Hunter absolutely knows it—is the narrow way down into the bowels of the would-be steel mill.

A side door stands open. Without slowing, the boy runs through it to a narrow staircase that leads to the first of the sub-basements. The stairs double back on themselves; at the bottom it's all metal conduits and white-painted pipes sprouting red valves and brass gauges. He has a choice: continue down a similar staircase to the next sub-basement or explore the narrow hall before him.

He looks back up the staircase and hears the footfalls of pursuit. Further descent would be predictable. Trying for obscurity. It would also be louder than a straight run, when he could try to soften the impact of his feet. Let it be the dim hallway, then. He runs along quietly, listening as the Hunter clambers down the staircase behind him.

The hall juts to the right, giving onto a slightly less narrow area and a three-way decision: a straight staircase up; another narrow, bending staircase down; or the continuation of the hall. The boy also sees to his right a gray metal door with a lockless knob. Sparing a couple seconds to open it, he discovers a janitor's closet with a utility sink and mop. He squeezes in and shuts the door, then in a flash of inspiration braces the mop handle across the knob.

Kneeling, the boy peeks through a square grate at the bottom of the door. He sees the Hunter arrive, then stop. He's scratching at his thin, almost-black hair; deciding between the three exits. The boy thinks: *He's thinking I'll go down to further hide myself. Then he'll think that I will have thought just that, and that I will have gone up. Then he'll think that I have thought that, too, and that I would never go up that long, straight staircase where I could easily be seen, and that I would take the straight path, deferring the decision whether to go up or down. Finally, he'll decide that since I eventually have to go up anyway, he would rather err to the side of safety. He'll go up. Dollars for donuts, he'll go up.*

The Hunter peers up the stairs. Then he goes to the twisty stairwell and looks down. He cocks his head; he listens down the hallway. In doing this, his face has been brought around so that he now spots the door to the janitor's closet. He walks over and stretches out a hand. He pulls at the knob; the broom handle strains, but holds the door secure. The boy can no longer see the Hunter's face—only a leg which now blackens what little light had been seeping in through the holes of the grate. The Hunter releases the doorknob and shuffles over to the upward stairs. He cups his hand to his ear. He has heard something. Like a shot, he races up the stairs.

Just as the boy had predicted.

He waits a few seconds, then emerges from the janitor's closet. Without further deliberation he descends the twisting stairs. The next sub-basement is identical to the last, minus the straight staircase up. With no need for further concealment, he casually wanders the hall, trying doors. The ones that aren't locked let onto small classrooms. He comes across another staircase leading down, and he takes it.

He expects another tight passage but instead finds a large, open room. Tables lie scattered about like floating islands, displaying models of high rises, bridges, and outdoor shopping centers. At the far end of the room is an arched passageway. Along the curve of this arch is painted, in a surprisingly delicate cursive, *All hope abandon, ye who enter in!* Beyond, the boy discovers a maze of interconnected rooms lit by vending machines. The odors of epoxy and room deodorizers thicken the air, and the place is cluttered with couches, metal folding chairs grouped around low tables, and workbenches piled with cardboard, empty potato chip bags and 16-oz Coke bottles, and all manner of hand-held tools. On a wall next to a blackboard dusty from drawings layered on top of erased drawings, someone has painted a window that appears to look out over a tropical beach. The shore is populated with taped-up pictures of bikini-clad women clipped from a *Sports Illustrated* swimsuit edition. Jesus. It's a whole 'nother school down here. These people—do they sleep? If so, where? Do they ever come up for air and real food, and if so, has he perchance seen one of them unknowingly in the dining halls? Inadvertently touched one? Who are these people? The boy tries to retrace his steps out of there but finds himself in another narrow hall. The next stairwell he comes across goes both up and down. Down it is.

In this next sub-basement (the boy now counts four), the first unlocked door he finds reveals a half-lit machine shop filled with dark outlines that recall that grinding and leering medical contraption from *The Exorcist*. He moves along.

Down the hall he comes upon a small window at eye level. Putting his face up to it, he sees at first only an inky black, then what appears to be a furnace along the back wall. An orange-hot glow comes from it, mesmerizing the boy. Exactly how far down has he come? A man stands before the burning glow. Though his back is to the boy, enough of the man's side is visible to reveal a body-length leather apron that ties around his neck. With a pair of tongs he pulls something out of the fire, so that the boy takes the furnace to be some kind of kiln. This man—he works here. Has always worked here, tending the infernal fire that, all this time, has secretly fueled the university.

The only exit is a straight flight down. All choices have been made; the straightforward path is fixed. The boy descends to find a room seemingly without shape and which exists for no discernible purpose. Here, at last, he has found the root of the building, the nadir of his flight.

It's as empty as a hole.

The boy sits on the floor, gathering himself, allowing himself to catch up. When this, too, has reached an end, he gets up and searches about the place. In the gloom, he finds a double door with painted-over glass panes. He pushes against the breaker bar and exits to a gravel lot.

The suddenness of the world stings; the boy squints and hugs himself against the night chill. As his eyes acclimate to the half-light, he realizes that Franz is built on the side of a hill and that his university backs up to a train yard. How had he not understood these things?

Ahead, gleaming train tracks disappear into the black maw of a tunnel. Behind him, a long concrete staircase climbs steeply uphill, skirting the backside of Franz. A curving metal handrail delineates the stairs from the encroaching brambles of the hill. The boy taps out another American Spirit from its pack and lights up. He considers the geometry of the situation as he climbs the stairs and calculates that he will emerge between Franz Hall and Ritchie Hall—the computer science building that, together with Franz, completes this length of the Quad. He finishes his cigarette just as he reaches the top.

His calculations prove correct. Almost the entire university now lies before him. To his left, the College of Fine Arts, looking like a museum, defines one width of the rectangle. To his right is Ungerschlitz Hall. 'Schlitz. A person, he reasons, could be forgiven for mistaking that hulking building for a factory. A single turret, massive and columned, sits atop like a smokestack. Forget the industrial motif; the university is a caravan of ships, commissioned during wartime, with 'Schlitz being the old-time steamer in the vanguard, pushing forward, prosecuting its unending campaign against ignorance, sailing its green enlisted men (and a few good women, too—not many, but a few) in stealth and steam, steadily toward the front.

Taking only a cursory glance around him, the boy sets off at nearly a full run. He keeps to the recently sprouted and already-trampled grasses, pivoting his head, watching for some shadow to suddenly move, striving to filter out the sound of his breathing in order to detect any stray rustle around him. He flies up the stairs to 'Schlitz and, with a final look behind him that reveals nothing, enters.

At the first elevator—obviously designed to haul cargo, with wide doors that lumber open and shut and a buzzer that screams angrily to indicate arrival—the boy presses the UP button. If the Hunter is waiting for him on the third floor, so be it. Unless Fred outright revealed the location of the quarry to the Hunter (or, more possible, the Hunter somehow tricked it out of him), there's no reason to worry.

The boy's reasoning proves sound, and he quickly finds the correct double-E lab.

There it is, sitting beside a flickering oscilloscope that no one had bothered to turn off. A Mountain Dew can. Hurrah. Someone (Fred, of course, who lately has been becoming more and more in danger of turning out to be a genuine jackass) has used White Out to redact the oversized capital M, the right half of the O, and the letters A, I, and N—leaving behind the message CUNT DEW.

Victorious, the boy grabs the can and sets off for his dorm.

His intent is to return under cover of Miller and Hobart Halls—the humanities buildings that lie along the length of the Quad opposite from Franz and Ritchie. But as the boy cracks open the front door of 'Schlitz, he sees a silhouette race across the width of the lawn, away from him, and enter Miller through a side door. Excellent. Perfect, in fact. The Hunter's location is known. A stroll through Ritchie will do just fine. Then a mad dash back to Carlsen, and he'll win the game before anyone's the wiser.

Entering Ritchie Hall, the boy practically sighs with repose as he imagines Muzak getting piped into the offices of the professors who are lucky enough to work in this building. Though connected to Franz by several breezeways, Ritchie bears scant relation to its brooding fraternal twin. One could not possibly imagine this building awaking one morning from uneasy dreams to find itself transformed into a giant steel mill. Here, in Ritchie, elevators politely ding, well-behaved classrooms sit off carpeted hallways, stairwells are neatly tucked behind closed doors, and lobbies are appointed with modern furniture designed around a motif of harmless brown and orange squares. Ritchie is a building conceived to be exactly what it is, and one would never think to descend it in search of an entrance to Hades. In fact, there is only one basement in Ritchie that the boy is aware of. It houses the school's sober and prodigious engineering library and is lit, during daytime hours, by natural light that streams in through a long line of nearly horizontal windows that skirt the medial side of the ground floor hall above.

It is down through these interior windows that the boy now gazes as he spots Mary Lou Kaminski studying at a table. He had met Mary Lou their freshman year at a barbeque during Greek rush—that last chance to get some pretty good meals in you before surrendering to four years of Kill-Me Café. For a while he and Mary Lou went together. Then she started seeing some guy named Bryan McCardell.

Maybe it was last year sometime when he'd heard that maybe they had broken up?

He takes the elevator down and gives a half-assed wave to the somewhat conscious student on graveyard shift behind the reference desk. He approaches Mary Lou from behind. She's wearing headphones and has her head down over a textbook. He peeks over her shoulder. From the vectored diagrams and accompanying second-order partial differential equations he sees on the page, he guesses that her final exam tomorrow (today, actually) will be in fluid dynamics. Or perhaps mechanics of deformable solids.

He plops down on a chair next to her.

"Jesus!" She pulls off her headphones.

"Hey," chuckles the boy.

"What are you doing up?"

"Same as you. Studying."

Dimples touch her cheeks. "Bullshit." She smiles and leans back in her chair, cupping her hands behind her head. She's small—all of five foot one—and her pointed elbows are like the tips of chicken wings.

The boy shrugs carelessly and smiles. It's nice seeing people one more time before everyone disappears. "All right, have it your way," he says.

She points to the Mountain Dew can in his hand. "Can I have a sip?"

The boy remembers the handiwork of his good pal, Fred the Nobel Laureate. "Um, no," he stammers. "It's … it's empty." He tries to shove the can into his jeans pocket. Naturally this fails, and he sets the can on the floor, turning it to hide the rude message.

"Whatever," says the girl. With hair the color of circus peanuts, falling in relaxed twists to her shoulders, and her flashing emerald eyes, Mary Lou Kaminski could easily be mistaken for Irish. But of course she's Polish.

"So," the boy observes.

She looks at him.

He finds a topic. "You got prospects?"

"3M," she says. She slips a sheet of paper into the book, marking her spot, then closes the book.

"Nice!" The boy is genuinely pleased. "Minnesota?"

"Uh-huh."

"Wow."

The girl's hand strays back toward her book.

He grasps for more. "Solids or fluids?"

"Huh?"

He points to the book.

"Oh," she says, understanding. She turns the book on its Z axis so that he can read the title: ADVANCED FLUID MECHANICS.

"Yourself?" she asks.

"Nah," he admits, "you were right. I'm not really studying. Just ..."

"I know," she says. "I meant about prospects."

"Oh!" The boy is unsure of the conversation's scope and depth, how much to say, how much she cares. Three weeks ago, he had accepted an offer from IBM. Silicon Valley, thirty-four thousand dollars a year. He's going to be part of a group that's working on something called the Internet. He's going to live in California.

He's about to tell her. He would have told her everything; a few moments is all it would've taken. But a stray motion catches his eye. He looks up to see the Hunter's demoniac grin leering down at him through the windows above.

"I've got to get out of this place," he simply says.

Mary Lou smiles. "You'll be okay."

The boy says goodbye and heads toward the exit. At the reference desk, he turns. Already, she has her headphones over her ears, her nose in her book. For a moment, maybe two, he stands there. Then he turns back to the kid behind the reference desk. He tips him a wave, and he runs.

Outside the library he tries a stairwell door, hears the Hunter racing down, chooses another. He goes up three floors, takes a connecting bridge across to Franz, jogs up the fourteen-degree incline of the hall to its top, clambers down two flights of stairs, and walks out the front of the building. He passes the Fence at a brisk but measured pace. He's holding back a little, wanting to save something. Coming to Mary Mattson on his left, he strolls along Hurley Street and arrives at last at the base of the driveway that leads uphill to Carlsen, his dorm. Here, at the end, the boy pauses.

Turning to gaze back the way he had come, he sees nothing of interest. The student union is still dark. In a few hours he can go get some eggs, a coffee, a bowl of cereal. They've got Cap'n Crunch—the kind made from peanut butter.

A noise is growing behind the boy, a kind of rattling, but it doesn't register in his mind: He's too busy wondering if a little sleep would be a good thing or a bad thing. Then he understands what he hears.

Too late, the boy turns around. The Hunter—Scott, his roommate of the last three years—is crouched inside a grocery cart that is rocketing down the driveway. In the few seconds before impact, Scott yells, "Class of 19-fuckin-88, mother*fuckers*! Yeeeaaaggh!!" He leaps out of the cart at the boy. The two of them, together with the cart, end up in a splendid crash that spills onto Hurley Street.

The boy stands up and brushes himself off. "You are one fine piece of work," he tells Scott.

Scott's already standing. "Nailed ya!" he yells. Then, "Woot!" as he punches the air.

Fred is walking down the driveway from Carlsen. "Give it here, Bill," Fred tells the boy.

Bill lobs the Mountain Dew can toward Fred, who doesn't quite catch it. The can clangs down the driveway and rolls to a stop somewhere beneath the upended shopping cart.

"Whaddaya say?" Fred asks. "One more?" He hands Bill a crumpled piece of paper ripped from a spiral notebook.

Bill flattens out the paper and reads: *Hobart computer annex. Mounds candy bar wrapper.* He turns to ask Scott if he wants another go. But Scott is already careening down Hurley Street and is soon lost among the cars.

Bill sees that they will indeed play one more time, and he sees that it is good. Dawn is still hours away, and it's the last day of finals—and then graduation and the creation of a new world. And they will all get out of this place: himself, Scott, Fred, Bryan McCardell, Jennifer Wallace, Mary Lou, all of them.

# for Jennifer

Where "This Do in Remembrance of Me" relates the story of an older man returning to the hallowed ground of his past, "He Would Have Told Her Everything" covers the opposite situation. Here we see a young man communing with the elements of his present stomping grounds one last time as he prepares to leave his college campus forever, peering with great trepidation out from the safety of his hidden but rapidly collapsing vantage point and into an unknown and hostile future, wondering how the choices he's made will affect that future.

When I find myself wandering around a building complex that I've never seen before, particularly if the buildings possess an interesting architecture, I'll sometimes entertain myself by imagining that I'm being pursued by a lone hostile tasked with my capture. I don't know if anyone else does this. Perhaps it stems from my tactical, chess-oriented mind?

Whether I'm the sole practitioner of this mental exercise or not, I hope it at least produced a fun read. The details of the college campus are lifted from Carnegie Mellon University, which I attended from 1984 to 1988. To one unfamiliar with the campus, the story might not be as compelling to read as it was for me to write. If so, apologies.

Whatever enjoyment you were able to glean from the tactical cat-and-mouse duel, I hope you at least were struck by the girl who sat at the inner sanctum of the campus and spiritual heart of the story. The beginning of the story gave no hint she was going to be there because the boy himself had no idea. Neither did the author. Yet there she was, an oasis of human contact and dialog in the middle of a story bereft of these things. My hope is that by the time you get to Mary Ann, you will have forgotten, as I did, that there are other humans around the campus.

Suddenly, the boy is confronted with a choice that is not merely part of a silly game. The girl represents all that is real—all that the boy is running both away from and toward. He could stop, break out of his silly make-believe crisis, and speak with her. Or he could ignore her and keep running.

I struggled with the title of this story. In my heart, I wanted the title I eventually gave it. But a lot of people didn't like it. Jennifer Baylor, however, liked it. Thanks, Jennifer, for the vote of confidence I needed to go with my heart on this. To think I could've named it anything.

# blue curtain

So Megalap's finally coming downstairs. About time. If he's thinking he's gonna share breakfast with Cold Hands, he's got another think coming. She's already gone, most likely to the gym. In those—what? gold lamé shorts? And pink leotard? Sure as shit better be the gym.

But listen. There's gonna be bacon now, and thank Skydog for that. Cold Hands was useless in the kitchen. I know Megalap's good for it, too, cuz I heard him. "Evelyn!" he'd yelled—humans have the most ridiculous names for each other—"Evelyn, I'm heading to the ACME to grab a can of WD-40, a pack of Trojans, and some bacon. Need anything?"

"Sure, Gene!" Colds Hands had yelled back. "Can you get me some Marlboro Red Pack 72s and two bananas? Thanks!"

That was just yesterday, while I was *trying* to nap on the La-Z-Boy. So he best not try holding out on me.

I greet Megalap as he descends the stairs. This is he who preps my food. Also, I've put him in charge of my pee outings. He's adequate to these tasks and has thus far not failed me. Skydog help him if he does. And, believe me, I will eventually want my pee outing. But first there must be bacon. What else? Either you like bacon or you are wrong.

Megalap's in the kitchen; opens the door to the treat cabinet. Here, he says to me, properly kneeling, have a treat. What he hands me isn't bacon. But it'll do for now. I guess.

He's checking the garage. Left-paw side empty? Yup, Cold Hands' Subaru Outback is missing. The whole house is quiet. Down below, Littermate sleeps in her basement empire.

Next, Megalap engages in the prime ritual: the brewing of the wakey juice. Fool tried to put the poison in my water bowl once. Take my word on this, pal, cuz I'm speaking to you as someone who regularly drinks water from puddles in the street: It's filth.

While the machine gurgles out its brown liquid nastiness, Megalap goes to his office, probably to check the news feed on his computer.

"Wait," I hear him say.

"No," he says.

"No. No. No!

NO!!!"

I'm interested. I walk over.

There's a blue curtain on his computer. That's all. Mind what I'm saying; I'm not talking a blue screen of death. I've seen how he reacts to those. This is different. I'm talking a *curtain*, framing the sides of his monitor, pulled back eerie-like to reveal the charcoal backdrop of an empty screen.

"This can't be right," Megalap says. "This can't be *happening*."

He's staring at the bottom of his screen. He's blinking at it.

I need to get a good look. Dammit, I think to myself, and not for the first time. Who put the tall things in charge of this world? I get up on my hind legs and set my paws up on his lap. It helps. I don't think the human even notices. He's still blinking.

On the bottom of his screen, a few miserable icons. Four, maybe five of the things that come with a new computer.

The taskbar? A mere clock and a volume control.

Desktop? A single orange-and-black Geek Squad icon, barely visible against the black void.

System tray? Or whatever they call that thing in the bottom-left-paw corner of Windows? A Start icon and a lame IE button. Nothing else.

"*Nothing?*" Big Guy cries. No Documents folder? No Libraries?

No, I want to tell him, nothing. Looks like it could be a ransomware situation. This is bad. Bacon is looking further away than ever.

"Nothing?" he says again, this time under his breath. Then he *screams* it. "NOTHING!"

That's when things get downright crass. "The fuckers," he says. "The FUCKERS!!!"

Whoever these fuckers are, they didn't even leave him his wallpaper—the one showing that popular horror author sitting in a gliding chair in front of an old typewriter, a bunch of crumpled papers at his feet. There's nothing. Nothing but that blue curtain.

It's not rage that I'm witnessing here. No, the smell I'm getting off Megalap is something else. Call it full-blown panic.

What came first, I wonder? Which realization of loss (each of them accompanied by a different but equally choice turn of phrase, let me tell you) was the worst? Most likely it was his written work: novels, short stories, works in progress whose ultimate form was yet to be determined.

Or maybe it was his financial records. Maybe his emails, bookmarks, and archives.

The situation needs to be resolved, and quickly. It's not that hard. You just put a few strips in the pan and fry it up. *Voilà*, bacon. I'd do it myself if I had hands. Who put the things with hands in charge of the world? It would also be nice, I guess, if Megalap got his computer back.

He calls out for Cold Hands. "Evelyn!" Never mind that *she's at the gym, bozo!* Remembering she's gone, he descends to the basement empire, bangs on the door of Littermate.

"Get up!" he cries. "Get up! Get up! We've been hacked!"

I think, What does this human think he's doing? He needs to sit at his computer and make such remedies as are possible. He needs to recover his life. What's Littermate got to do with any of this?

Littermate ignores him. Probably still asleep. Eventually Megalap goes upstairs and sits down at his computer.

First line of defense: that Geek Squad icon. At least the bastards left him that. Although …

… he clicks on it. Alas, the brain-wrecked computer will need an internet connection in order to accomplish this task (duh!), and apparently this too has been wiped. Computer's asking some idiotic system question that Megalap has probably never seen before, not even when he first got the thing. These kinds of details would have all been set up for him at time of purchase at Best Buy.

Fine, he seems to conclude. No Geek Squad.

Meanwhile, I'm thinking to myself, *Geek Squad*? Really? Why would he even want them? This was their fault! Last night, because of absolutely nothing Megalap had done, he had this whole online session with them. Some "key validation" issue with his antivirus software, some glitch that wasn't his fault, unless you wanna go ahead and argue that if he'd just kept his subscription active, he wouldn't have needed a different key in the first place. Tech had given him a number to call and said in the meantime they'd set Megalap up with a backup antivirus package. It'd hold him over, the tech had said.

Total bullshit, of course. And now Megalap's been hacked. To be frank, I'm starting to feel a little bad for the human.

But wait, his body language seems to be saying, all is not lost. A sharp intake of breath, and he's mumbling about cloud backup service. Myself, I'd always considered that to have been a wise purchase on his part. Of course, once he realizes …

It doesn't take long. "But … no internet connection!" he yells at no one.

The panic is almost complete.

Now, I happen to know that Megalap has a friend. Friend's a really good IT guy. I know this for the same reason I knew about the antivirus package and that Ben Affleck was going to (ahem) screw the pooch with Jennifer Garner and that Barack Obama was a shoo-in for the White House. I know this because, quite frankly, I have absolutely nothing to do. Day in, day out—nada. Zilch. Bupkes. Life is unbelievably boring when you don't have hands. You've no idea, pal. So I may as well pay attention to my social media feed. You know, YipYap? 1.9 billion WAGs (Weekly Active Growlers) and counting? You just wouldn't believe how many different smells can be communicated by odormoji. A single "growl" can pack as much information as a week's worth of piss at the base of a street sign.

I digress.

Friend, he lives a few hundred miles away. So, look. I realize there's nothing Friend will actually be able to do. But at least Megalap can give him a call. Talk to someone. Someone with hands and vocal cords. I wish to Skydog that I was tall, that I had hands, and that I had vocal cords. Because, really, I've got a pretty good idea how to fix this issue. I mean, the one with the computer. Bacon, it seems, has been relegated to the back burner. (Pun. Sorry.)

Megalap picks up his phone. He's remembered his friend. He makes the call. It goes to voicemail. Perhaps Friend is still sleeping. But halfway through Megalap's frantic message—I'm totally fucked! I've lost everything!—Friend must've picked up.

It doesn't take long for the panic to make its way across the wire.

"What happened?" is what I hear coming through the phone. "Are you all right?"

Megalap walks as he talks. Tells it in spurts. He's gotta back up a lot, answering a few basic questions from Friend.

I, meanwhile, wander off to the hall closet. I'm on a mission. Humans are tall, they have hands, and they've got vocal cords. But Skydog only knows what He was thinking when He made their brains. Some of my woke pals argue that humans are just as intelligent as us. A pawful of philosophers—Bark Spinoza, Dogenes, Pluto—even claim that humans have *souls*, for Skydog's sake. I dunno.

No, I can still hear Megalap saying as I head to the foyer, everyone is alive and fine. Yes, the house is still here. No, it hasn't been burglarized. Yes, he is being calm. Well, no, he agrees, he isn't being calm. Yes, it's the damn computer. This is what he's been trying to say this whole time: His computer's been hacked.

"What?" Megalap says to Friend. "What's on the computer? You mean, like, right now? A curtain is all. A blue curtain. No, not the blue screen, dammit! A *curtain*. As in: *It's curtains for you, pal!* That kinda thing." Kinda thing a hacker would leave behind on your screen after they toasted your computer. A calling card. Then Megalap rattles off the few other crumbs that the hack-bastards have left behind.

While he's talking, I discover that the door to the hall closet has been left open. Just a crack. (Do humans ever learn?) I easily paw the door open and start digging through the pile of footwear that's always on the floor inside. I know exactly what I'm looking for....

Wait. Megalap is on the move! I abort mission, find him in ... the kitchen! Thank Skydog, there will be bacon!

Megalap opens the fridge. I stand *directly in his path* so that he practically has to trip over me to move. I loll my tongue out of my mouth like I'm a complete idiot, and I cock my head at a 45-degree angle. I hate it with every bone in my backyard, but it *always* does the trick.

But no. He grabs wildly at a pitcher of water. Pitcher falls to the floor. He goes to the sink, gets a rag, nearly slips in the puddle on the floor. Then he flees back to his office. He looks around at nothing while he rattles off a bunch of stuff so quickly that I doubt even *he* is able to follow what he's saying.

Friend tries to help. I hear him over the phone. "Okay," he says, "you've been hacked. This is going to be hard. You can do this, though. You can. You just need to be patient. You need to adopt the right frame of mind."

The right frame of mind, I think. Yes. This Friend person, he sounds very wise. Perhaps humans—some of them, at least—have intelligence, if not souls. Perhaps Friend is one such as these.

I trot back to the hall closet, dig through some more footwear: Vans, Birkenstocks, Crocs, Teva Pajaros—Skydog, what *do* humans do with all the shoes?

Ah. Here's what I was looking for. I grab it with my teeth and drag it over to the office.

Megalap and Friend are agreeing that what they need right now is the right frame of mind.

I drop what I'm carrying at my human's feet.

Megalap, still on the phone, picks up what I brought him and tosses it into the hall. Idiot thinks I'm playing a game. I grab it again. Drop it at his feet.

*Boot*, I think at my human. *Boot.*

Again, the human tosses the boot into the hall. He's not in the right frame of mind, and that's a damn fact. But what else to do? I pick up the boot again, drop it at his feet. *Boot, idiot! Boot!*

Of all things, *Friend picks up on it.* (I wonder: Does this one have bacon?)

"Wait," I hear Friend say over the phone. "You ... *have* tried restarting your computer, right?"

"It won't do any good," Megalap says. He's been hacked, he reminds his patient pal. But, yes, he can go to the Start icon and select Restart.

He clicks on it. While the worry circles on his screen start to churn, I'm sitting there thinking: Human. Why didn't you just pay to renew the antivirus subscription last week, like you told Cold Hands you were gonna do?

Megalap, pacing, swears that if he ever gets his files back again, the very first thing he'll do is renew that subscription.

Enough time has passed for the restart to have finished. Meanwhile, Megalap has walked away from the office and has been roaming the house like a maniac, moving things around as if the missing files might be hiding behind the couch pillows. I've been following him. I'm really starting to worry.

He strides back into his office. He sits at his desk, holds his head in his hands.

The horror author comes back on the screen. He's sitting there on his glider, perfectly calm, typewriter on his desk, crumpled papers at his feet.

With a trembling hand, Megalap clicks on the Documents icon. A window pops up, loaded with files. He goes to a folder. Inside this folder, he goes to another one, and then another and another. Again and again, the screen fills with icons. Lovely, beautiful icons.

Megalap tells Friend everything is fine. He hasn't been hacked. Everything is there. It's all there. He thanks Friend twice, maybe a third time. Hangs up.

I know that look on his face: He's got a story to write. For the next few hours, he'll be useless.

I plop myself on the floor behind his chair. I'm trying to sleep when a noise comes from behind me. The door to the basement is being opened.

I get up and turn around. Littermate is in her pajamas, the ones with the soft pink bottoms perfect for curling up on. Right away, she spots me. She picks me up and holds me belly-up in her arms. "Aww!" she coos. "You're just a *baby*, yes you *are*!" She takes me into the kitchen and falls into a swivel chair. She rubs my belly and gives the chair a spin and says it again, "You're just a *baby*, yes you *are*!"

Then it comes to me: Philosophers are asking all the wrong questions. I just hope Megalap remembers to renew that damn subscription.

# for Daniel and Rosie

As I said, some stories are based on real-life events. But not this one. Nope. No idea where this story idea came from. Schenectady?

Now, as this story—which greatly taxed my imagination to write because it in no way bears any relation to anything I've ever experienced—is narrated by a dog (whose dog? no idea), and because Daniel and Rosie are such terrific animal lovers, I'm naturally dedicating it to them. Daniel and Rosie, your wedding was beautiful. Thanks so much for being a part of the circle and for including me in your special day. Keep on writing!

# crapperclysm!

*Some see a cool blonde in a red Ferrari—a Christie Brinkley catching up Chevy Chase on an open highway, cutting through a forgotten wheat field in Nebraska. Others recall a Diana Rigg behind the wheel of a '62 Lotus Elan—an avenging femme fatale suited out in black leather. A small but vocal minority, coping with the world's complexities through means of conspiracy, speak of Jackie Kennedy, driving the very same '61 Lincoln Continental that once cradled the shattered form of a bleeding American president.*

*What all agree on, the very few who remember anything at all and don't relegate to dream the rumors of wreckage and fury, is the license plate: MDMDRVR.*

*And that she drives,*
*and she drives,*
*and she drives.*
*And no one has ever seen her stop.*

Way up on an I beam, legs dangling over the scaffolding high above the I-23/I-16 interchange project, was no place to be taking lunch. Whether Mack had lost a bet or the crisp October air had filled him with a sense of daring or he was responding to some unearthly summons, the circumstances that led Mack Dinsdale, second apprentice welder, to a spot where he could bear perfect witness to what would initially be called The Interstate Incident, then, for a time, The Great Blue Goo Snafu of '22 before finally settling down in the history books as simply Crapperclysm remain unknown to history.

Mack set his brown paper bag lunch on his lap, craned his neck, and used his welders' chipping hammer to wave to the fella who drove the Honest Jons tanker truck. The fella waved back with a channel lock. Every third day for the last month that truck would drive up onto the I-23 overpass, behind and a little above where Mack now sat, to syphon human excrement from a dozen green porta-potties, all standing in a row, lined up north to south along the shoulder of the newly built highway, directly over I-16. The side of the truck bore the Honest Jons business motto: WE TAKE SH*T FROM EVERYONE! Mack would wave to the fella, and the fella would wave back. The two had become friends.

As for the channel lock, it was probably just an ordinary one, but Mack's chipping hammer was something special. Its nose was cone-shaped and sharp for chipping away at slag, the tail dual-beveled to get at build-up from any angle, and the handle coiled into a spring to absorb the shock of each blow. In these respects, it was like any other welders' hammer. But this one rang every time it hit, and that's what made it special. It is also what made the salesman toss it in for free, decades ago, when Mack's grandfather bought himself his first set of welders' tools. The ring wasn't terribly loud, but it was high-pitched, and not many welders want to hear that every time they take a swing. Mack's father had no interest in welding and became a successful patent attorney. But he let Mack play with all his grandfather's tools, and that hammer had been Mack's favorite for as long as he could remember. Over the next twenty years it became Mack's lucky hammer. When it was not in use he would secure it by pushing the handle through a belt loop and giving it a full-circle twist. If several minutes had transpired since Mack last felt the hammer push against his thigh, his hand would stray to it, verifying its existence, as if fearful it might someday willfully free itself.

Mack opened his brown paper sack lunch and looked inside. He smiled. His wife had packed his favorite: Oscar Mayer and Velveeta—four slices of each—interleaved and slid between twin slabs of Wonder bread, crusts removed. Also, a bag of Fritos and a few sticks of celery. If Mack was particularly hungry, he would eat the celery.

Mack looked down at the I-16 traffic coming toward him and moving away from him, flowing eastward and westward. His hand drifted to his lucky hammer. His hand found it, and only then did Mack start eating his lunch.

Behind the wheel of her husband's Mercedes Benz SL-class convertible, state senator Barbara Stanton drove down I-16 under the influence of inviolable destiny. Indeed, Senator Stanton had not felt this level of righteous providence since the primaries, when her campaign manager, Corey Blackburne (the man was a legend; worth every donated campaign dollar), leaked a story that her opponent was "involved" with an elementary-school-girls' soccer coach. In the end all that could be shown was that he had given the skank a gym member-ship—but the man had simply been no good. *That* was the bottom line for the voters to keep in mind, and by gum they had kept it. Corey had meant well, and no harm done. Barbara Stanton's upper lip quivered with significance as she drummed her ballerina-slipper-pink fingernails against the black, leather-wrapped steering wheel, and the wind lashed ineffectually at the stiff blonde bob hugging her skull, shielding the world from the sticky emissions of her thoughts like the tip of a banana-pudding-flavored condom.

To attribute the adrenaline that coursed through the senator's overstimu-lated veins to the fact of her husband's having lent her his car for this special mission (her own Mercedes was a mere S-class, non-convertible) would be to miss the point. The great state of Alabama had not only elected her, it had re-cently elected a new governor—one truly dedicated to the United States Con-stitution. It was time to rein in government, to increase personal liberty, and to once again respect the rights of all the right people.

It was time, in other words, to lower taxes on rich folks. The mere thought of it sent a tingle across Barbara's skin and seemed to pull her blazer tight across her chest, her nipples hardening most irritatingly underneath her J. Jill pussy-bow blouse. (Power had its benefits and its detractions.)

All at once the Mercedes's self-nav system took over, decelerating the car sharply behind a Jeep with a pair of American flags flailing patriotically behind it. She lurched the car into the other lane, where she came up behind the tail end of a trashy VW bug convertible. The license plate said MDMDRVR, and the car was driven by an equally trashy-looking woman, her visible arm bare but for a smothering of tattoos, the skank leering like a low-class slut across her graffi-tied shoulder at the driver of the Jeep. Disgusted, Stanton veered back into her original lane.

People deserve to keep more of the money they earn, she thought to herself. Not the poor, of course, who don't pay any taxes and don't work and have ev-erything done for them. No, it was herself she was thinking about, born into an expensive world where the price of everything—sedans, beef, power—was on the rise.

And the cause? The reason, precisely, that too many dollars had been sent chasing too few 6,000-square-foot new-construction homes in too few planned unit developments? Was the answer not that, during the glory days of Ronald

Reagan (here, Barbara mentally genuflected and praised the one economics class she had taken at Ole Miss), women had refused to stay in their place? That they had insisted instead on careers, ending the era of the one-working-parent family?

But today was not for Senator Stanton to singlehandedly bring justice to the tax system. Such things would be handled by men in DC, men whose wisdom would prevail over the reckless forces of socialism and state totalitarianism that tore at the great moral fabric of America. No, today, this long and long-looked-for day, Barbara had a much more pressing duty, a more dire mission, a more manifest destiny. For today was the day that, in the name of life and liberty and the pursuit of happiness, the Alabama State Senate would be voting to restrict access to abortion.

How long had this imminent liberation from the bondage of poor judgment and immoral self-determination been in the making? How many more women would be permitted to escape the consequence of their decisions?

Let not the good, natural-born citizens of Alabama misunderstand: Barbara Stanton was not without compassion. There were exceptions. *Things* happened. Things against the intended order of the universe. For such exceptions—in cases of true emergency—one could always "make arrangements." A few days off work. An out-of-state flight, a few nights away from the comforts of one's parents' home … in a cheesy, horrible Motel 6, paid for with a clutch of hastily grabbed cash from her father's cigar box (the few hundred dollars was never missed, and she had only been sixteen, for sweet Jesus's sake—was she supposed to have come up with it on her own?); a hushed conspiracy, where motorcycles pulled up outside your ground-floor room at all hours of the night, headlamps glaring through beige curtains; a motel where, perhaps, the teenage girl's boyfriend (pregnancies can only happen one at a time, after all) could come stay the night. Bring along her favorite Oreo Double Stuf cookies. Provide … comfort.

One could always, in other words, "work around." Such delicate situations were private and bore no resemblance to the sorts gotten into by sluts who can't keep their knees together when with a man. Sluts such as, say, the woman in that VW bug that Barbara Stanton had seen only a few moments ago.

Compulsively, the Senator veered around the Jeep to the right. She was in search of that woman with the tattooed arms. Coming around the Jeep blind, her nav system blared shrilly as she nearly struck the tail end of another car—

this one nauseatingly chartreuse and obviously out of control, heading to the shoulder of the road and somehow giving the impression that it was falling apart.

Recovering from the near miss, Senator Stanton searched again for the tattooed skank. But she must have put on an incredible burst of speed, Barbara thought, for the highway was visible for at least two miles ahead. The license plate that said MDMDRVR was nowhere in sight.

His sandwich was finished, the Fritos a mere afterburn of salt. Mack watched the cars below and mindlessly fingered a stick of celery. Fact was, he didn't care for celery too much. Perhaps it was time to get back to work.

Still, it was nice up here. Most of the work that day had been going on at street level. Viewed from above, it seemed irenic, almost passive, the only sounds the gentle whine of the traffic below and the hum of the Honest Jons' pump behind him. Mack watched a group of hard hats take a break from setting a streetlamp into a cement foundation. He watched Hank Giffords climb down from his bulldozer and begin a long, lazy walk over to where Mr. Skeet, the crew foreman, stood—a clipboard dangling from his hip like he'd put it on that morning along with his pants and then forgotten all about it. Mack watched some new grunt he hadn't met yet work a rope, hand over hand, hoisting a bucket of bolts high up on a pulley. Even the sky at that moment seemed a silent observer. It was the color of turmeric, and although it was much too early for it, a handful of stars was poking through like the sky had lost its top.

Then something happened that brought Mack back to earth. Several miles down the highway, where a mere dash connected the road to the sky, there was a disturbance. Perhaps a vehicle had swerved onto the shoulder. There was a thickening of shapes out there, as if several cars had clotted themselves together into a pack. It also seemed to Mack that one car had suddenly sped up and separated itself from the rest.

He watched, transfixed. The dude had to be going at least a hundred. Mack's hand strayed to his hammer and found it. He brought the stick of celery to his mouth and was surprised to discover he had already eaten half of it.

Speeding down I-16 like Paul Revere riding into Concord came a Jeep Wrangler. Its top was open and the doors were missing and twin six-foot American flags waved off the Jeep's exposed back. The wind crashed all over the body of the driver, a man named Lou "Da Loo" Dellucci. He, too, was six foot, and he weighed a fuck-ton more than both of his flags put together. The middle-aged club bouncer was on his way to a combination gun show and political rally when he spotted a mane of blonde hair streaking from the front seat of a red '89 Ford Mustang convertible that was weaving all over the place just ahead of him.

Lou "Da Loo" Dellucci shifted lanes and pushed down on the pedal. Coming up behind the Mustang, he spotted the license plate, and his thoughts went along the following lines:

*M-D-M-D-R-V-R? What the fuck is that? Made me drive her?*
*Am dumb driver?*
*Oh, I got it now. Me dumb driver. Wow, what a dumb fuck she must be.*
*Let's get a look.*
*Oh, yeah, she's looking good. Nice rack. I'm gonna get her to look over.*
*C'mon, baby, look over.*
*Look over,*
*look over,*
*look over.*
*Oh, yeah. Not bad, not bad. Semi-hot I'd say. I've seen better. Hell, I've had better. Like that slut*
*Last week outside Dan's Wheezy Shack. What a blow. Cleanup in aisle 3, bitch!*
*Still, this one? Nice rack. This one's the kind you can do things to. Get her into my Jeep. Get her ankles up.*
*I know what.*
*I know just the thing.*
*I should get that into a voting booth. A nice, fucking, voting booth. I bet nobody ever once fucked*
*In a voting booth. God, that would be quite the fuck. It would have to be the right kind*
*Of voting booth, of course. Not one of those namby-pamby things they make nowadays,*
*With the blue touch screen "ballots." Those came around during the Florio years*
*And NEVER LEFT.*

*Fucking Florio.*
*Liberal fucking Florio.*
*Only a liberal fuck like that*
*Could fuck in a voting booth like that.*
*I'm talking a real voting booth. The ones we used to have*
*When we were a country that did things.*
*When we were great.*
*The kind of booth you get into. You close a curtain, and you shut yourself*
*into conclave*
*With God.*
*And you don't have pens, either. You have levers. Real levers,*
*Like the kind they have on nuclear subs.*
*Tactile.*
*Tactical.*
*Like the kind Gene Hackman pulled in Crimson Tide when he launched the*
*nukes and he took out the fucking godless Commies, except that they didn't*
*launch, don't forget THAT, assholes, the missiles DIDN'T fucking launch,*
*because that namby-pamby black faggot Denzel Fucking Washington scuttled*
*the whole thing. Don't forget THAT.*
*There were names next to each lever,*
*And you grabbed the right one,*
*And you fucking PULLED.*
*I'm talking about a voting booth like that.*

Lou "Da Loo" Dellucci had much more to say, none of it amounting to anything, but at some point he looked around and realized that MDMDRVR had disappeared.

Mack Dinsdale squinted into the distance. The car that had sped away from the others a minute ago was a convertible; on that point he was clear. And although he still didn't have much more than a fleck of light off a hood, Mack would've laid odds that the make was foreign. He also imagined it was a woman he saw in the driver's seat. *Guys*, he thought to himself, *don't drive so saucily*. Although if someone had asked him what he meant by that, he couldn't have said.

The next three-quarters of a minute proved both of Mack's convictions true. The car was indeed an Alfa Romeo: silver, a bullet speeding just above the ground and *far* above the posted 70 mph speed limit. Every single car and truck that had stood between Mack and the Alfa had been passed, and none of them had yet passed below him. What was more, the car was accelerating.

As for the driver, Mack was still only getting a smudge of light reflected off the windshield. But the license plate at least was clear: MDMDRVR. *Madame Driver* ... Mack whispered the words out loud like a chant. An invocation. A prayer. On cue, the woman passed underneath him and looked up. *A face to launch a thousand ships*, thought Mack.

His hand reached for his lucky hammer.

It wasn't there.


With no one to mutter to, Ronald Kirby muttered just the same, and the color of his twitching goatee was something out of a kit. From time to time he'd lift his eyes to the rose-smeared heaven above him, then return them to the highway traffic. His head bobbed up and down or shook violently in response to whatever opaque thoughts gummed his brain. "Pastor Ronnie" (the kids at Happy Hands Super Mega Bible Church loved calling him this) was deep in one-way conversation with his Lord.

Not that Ron Kirby was an actual pastor. He was pretty sure the Lord had not called him to *that*, and if there was one thing Ron excelled at, it was discerning the Lord's voice.

For example, he had heard the Lord one dark and horny night during his sophomore year at Bowling Green tell him to go to the Tri-Delt sorority party. Where, all praise to Jesus!, he had met Sarah, the woman he was now blessed to call his wife. Ron had also heeded the Lord's call to go ahead and buy a '69 Fiat Spider convertible off the Used lot. That car now surged and hummed underneath him as he drove to his happy hands church for a happy hands Wednesday night youth lock-in. (Tom Doflin, the salesman at the used car lot who had prayerfully guided Ron into his purchase, was none other than Pastor Tom, the *real* pastor of Happy Hands Super Mega Bible Church. A busy man and laden with many spiritual gifts was Tom Doflin.)

If there yet be any skeptics regarding the spiritual acumen of our subject, Ronald Kirby, let us not overlook how, just the other day, Pastor Ronnie had felt the gentle tug of the Lord telling him to go check out a magazine that an old man had tossed into a wastebasket outside a McDonald's. Hear ye and believe, the mag was indeed porn, *just as the Lord had suggested it might be!* Ron took that magazine home and, sacrificing his Tuesday movie night with Sarah, spent the entire remains of the evening by himself with the magazine, feeling the tug of the Lord as he struggled for that old man's soul.

Recently, the Lord had led Ron Kirby to work closely with youth. The Almighty had even been so kind as to single out to him one girl, Amy Freestone, as an especially worthwhile teen to spend many a good hour with. Poor Amy, struggling at home, her father dealing with depression. The man rarely came to Bible study anymore. The Lord knew Amy could use a good, firm father figure about her.

It was naturally, then, Amy Freestone whom Pastor Ron happened to be thinking of when a purple brassiere flew out from the car ahead of him and smacked into his windshield. Ron flipped the wipers, sending the bra over his head, flapping like an exotic bird into the distance behind him, where it passed out of the knowledge of men.

Ron thought, *Is it her? Could that be Amy Freestone in that hot little Mazda Miata convertible ahead of me? The car doesn't look familiar. Neither does the license plate. MDMDRVR? But the driver sure does look like Amy. Those long, curly brown locks of hair; that cute little button nose. She's looking over at the carload of boys in the lane next to her. Why, they're shouting at her. How rude! Should I speed up and over-take her? She sure seems to be missing a bra. Maybe I can investigate. Help a little?*

"Great idea, Ron. Do it."

The sudden voice startled Ron. He snapped his head to the right, where something was hovering over his shoulder.

It was Jesus. Again. Fuck.

*Drat that Jesus*, Ron thought. *Would it kill Him, just once, to appear like He does in all the portraits? The way He's supposed to? Gentle, flowing hair? Knowing eyes? How come all I ever get is this round, grinning yellow face like the ones they put on grocery bags, telling folks to Have a Nice Day? For all I know, it's Satan floating over my shoulder.*

As soon as he had thought it, Ron braced himself for what he knew was coming next. He only had to wait one second.

"Good question, Ron. How *do* you know that that grinning nincompoop over there isn't Satan and that *I'm* not the real Jesus?"

There it was. The *other* voice. A second round, yellow face—this one floating over Ron's left shoulder. Just like the first, but with the smile upside down. No—not just the smile. The whole goddamn face. Ron let out another sigh, longer than the last. He hated when this happened. Surely life had lost *something* on the day that the demiurges (or whatever) who rule Creation and drive the hearts of men had turned out to be a pair of emojis.

Ron let the yellow faces debate, trying to discern which was the Lord.

☺ spoke. "I have Ron's best interests in mind. What have you ever done for him?"

"Well, for starters, I try to shut you the hell up," said 🙃.

Was it Ron's imagination, or did the smile one flatten just a little? It said, "There, did you hear that, Ron? A cuss. I wouldn't use that kind of abusive language on you."

"Let your no be no, is that it?" countered 🙃.

"Even the devil can quote Scripture," said ☺.

This time it was the frown on 🙃 that seemed to lift, moving closer to a flat line. It said, "Just what, exactly, would you have our friend Ronald, here, do?"

"Why, he wants to go minister to that young lady, Amy Freestone, who drives yonder ahead of us. Those young men in that other car are taunting her."

"Bullshit. Ron here thinks the girl threw off her bra. He only wants to see her tits."

"Language!"

"Ron." Like a coin that balances on a table, 🙃 turned slightly on its axis toward Ron's head, revealing the two-dimensionality of its non-existence. "Ron," it repeated, "look at me." Ron spared a glance from the road to see the pale yellow disc that addressed him. "Confess thyself to me. If we claim to be without sin, do we not deceive ourselves?"

"Blasphemer!" cried ☺, and now Ron looked at it and saw that its smile had definitely been squashed flat. "Confess to *me*!" ☺ cried. "I am faithful and just and will purify you from all unrighteousness!"

"I ... I ..." Ron stammered, looking from one emoji to the next, "I never had an unrighteous thought about Amy in my life!"

☺ and 🙃, in unison: "Yes, you did, Ron! Yes. You. Did!"

They were indistinguishable now, the 🙂 in their single-minded judgment, their countenances utterly flat as they spun about Ron's head. After several orbits, each landed on a shoulder, and Ron had no idea anymore which was which.

"He's going to jump her bones!" one of them said. "She's only a kid!"

"She's eighteen, for Christ's sake," said the other (potentially invoking an unsettling self-reference).

"Don't give me any of your According-to-Hoyle definitions. Ronald Kirby is a predator!"

"Ron is a regenerate creature, unblemished in the sight of God!"

"Uh-huh. And I suppose the next thing you're going to do is remind me that Ron and Sarah have prayed for Amy every night."

"That's right."

"And that, therefore, everything Ron does to Amy is on the breezy side of your grace."

"He is doing the Lord's work."

"You're a piece of work."

And on it went. Ron never did figure out which of the emojis was the Lord. But it was the *voice* of the Lord that mattered, and in the end, discerning *that* was never much of a task for Ronald Kirby. It was always the voice that put Ron's feelings first and told him to do and believe whatever it was he had wanted to do and believe in the first place.

Ron revved the engine of his '69 Fiat Spider to catch up to the girl with the missing bra, but he never came even with her. Everything below his shoulders wanted that girl to be Amy Freestone. Everything below his shoulders wanted Amy Freestone to be at the lock-in that night. And maybe *something* that had been *on* Ron's now-empty shoulders would have told him that that wasn't such a great idea. But to Ron's great relief he discovered that everything above his shoulders told him he just didn't give a fuck.

Mack Dinsdale's hammer has been cut loose from space and time.

*Ping! Ping! Ping! Ping!* The hammer tumbled down the rungs of the 12-foot A-frame ladder that connected the scaffolding below to the I beam Mack sat on. The hammer reached bottom, took two more bounds, and disappeared over the ledge. For a few breathless moments the hammer went incommunicado until, with a final, declamatory *PING!*, it hit the pavement below and rebounded into view. Following a tremendous arc, the hammer lodged its pointed head into a sandbag that was serving to weigh down a pulley system on a second set of scaffolding. Immediately, sand began spilling out of the punctured sack. From his perch, Mack could see across to the top of the pulley, where a bucket of bolts hung from a hook. As the sandbag lost weight, the heavy bucket began to descend—slowly at first, then accelerating as the sandbag turned into a flapping flag of burlap, with Mack's hammer, still stuck in it, going up for the ride ... becoming a projectile....

The bucket smashed to the ground, bolts spilling everywhere. In the same instant, far overhead, the hammer struck the wheel of the pulley. The wheel, spinning madly, came loose, as the armature that had held it in place snapped with the impact. The burlap wrapped itself around the broken and limp armature while the hammer, clinging to the end of the ripped bag, swung back and forth like the pendulum of a clock.

The wheel, however, fell to the ground; where, still spinning, it raced across an open patch of raked gravel to the base of a plank of lumber that formed a ramp to the top of a line of cement highway lane dividers. The wheel sped up this ramp and careened, perfectly balanced, along the tops of the dividers. Sitting on top of the last divider was a road sign. The sign—a white triangle bordered in red—was an extra and hadn't been installed. It depicted the silhouette of a car driving under falling clumps of some amorphous matter that was falling from a cliff. The wheel struck this sign, knocking it off the divider and onto the end of another plank of wood, this one with its center balanced atop a sawhorse, forming a seesaw. On the opposite end of this seesaw someone had placed a large, metal toolbox. The sign collapsed onto the plank, flinging the toolbox across the work area and into the open cab of Hank Gifford's bulldozer.

The bulldozer was unoccupied, and its engine was running. The toolbox hit the driver's seat, took a healthy bounce, somersaulted in the air, and lodged itself directly on the gas pedal. A billow of black smoke discharged from the vertical exhaust pipe, upon which rested a red-tailed hawk. The hawk, displaced from its perch, half-flew and half-rode the warm updraft of exhaust until it settled again, this time on the burlap bag from which swung Mack's lucky hammer. As soon as the hawk landed on the hammer, it came free of the burlap bag and fell into the open cab of the bulldozer, where it hit the stick shift, putting the thing into drive.

Mack Dinsdale now sat watching a bulldozer drive itself up the unfinished road that would one day become the onramp for I-23.

The kid was upset, and why not? He was, after all, riding in the backseat of a puke-green modified Dodge Challenger with its top sawed off and bolted back in place with a handful of metal hinges. The others in the car with him—the usual suspects, chumps all three—were Thebes. His "brothers." Theta Beta Delta. He had rushed his first term, hoping for friends. He ended up pledging, just to make sure he wouldn't live the next four years alone. His name was Schlomo Hazzan: creative writer, dreamer, reader—lost in a world of other people's making (or sometimes, better yet, his own making). But one way or another, lost. Out of place in the routine world of objects, demands, people. People who, he recently had come to realize, would never, ever, stop calling him Slow Mo. And there had been a second realization: he would never, ever, stop minding.

And other things. Things he hadn't signed up for. The humiliation of hazing, the parties that don't finish up without some girl in a tit sling and a pair of crack-clinging sweats saying no and everyone pretending it was yes, and the skits that were of course only meant as satire, because who doesn't laugh at white boys in brown shoe polish?

He quietly mocked himself as he sat there, looking out the window at the big orange signs warning of impending road construction in large capital letters, recalling his naïve belief that college would fetch him some story ideas. *Story ideas*, he mentally repeated to himself, holding the words out at arm's length like so much rotting fruit.

More than upset, the kid was worried. Worried that someday the name Schlomo Hazzan would show up in a newspaper alongside Greyson Mattock, Chaz Holt, and Travis James III.

The kid wanted out, and why not? With all his heart, he wanted out. Out of the frat, possibly out of the university. But most immediately, the more he looked through the windows and the more he saw what was going on inside, he wanted out of that car.

"Fuck!" observed Greyson. He was driving. The car jolted to one side as he grappled with his seat belt, which had clamped itself down on his shoulder. A vein bulged angrily through the fade of his crew cut.

"Snap, brother! What shall I fuck?" said Chaz, sitting shotgun. He pretended to work the button fly of his jeans.

"Fuck … this … fucking … *fuck*!" Greyson clarified, pulling repeatedly at his seat belt, which was now firmly locked in place, probably due to his yanking it while simultaneously accelerating the car.

Travis, sitting next to Schlomo in the back seat, chimed in. "Slow Mo the Homo! Chaz is in need of your phallic services. Greyson is driving, so him and Chaz can't homo right now. Sorry, girls." Travis leaned over the seat to pinch Chaz's left nipple through his Vineyard Vines oxford shirt, its powder puff blue dotted with the outlines of little lobsters and its sleeves rolled up to the elbows to reveal fronds of blonde hair that streaked Chaz's tanned forearms and matched the twists of his braided goatee. "Chaz? Can it reach from all the way up there? Come on, Slow Mo, don't be such a Jew. Push up a bit, Chaz's dick isn't quite as big as mine."

Greyson yelled, "You're all a fuckin' bunch of fuckin' asshole queers!" thereby bringing this segment of the colloquy to its logical conclusion.

"Hold it, Chaz," said Travis, his voice earnest. "Don't put that dick away yet." He pointed through the windshield. "What's *that*? Pedal to the metal, Greyson!"

Greyson came up behind a Corvette convertible. It was pink, like cotton candy, and the top was down, and the redhead inside gave the boys a little wave of her hand through the rearview mirror.

"Well fuck me with a cigar and don't forget to make it moist, Travis," said Chaz. "I can't be sure with all the clothes she's got on, but I think it's your mom!"

Travis had been eating a stick of celery. Now he took it and stuck it in Chaz's left ear. He had time to swivel it around a little in there before Chaz batted it away.

"Knock it off, you faggots," Greyson said. "What's that on her license plate?"

Travis spelled it out: "M-D-M-D-R-V-R. Slow Mo, you pulled a 400 on your SAT verbals, right? What's that license plate say?"

Schlomo sighed. 400? That'd be a 740 to you, pal, and there's a fact. But— facts? Oh me! Oh life! (Had not someone—a poet, certainly; Whitman?

144

Frost?—once advised that we re-examine life and dismiss all that insults the soul?) Oh me, of the endless taunts of the witless, of houses filled with fuckery, what good amid these, oh me, oh facts, oh life?

*Answer.*

The Shiskebloyshtilkayt. Yes. When things got bad enough (and things were getting pretty bad, here in the car) there was always the 'Bloyshtilkayt. The BS, for short. It was a skill—a trick, really—that Schlomo had discovered a few years back at a party where there had been a few too many leaves of grass being passed around. The skill itself had seemed to come from outer space, but the word for it he had made up himself. From the Yiddish, *shishkebloyshtilkayt* roughly translated to "cone of blue stillness." It was a shield—a way to withdraw from a world of excess stimuli, to take refuge from the constant shit that people were forever trying to give him. Lately, he had even discovered that the BS provided a good mental state from which to engage in his creative writing.

So. The 'Bloyshtilkayt? Things were indeed getting pretty bad in the car. But had they progressed (regressed?) enough, yet, for the BS?

Schlomo felt not. Not yet, anyhow. The psychological maneuver could easily be taken for a retreat (which, in fairness, it pretty much was). Painfully, he had learned that the old schoolmarm's adage of "just ignore them" all too often backfired. Bullies were mean and often stupid, but usually not quite stupid enough to not know when they were being deliberately avoided.

For the time being, then, the BS, in its fullest form, could wait. Still, one could tap into it a little bit....

Schlomo had been asked a question. "M-D-M-D-R-V-R," he repeated. Instantly, the answer came to him. He inhaled deeply, then said: "Madame Driver."

"Ma-Dame-Dri-ver," repeated Travis. He emphasized each syllable like it was a dream come true. "Greyson. Pull up next to her."

The Dodge Challenger approached the Corvette, a supplicant sidling up to the hallowed image of its metallic god, the driver its high priestess. She had on a pair of sunglasses so big they made her eyes seem everywhere at once. She looked over. Her ruby smacks curled up into a grin so vicious it burned the air. With one hand still on the steering wheel, the other reached for her blouse. She started playing her fingers over the front, miming voluptuous, airy curves. Then she pointed to the top of the Challenger and jabbed downward with her finger.

"What's she doing?" said Greyson, the pink of his fingers drumming with interest against the black steering wheel.

Schlomo said, "She wants us to take our top down."

Chaz put it together. "If we take off our top, she'll take off hers!"

"Je-zus!" Travis said. "The hatches, boys! Un-batten down the hatches!"

"Like hell we are taking off the top of this car," Greyson said.

"Why not?" Travis inquired.

"Fuck!" Greyson explained.

But Travis was already at the hinges, flipping them up, motioning to Schlomo and Chaz to do the same. (Schlomo, refusing to budge, was treated to a whiff of Abercrombie & Fitch Fierce cologne as Travis leaned across him.) "Sorry, Greyson," said Travis. "You lose this one!"

Greyson tried again. "Like. Hell. We. Are. Taking. Off—"

Too late. The wind was already whistling in through the crack of light that now appeared at the doorline all around the interior of the cab. Only the hinge that was over Greyson's head, to the left of the windshield strut, still connected the roof of the car, and it was starting to give.

"Fuck!" Greyson reiterated.

"Get over to the shoulder!" yelled Chaz. "The roof is about to go ballistic!"

Greyson swerved onto the gravelly shoulder of the road, barely missing a Mercedes convertible in his blind spot. For one final moment, the top clung to the frame. Then it flew off the car. It hurtled backward with amazing speed and made a horrific sound as it hit the pavement. While Greyson, Travis, and Chaz cheered on the redhead, who had tossed her bra into the wind, Schlomo was realizing two things: that he had finally gotten his story, and that, somehow, everything he just witnessed was merely the prelude to an awful, mind-blowing, beautiful, climactic catastrophe.

Now, finally, it was time for the full BS.

Again, Schlomo inhaled deeply. The key was always just to *get started*, and the key to *that*, Schlomo had discovered, was to find some focal point on which to center one's attention. Doing this allowed the world to become ... flexible. Fiction was non-fiction, reorganized. For this purpose, Schlomo would often light a small votive candle in his room. All too often, however, the BS demanded that fealty be paid in inconvenient places. Schlomo looked around for something to gaze at and discovered that the bulging vein in Greyson's temple would get the job done. After that, it was simply a matter of pulling in some elements from his surroundings and seeing what would come out of his pen.

Schlomo pulled out his writer's journal and got to work.

Up the half-built I-23 onramp came the yellow bulldozer. It growled as it crawled along, a splotch of oily exhaust belching from a shiny chrome pipe into the air above the driverless cab. The dozer's blade was down, spattering gravel to either side as it came on. From where Mack Dinsdale sat, the stones sounded just like hail.

Mack took his gaze from the bulldozer to search behind him for his friend in the Honest Jons tanker truck. The tanker, its engine idling, its pump humming away, was syphoning out the last of the twelve porta-potties. The driver himself was leaned up against his truck, one foot planted toe-first in front of the other, heel to the sky. He was puffing on a smoke.

Mack caught his friend's eye. He pointed to the dozer. His friend smiled, lifting the cigarette toward him, not understanding the gesture. Finally, he looked the way Mack was pointing. He saw it. The dozer was halfway up; its path would take it very close to the far end of the line of porta-potties. Too close.

Both men looked at each other, then again at the approaching menace. There was no direct way for Mack to get to the onramp; the scaffolding he was on was built against the old overpass, which was being systematically demolished. But Honest Jon could make a go of it, and he did.

He ran along the southbound shoulder of the road, his cigarette leaving a wispy trail of white in his wake. Past all twelve porta-potties, then down what little ramp remained between him and the vehicle. Sashaying alongside the thing, he searched for a way to hop onto an eighteen-ton moving bulldozer. It moved on wide tracks that allowed it to climb over or destroy anything in its way. Mack thought: *He's crazy.*

Man and machine were almost to the top of the ramp. Mack watched Honest Jon allow the dozer to get ahead of him. *He's given up*, Mack thought. Then, running up from behind and pushing off with one foot, arms flung skyward, Honest Jon leaped onto the rear of the turning track. His momentum, together with the upward motion of the track, proved just enough to keep him upright. Then he lurched forward, and Mack thought things were going to go the other way. *That's it*, thought Mack. *He's jelly.* Honest Jon threw his arms backward,

147

flailing, and all the while the cranking track cranked, pushing everything forward, bringing him closer to the open door of the cab.

The bulldozer leveled itself out at the top of the on-ramp just as Honest Jon grabbed one of the black bars that framed the cab. He climbed inside. Mack could see his face through the plexiglass window as he hunted for the necessary controls, miraculously still in possession of his cigarette. Just as the bulldozer was about to hit the first of the porta-potties, Honest Jon's face lit up. His hand reached for something, probably a gear shift. For a second, Mack believed he was going to make it.

But Honest Jon was too late. The right side of the bulldozer encountered a jumble of extension ladders, lumber, and excess scaffolding that sat in a heap on the ground. The dozer—but only its right side—began to climb this mound. The thing tilted left. "Get out of there!" Mack cried as Honest Jon leaped free of the vehicle.

The bulldozer crashed onto its left side, knocking into the nearest porta-potty. Then one by one, like dominoes, the porta-potties fell across the entire stretch of road until the last one, next to the offramp for I-16 West, yanked free from the tanker truck that was emptying it and tumbled over into an orange-and-white-striped barrel.

The barrel was filled with sandbags and very heavy. It teetered toward the ramp that descended from what would one day be I-23 southbound to the freeway below that currently was I-16 westbound. The barrel came to the middle of the ramp, almost stopped, rotated a complete 360 degrees, and then found its groove.

With a rolling thunder, the barrel careened down the runway. A sign (WRONG WAY—DO NOT ENTER) stood at the base of the ramp. The barrel crashed through the sign, sending it harmlessly, fortuitously, to the shoulder of the road on its right, away from the traffic. The barrel came to where a crew, now on lunch break, had been in the process of securing a streetlamp to its base. The lamp was fifty feet tall, with dual arms extending east and west, each bearing a pair of 1000-watt fluorescent lamps. Into the base of this towering structure the barrel invested the full measure of its fury.

Like a battling giant whose shin just got busted by some nuisance of a dwarf landing his blows scores of feet below him, the lamp groaned, then moaned as it strove to maintain its balance. Finally, with a sickening clamor, it fell from its base and crashed westward—toward the next streetlamp.

It was the porta-potties all over again, the dominoes this time scaled by a factor of ten. The tilting, falling, and crashing of each street lamp—down I-16 for a mile and a half, then the trajectory of destruction pivoting as it hit an exit sign, knocking over the streetlamps that lined a north-south bridge, then pivoting once more upon encountering a sign for a rest stop to advance, eastbound, like a perpetrator returning to the scene of his crime—was so exaggerated, so surreal, so deliberate, that many of the cars that traveled the highway didn't seem to notice and sped underneath where Mack stood, watching the noose tighten around the oblivious traffic.

Only as the final two or three streetlamps fell, very close to the construction site, did a group of cars begin to slow down and squeeze into a knot. The last streetlamp, as it fell, clocked the exact center of a wrecking ball that hung from a chain affixed to a turret that was positioned to take down the old I-23 overpass. The streetlamp, now deflected off the wrecking ball, fell into the road, blocking all lanes. The knot of four cars—Mack noted they were all convertibles: a Mercedes, a Jeep, a Fiat Spider, and something nasty done to a Dodge Challenger— were brought to a stop almost directly beneath the new overpass.

The wrecking ball, meanwhile, had taken a wide, circular flight above the interchange. It flew high into the air, testing the strength and limit of its chain tether. It arced around ... and slammed into the side of the Honest Jons tanker truck. The truck tipped over, the tank burst, and two thousand gallons of sewage, turned blue by the chemical toilets, fell onto the four convertibles that lay below.

Mack felt a tap on his shoulder. He turned around. It was Honest Jon, a cigarette dangling from his mouth. He was holding something out to Mack. His lucky hammer. The fella said, "Lester."

Mack took the hammer, shook Lester's hand, and thanked him for the hammer. "Mack," he replied.

Lester looked around at everything, then down at the people climbing out of their cars, soaked in blue.

"Well, Mack," he said, "they say shit happens."

**Catastrophe on the Interstate** (UPDATE 10/13/22, 10:04:53)
by Christopher Matteo for the Associated Press

ILIUM—In yet another freak twist to our continuing coverage of what some are calling The Interchange Incident, we caught up to an occupant of one of the four cars struck by chemically treated excrement that fell from an overhead porta-potty tanker truck.

The man, Schlomo Hazzan, had been sitting in the back seat of the Dodge Challenger and claims to have been completely missed by the deluge.

"I don't know how to explain it," says Hazzan, a self-described creative writer. "I was sitting there, writing out some lines that had just come to me, when [the driver] suddenly slammed the brakes. The next thing I know, everyone is covered in blue goo. I mean, head to toe. The thing was a total snafu. They were yelling and spitting the blue out of their mouths, and it was dripping from their eyelashes and everything. And then we all noticed this clean circle that surrounded me. I was completely untouched. I don't know what else to say about it."

When asked about the journal he had been writing in during the moments that led up to the catastrophe, Hazzan offered the following:

*Some see a cool blonde in a red Ferrari—a Christie Brinkley catching up Chevy Chase on an open highway, cutting through a forgotten wheat field in Nebraska. Others recall a Diana Rigg behind the wheel of a '62 Lotus Elan—an avenging femme fatale suited out in black leather. A small but vocal minority, coping with the world's complexities through means of conspiracy, speak of Jackie Kennedy, driving the very same '61 Lincoln Continental that once cradled the shattered form of a bleeding American president.*

*What all agree on, the very few who remember anything at all and don't relegate to dream the rumors of wreckage and fury, is the license plate: MDMDRVR.*

*And that she drives,*
*and she drives,*
*and she drives.*
*And no one has ever seen her stop.*

# for Eric

Nobody can take a character from 0 to 60 in 2.3 paragraphs like Stephen King. There you'll be, letting Steve do the driving as you watch the plot slowly roll past outside your window. All at once, he'll spot a hitchhiker on the side of the road—a character you haven't seen before. If there's anything remotely interesting about them, it's a sure bet Steve'll pick 'em up. He'll know where they're going without their having to say. Then the fun begins: They'll start thinking out loud. And by the time you're ready to turn the corner (or the page), you'll love them or you'll hate them; you'll be laughing at them or with them; you'll be shaking your fist at them in anger or tearing your hair out in frustration—all from hearing their thoughts, and all within a shockingly small amount of writing.

So I was listening to KISS one day—probably randomly, probably on Spotify—when the song "Baby Driver" came up. I'd certainly known about this song ever since fifth grade, but I hadn't heard it for a long time. Sometimes when I hear a song that grabs my imagination, I put it on loop and let it play over and over again. Sometimes, a lot. (For example, I discovered Leonard Cohen's "You Want It Darker" a couple weeks ago. I can't tell you how many times I listened to it that day and the next, mesmerized. Another recent example was my re-discovery of Kate Bush's "Under Ice." Chilling.)

Anyway, I was listening to "Baby Driver," and boy, was my imagination in overdrive (sorry). There was good stuff here. Who *was* this driver Gene Simmons was wailing about? Why *didn't* anyone know where she (yes, definitely a she) was going? Why did nobody care where she'd been? Why didn't she ever need to know directions? And what exactly were all these stories she was getting herself into?

I listened and imagined. I strayed, like Gandalf the soon-to-be-White, out of thought and time. Images started coming: the rusty old rig from the movie *Duel* and the faceless menace behind it; Christie Brinkley passing Chevy Chase in the movie *Vacation*; Stephen King's own demon-possessed car, Christine, that drove itself and killed anyone who badmouthed it; Emma Peel and her sleek and sexy Lotus Elan. Could these ideas be blended?

I didn't have a story, but I was beginning to get a concept—and it was a little ... supernatural for my usual MO. I'm not one for supernatural plots, but as long as I'm not baited and switched halfway through, like in *The Stand*, I don't mind them. What if there was a demon woman who eternally rode the open highways of America? What would be her crusade? I didn't take the subject of "Baby Driver" to be evil—merely a badass. A badass with an agenda.

This was going to be fun! Next thing I needed was to put on my Stephen King hat and start taking characters from 0 to 60 as fast as possible. They were all going to be gross. It didn't take me long to come up with my menu of cretins: a woman who deliberately centers political power in the hands of men, knowing all the while that, in her privileged state, she has the means to get what she wants—and too bad for all the rest of you women out there, suckers; a misogynist; a sexual predator; a bunch of frat boys who represent the next generation of chauvinists.

Next, knowing that I was going to take the reader into each of these drivers' heads, I needed a method for MDMDRVR to exact her vengeance on them. What better than a porta-potty truck loaded with chemically treated excrement? (*Boy*, was this gonna be fun.) I don't remember at what point I decided to make a huge and utterly impossible Rube Goldberg contraption out of the porta-potty situation, but as long as I had come this far, I figured I may as well go for it. I hoped that if it was fun enough, the reader would forgive the obvious absurdity of it. Was I right?

When I got to the frat car, it occurred to me that one of the boys could be made sympathetic, at least to some degree. This represented a refinement of my understanding of the story. Like Stephen King, I generally write as I go. I don't first create an outline or a dossier of characters and their traits. I try to let the characters show me their deal.

And that's the story behind "Crapperclysm!" I'm dedicating it to Eric Bertsch, who is one of our circle's best world builders. I haven't had to do that yet, build a world. Not in the sci-fi/fantasy sense. But this story *does* break the laws of nature, and perhaps that's adjacent. If I ever need to build a world in earnest, I'm hoping Eric will be there to help me out.

# the innkeeper's husband

Not more than two hours outside Baltimore, the orange VW Bug hummed pleasantly along roads that defined entire villages; bisected fields of undifferentiated crops freshly poked through the mud in a blur of green rows; and offered stands selling April flowers, shellfish, and locally sourced fried chicken. Bishara had no need of a dashboard to tell him their speed: David was driving, and that meant they were traveling at precisely whatever the speed limit happened to be way out here in the middle of resplendent nowhere. Had their modest car been equipped with a thermometer, David's relentless desire for exacting regularity in his environment would have allowed Bishara to predict with unswerving confidence an interior temperature of precisely 72 degrees Fahrenheit. Had the correct mathematical tool (a protractor? a compass? why retain facts one has no use for?) been available, Bishara's faith in his husband's ability to use that instrument to demonstrate that the steering column was tilted to exactly ten degrees off the vertical would have been unshakeable.

Not that any of these metrics were important.

With his favorite bookmark (an inspirational quote from Rumi flowed in the color of ripe plums across the length of an orchid-hued strip of tasseled, cardboard-reinforced silk), Bishara marked his place in the book he had been reading out loud and set the hardback on his lap. Leaning a little toward his husband, he placed a gentle hand over his on the gear shift.

Poor David. This weekend trip to the beach was meant to be a celebration for him—and why not? The advance he had received on *Ded Reckoning* was his biggest ever! As was only fitting for a novel as brilliant as the author himself! Why, the plot was a veritable tour de force of extreme cleverness on the part of that wily Merit Badge, who once again saved civilization (or New York, anyhow) from some sinister threat or other. David had completed the book on schedule; they had planned this trip. Then they'd received a phone call: David's elderly father had taken ill again. He would be transferred to a nursing home tomorrow. This time, David would not be there for him.

It was therefore only reluctantly that Bishara brought up a mundane, yet more immediate, concern.

"I'm hungry," he said.

Beneath David's meticulously manicured blond mustache, Bishara saw his husband's lips begin to quiver. Then they pursed into something that Bishara at first took for the onset of tears ... but, no. It was turning out to be a wry smile. Thank god. That brain of David's was getting ideas. He was self-distracting, and Bishara knew that this meant something—something probably quite clever—was on the way.

Presently, David said, "I don't think stopping somewhere for a bite to eat would have too much of an *impac* on our arrival time."

Bishara paused, caught off guard even with the foreknowledge that something like this had been coming. Then: understanding. He rolled his eyes back for a think, then said, "We could stop and get some fried chicken. Show one of these road stands a little *respec*."

David said, "I'm sorry we didn't stop sooner. I didn't mean to *neglec* your appetite."

Bishara chuckled, then shifted in his seat as the strain from the elastic waistband of his cargo shorts (perfect in any weather, and those who were wrong could keep their opinions to themselves!) pinched at his ample belly—jiggling as he laughed, yet held at bay by a bright floral button-up (they were going to the beach, dammit!). He was thrilled; with David, there seemed no end to these sorts of verbal games. "You choose, David," Bishara said. "I will abide by your *verdic*."

David, utterly beloved and equally short-sighted, pushed his copper-framed glasses up on his long nose. He cleared his throat. This was going to be a good one. "I'm surprised you would grant me such latitude, given my *circumspec* disposition when undertaking novel endeavors."

But this was a little too much. Bishara squinted sideways at his husband, who was clearly showing off. "Nonsense," he retorted. "You're ... *perfec*."

This caused them both to chuckle a little, David presumably out of embarrassment, Bishara because David really was perfect.

"Rob Halbert," said David.

"Rob Hal*ber*," Bishara corrected, still giggling.

David sighed. "He was a fantastic wedding planner. But ... those *T*s at the ends of his words. What *happened* to them?"

Bishara thought for a moment. "He wanted to sound French?"

Now they both laughed in earnest. After a time, things settled down, allowing a concern that had been lurking in the back of Bishara's mind to now take full possession of it. "Rob was nice, though," he said. "I liked him."

"I liked him, too," said David.

"We're paying him adequate respect, aren't we? When we play that game?"

"We are paying him adequate respect," replied David.

Bishara relaxed. For the next half hour, the two of them played variations of this game, paying adequate respect to the manager of a hotel they had once stayed at who turned every sentence into a question, a motivational speaker who insisted on preceding every adjective with an adverb (most of them decidedly redundant and all of them abundantly unnecessary), and a tour guide who replaced a great deal of her short vowel sounds with long ones.

They had just finished paying adequate respect to one of David's college professors, who used the phrase *to wit* in the same manner and frequency with which some people use *umm*, when it became clear that dinner could no longer be put off. They stopped at a greasy spoon, where David ordered a BLT (his safe choice, Bishara had observed, when in strange places), and Bishara braved the meatloaf.

David's phone bleeped. It was a text. "It's Frieda," he told Bishara. "The innkeeper. She wants to know what time we'll be arriving."

"What time is it now?"

David pushed up his glasses. "It's 7:18." His gray eyes glossed over and he scratched at the smooth underside of his chin. "I'll round, and tell her 11:05."

After a few more texts, David said, "Frieda says they don't actually live in the B and B. They're down the street. She says she'll have Ron there waiting for us."

"Ron is her husband?" asked Bishara.

"Yes," David said. "The innkeeper's husband."

The last coral sliver of sun surrendered to the night, and the earthy farmland air gave way to a briny smell that announced the nearby sea. David started seeing harbingers of an impending small town: an outlying gas station and convenience store, a billboard (JOEY SELLS HOUSES!), a Perkins. Bishara had read himself to sleep and was softly snoring, his head lolled over onto his right shoulder.

Stopped at a traffic light, David reached over and closed the hardback on Bishara's lap, being sure to first mark the place with that bookmark of his. A tattered thing, it was—frayed at the edges and its color mottled, as if the words of countless pages, in protest of being held in check, attacked the silk, oxidizing it according to the subtle chemistries of their various meanings. Some doubtless uplifting piece of purple philosophy ran the bookmark's length in a flamboyant cursive. Seriously, the thing needed to just turn up lost someday.

And the novel itself? It was as insipid as the bookmark. Vapid in its build-up and cluttered with characters cut from a uniform cardboard, the plot relied on any number of hackneyed devices. It was obvious who did it. Worst of all, the author had a maddening habit of drifting into the passive voice.

Still, Bishara was enjoying it.

But what *wouldn't* Bishara enjoy? He was far too easily pleased. How many times had he, David, tried to explain to him that not everything is good? That if everything was good, nothing would be good? Half the drivers on the road are below average! There was a scary thought! (Or was he now just being … mean?) There is value in reserving one's praise. People coveted David's praise for a reason. That which is scarce has value.

Take that meatloaf Bishara had ordered tonight. (Please!) It had looked dry. (What is so difficult about meatloaf, that so many cooks screw it up?) Which is surely why Bishara had kept smothering it with ketchup. David had researched their bed and breakfast thoroughly, because he *cared* about things. After checking TripAdvisor, Yelp, Kayak, and Hotwire, he had called the innkeepers directly. Frieda had answered, and he'd interviewed her exhaustively—ostensibly in reference to the amenities, but in reality to gauge her temperament. He'd had enough of discourtesy (to say nothing of … darker attitudes) ravaging otherwise wonderful getaways. He deserved better. Bishara, too. *Bishara* deserved better. Not that Bishara would ever complain—not when he, David, organized the trip, made the reservations, notified all their friends of their plans, and packed everything short of Bishara's underwear. Hell, there had been trips when David had packed even that. In fact, David wondered, neither for the first time nor, probably, for the last, how they would be getting on, *right now*, if he had just left everything to his husband.

And then there was the matter of Dad. But that would have to wait, for David had spotted their bed and breakfast. He couldn't think of his father right now.

The street was dark and deserted. A pair of lamps hung over a clapboard sign, illuminating in a pool of white the inn's name: The Music of the Seas.

Beside him, Bishara stirred and awoke. He rubbed his chestnut brown eyes (oh, boy, was he going to have such bags under those eyes some year) and smiled at David. "Are we here?"

David, all at once chagrined by the internal torrent of whining that only then impressed itself onto his conscious mind like a lightbulb that buzzes overhead and is suddenly noticed, took Bishara's hand and kissed it. "We're here," he said.

It wasn't clear where to park, so David activated the four-way flashers and stepped out onto the sidewalk. The front door of the inn, unlocked, opened onto a glass-and-white-rattan sunroom that dragged the tropics into the cool pastel weather of April. David and Bishara walked through it and into a parlor. This room was dim and empty, lit only by a small lamp that sat on a desk in a corner.

"Oh, God," whispered David. "Please tell me we haven't walked into the wrong house."

But Bishara gently elbowed him and gave a nod into the dark room straight ahead, where stood a man, large and slightly stooped.

The man blinked: two pallid circles—a pair of marbles—disappearing and reappearing in the dark. He took a halting step forward. "David?" he said.

David didn't believe in ghosts and would never write about such things. *But*, David thought, if he *were* to give a ghost a voice—just because something doesn't exist doesn't keep it from possessing qualities: Rudolph's nose is red; vampires detest garlic—if a ghost *had* to sound like something, David thought, he supposed it would sound just like that.

Bishara was already halfway across the room toward the man. "I'm Bishara. Your inn is lovely. Charming! So ... comfortable ..." He glanced around as he spoke, searching for some concrete object to receive his praise. "I love what you've done with the fireplace," he decided. "David, look at the fireplace. Isn't the stonework gorgeous?"

"Yes," agreed David, who was still in the parlor, not really looking at the stonework. "Yes, it is very nice." He went forward to greet the man, who must be Ron.

Ron stood there, hearing Bishara out, having his hand pumped, content not to say a word. He was, David decided, perhaps the age of his father; in fact, rather similar to him in appearance, but … able-bodied. Yes, David decided he was looking at an *able-bodied* dying man who wore the practiced smile of one employed in the art of setting strangers at ease and whose firm leaning-in suggested a readiness to give himself to the tactile needs of the weary traveler. With no trouble at all, David imagined a not *too* much younger Ron, with those broad but stooped shoulders and brawny hands, hoisting up his guest's luggage and running it up the stairs to their rooms, seeing to any disturbance in the night from an unruly guest, or solving an annoying drip in the bathroom with a twist of a wrench.

David looked all the way back through the inn, barely discerning the flashing orange lights of his car outside. Perhaps Ron could park their car for them? Adjusting his glasses, David returned his attention to the one-sided conversation. Ron was holding a ring of keys out into the space between David and Bishara, unsure of the proper recipient. David took them.

Ron said, in a voice David now perceived as not so much sepulchral as infirm, "The silver one is for your room. The one with the yarn unlocks the front door."

"Thank you," said David.

Only now did he give his attention more fully to the room's appointments. A gilded clock, centered on the mantlepiece, showed the time as 11:13 (as accurately as he could determine from the minute hand, which lay somewhat closer to the Roman numeral III than the II). Within a massive armoire framed in carved wood hulked an ancient CRT television, respectably large for its time, probably 32 inches. David breathed a sigh of relief to see a set-top converter box on the shelf below, giving him at least a guarded optimism that both necessary channels (CNN, PBS) would be available, as advertised. On the far side of the couch, where one would expect an end table, there stood a strange apparatus— all posts and ledges and alcoves. This confused David until it registered in his mind as a kitty condo, and he recalled the moment in his interview with Freida (the tone of her voice over the phone had palpably constricted, as with one who fears to speak but must do so) when she had explained that the inn was "pet friendly." He'd stated his approval, and Frieda's voice had returned to normal.

The place, David now concluded, was dated but maintained; lived-in, yet not without a sense of refinement. It was, in other words, precisely how Frieda had painted it during their interview, and it was this fact of clean honesty that produced from David a slight exhalation as, finally, he allowed himself to be fully present.

"Freida usually serves breakfast at nine o'clock," said Ron. "Will that work for you?"

David and Bishara looked at each other. "That will be wonderful," said David.

"Would you like something brought up to your room before? Frieda could bring you coffee. Or tea?"

David gestured to Bishara, who said, "Oh, no, you needn't do that."

"Just with breakfast, then?" asked Ron.

"Yes," said Bishara.

Ron shuffled across the room to an open archway. "Let me show you the dining room. It's right here." He reached around the wall and flicked a switch. The room inside was large enough to seat upward of twenty people, but only a single table had been set—for four. Heavy-looking silverware surrounded a central floral arrangement on white linen. The napkins had been folded into swans.

"Frieda is a quite good cook, if I may say," Ron said.

"Low ebb," mumbled David absently as he eyed the other tables, out of service, shrouded over with white.

Ron questioned David with pale eyes.

"Off season for visiting the music of the seas," Bishara explained in his husband's stead. "The table here is set for only one other couple."

"None," said Ron. "It will be just the four of us in the morning."

David, having failed to imagine the possibility that he and Bishara would be dining with their landlords, adjusted his glasses in an effort to cover any show of surprise. Bishara, meanwhile, looked more pleased than ever as he said, "I love what you've done with the napkins!"

Between Bishara's exclamations over the decor, David asked about the parking. Ron pointed out a small lot behind the house. They all went outside to the car, and David unloaded the suitcases—three of them—from the trunk. He then parked the car out back. When he returned, Bishara and Ron and all three suitcases were still there, Bishara chatting away, Ron faithfully listening.

David asked Ron for help with the luggage. Ron steepled his fingers together, his eyes taking on a certain vacancy as he looked down at his shoes and made a noise that sounded like *hoom?* David looked at Bishara, who looked back at him with a shrug. The two of them each grabbed a suitcase, and David picked up the third. Ron then led them up two floors—four flights—of stairs to their room, at the end of a hall. David waited for Ron to open it, but Ron just stood there. Then David recalled that he had the keys. He set down the suitcases and unlocked the door.

Inside, Ron pointed out the bathroom and the closets. The room was freezing. The air conditioner was running. In April. David began to ask Ron for assistance, then thought better of it. He would take care of it himself.

But Bishara had apparently thought differently. (More likely, he had not thought at all.) He asked Ron to warm the room up a little. Again, Ron made the *hoom?* sound, this time selecting a picture on the wall to stare at through his vacant eyes.

*Shrouded in white*, thought David. *Out of service*. Then, unbidden—*Dad*.

Bishara, clearly wishing to gloss over any embarrassment, declared that he rather enjoyed a cold room when he slept. (True, that.) Ron then left them for the night.

The two of them were finally alone. Bishara was playful, bordering on giddy, as he said to David, "Ask me to unpack your suitcase."

David, busy at the thermostat controls, sighed. "Just this once."

"Just this once," agreed Bishara.

"Bishara," David said, somewhat mechanically, "could you please unpack my suitcase?"

"*Hoom?*"

Bishara sat down on the edge of the bed and laughed, holding his shaking belly, while David (closed eyes, deep breath) resumed his inspection of the thermostat.

The air conditioner finally stopped. "I've worked out the controls," said David, sitting down next to Bishara. The annoyances of travel were, with luck, past them. He needed to unwind—and he knew just the thing. He placed a hand on Bishara's back. "I was thinking we could ... celebrate?"

"Oh, yes," said Bishara. "But ... aren't we at the beach?"

"Yes?" David's face contracted. He *thought* he understood where this was going...

"I don't *feel* like I'm at the beach. I'd like to feel that we're at the beach." Bishara winked.

160

Excellent. David smiled, then got up. He went to the window and pulled aside the lace curtain. The window was the type that lifts straight up and must be braced with a stick of wood. David did this and stuck his head out a little. They were on the third floor. Below him was the backyard of the inn and a garden with a pond. A fountain rippled the water and folded the moon into a thousand pleats of white. Above the trickle of the fountain, David heard the nearby surf rhythmically crashing, then receding again, and crashing once more. In the morning, he imagined, these sounds would be drowned out by the cawing of gulls.

Retracting himself back inside, David asked Bishara if everything was all right now, with the window open, and Bishara said that it was, and that they were now officially at the beach, and they could celebrate, and they did, and the water rippled and the moon folded, the garden grew and the surf crashed, and David fell asleep and dreamed of gulls that screamed at the light.

But although Bishara had gone to bed with David, he did not go to sleep with him. David had asked if everything was all right, and he, Bishara, had said that it was. But Bishara knew that *David* was not all right, and that meant that *all* was not right. It also meant that Bishara had lied when he said that it was.

He waited for the soft, even pulse of David's breath, indicating sleep, then sat up. It was obvious what was bothering David: his father. Dad, as Bishara sometimes tried to address him, to tepid reception. It didn't help that Ron looked like him. In fact, the innkeeper's husband reminded Bishara of David's father in any number of ways: the once-sturdy stature in decline, eyes that sank into the skull, a mistrust in his gait. Here was a man once accustomed to being useful now unaccustomed to being unuseful. A pang of guilt fell over Bishara's heart for making fun of Ron earlier. It would be okay, though. It was all so much adequate respect, right? David didn't seem upset by it.

But, what *did* upset David? Ever? Beyond the trivialities of material existence? David had quite definitely flashed a look of contempt upon the meatloaf that evening. Perhaps it had been dry—a little— but what else was ketchup for? David had probably spent hours researching the bed and breakfast, when, in point of fact, Bishara had never met an inn he didn't like. (Goodness, Bishara wouldn't be surprised to learn that David had *phoned* the innkeepers to *interview* them, the poor souls.) But the larger of life's tribulations? David seemed normally unshakeable—lost (or perhaps not lost) in the worlds of his own making that were his books.

Bishara needed to think. He looked at David. A point had been made earlier that David hadn't taken notice of—one that intrigued Bishara to no end but that he feared David would have no use for: *There were no other guests*. Not even the innkeepers, who David had said lived down the street, were here. They were alone in the inn.

So he got up, put on a pair of slippers, and buttoned the tops of his pajamas. He wanted to wander. What, exactly, he was after, or why, he wasn't entirely sure. He went for the door keys that David had stowed on the tallboy, then let them be, relishing their inconsequentiality. He went out into the hall and quietly shut the door behind him.

The guest rooms were named after musical composers, with attempts at alliteration that enjoyed varying levels of success. Signs on the doors read BIZET'S BEDROOM and THE SHOSTAKOVICH SUITE. Bishara assumed the guest rooms would be locked, but he was wrong. One by one he looked through all of them and decided they were all equally cozy as their own, but none quite as large. Wall sconces in the halls and common areas provided enough illumination that he didn't need to turn on any lights. This relieved Bishara, somewhat, for this wandering around had gradually begun to feel questionable to him, and it would do no good, he thought, advertising his movements to anyone watching from the street by flicking the room lights on and off.

Downstairs, he explored the parlor and dining room, but there was little more to discover. The office door stood ajar; that at least was something. Books filled the walls, tempting Bishara to enter, which he did. There was a laptop here that, surprisingly, was still on. He decided that entering this inner sanctum had crossed a line. He left immediately. To reward himself for this act of discretion, he allowed himself a poke around the kitchen. He found it behind a swinging door off the dining room. That room was quite dark, and he left quickly.

With a feeling of incompleteness, Bishara returned to the third floor. He reflected for a while and discovered that he wished to be outside. At the beginning of his exploration, he remembered he had seen a door with no name on it. Primarily interested in the guest rooms, he had let it be. Now he opened it, revealing a laundry room. On the far side of the machines was an exterior door, its glass panes blackened by the night. Perfect. Opening this door, Bishara stepped out onto a small wooden landing, remembering at the last moment, as the door was swinging closed behind him, to unlock it.

Steep, narrow steps led down to a garden, the branches of an oak tree caressing the banister most of the way. A fountain here collected the moonlight, then shattered it into a thousand shards. He opened a wrought-iron gate and found himself on a back road. Perhaps, in this town, *all* the roads were back roads? He wondered if he could find some shops and what kind of shops they'd be. He walked along until a turn took him to a blinking amber traffic light marking the main thoroughfare.

This, too, was deserted. A row of art galleries was broken up by a sandwich place, a few gift boutiques, and the kind of shop found only at beaches like this one, where, in two short months, the salty crowds would purchase bikinis, boogie boards, live hermit crabs, and overpriced suntan lotion. Even the police car that slunk like a cat down the alley between a barber shop and the post office moved along like there was nothing to see.

Bishara walked back a different way, turning off the main road into a patchwork of Cape Cods and small Victorians stitched together with white picket fence. Stopping in front of one house—pink with sea green trim—he saw a woman in a lighted upper-story window. The front yard was shallow enough that he could see her clearly. She was bending over something. Now she was backing up, strong arms extended in support, as a shape—a head, a man—came up the stairs from below. Her job finished, the woman turned and left. The man, exhausted and spent, stood at the window. It was Ron. The light went off, but not before Ron and Bishara saw one another.

A few minutes later, Bishara quietly entered his and David's room.

David was awake, sitting at the edge of the bed. This was good. Bishara had finally understood the motivation behind his wanderings, and there was something he needed to tell David.

"I went for a stroll—" began Bishara.

"We should go," said David. "Dad needs me. We can leave a note—"

Bishara sat next to David and placed a hand on his shoulder. "Of course we'll go. But you're going to get a nice breakfast in you first."

David's eyes, unguarded by glass, sought in the grey light some focal point and eventually settled on Bishara's face. "You're okay with ruining our weekend?"

"One thing I'm pretty sure of," Bishara said, "this is not our last weekend. But right now, you're going to go back to sleep, and in the morning take a shower. Then you'll go down and have a nice breakfast cooked by Frieda and have a scintillating conversation with Ron."

"I can't do this by myself, Bish," said David. "Promise me you won't let me do this by myself."

"Of course," said Bishara. "Now go back to sleep."

"Are you going to sleep?"

"Soon. Right now, I'm going to pack."

An hour outside of Absolutely Nowhere, Pennsylvania, the orange VW Bug sped along roads that kissed the sky, stank of manure, and offered billboards advertising clubs that no true gentleman would patronize. Without recourse to the speedometer, David knew that his husband was driving a bit heavy on the foot. Yet they were surely within five MPH of the law, and David supposed that that would be okay. Soon, they would be with Dad.

The book Bishara had been reading aloud earlier was turning out to be quite interesting. David's presumed culprit had come down with a bad case of dead, and certain phrases David had taken for cliché turned out to possess a double meaning. Even the occasional lapse into the passive voice David forgave, as it became clear that the author was trying to create a sense of distance between the reader and some of the more covert action.

Nevertheless, David was getting sleepy. He laid a gentle hand on his husband's, on the gear shift.

"Do you have the rest of this drive?" he asked.

"You bet," said Bishara.

"Okay," said David. "I'm going to take a nap, then." Before shutting the book, he reached for his husband's favorite bookmark and read it:

*Yesterday I was clever, so I wanted to change the world. Today I am wise, so I am changing myself.*

David slept.

# for Karla

I had no intention of writing about a pair of gay men, but the banter between what had begun as a husband and wife wasn't quite working. Somehow, I thought to change the wife from a woman into a man—then the whole thing clicked. This is another example of my not knowing what happens in my own stories until I like the words on the page.

Stephen King refers to writing in this manner—when you discover the story and characters as you go—as pantsing. As in "writing by the seat of your pants." When it comes to any creative endeavor, there's never just one way of doing things. Some people in our circle are pantsers, while others outline their stories and collect facts about their characters before ever setting pen to paper. Some, like me, begin at the beginning and write their way through to the end; others, like Janet Hicks, write scenes as they occur to them. To anyone who is trying to write, I suggest experimenting. Every method has pros and cons. However you write, it shouldn't be hard, if you want, to find a mentor who works in a similar way.

I'm dedicating this story to our resident romance author and fellow pantser and beginning-to-ender, Karla Kratovil. I don't think anyone has used our circle of writers to greater advantage than Karla. She joined us about six years ago, wanting to finish a novel she'd started. Now she's got a publisher and everything that comes with it. Check out her work at KarlaKratovil.com.

Karla, some year I hope to write my own gothic romance. I don't know much about the genre, other than that it must—I will be absolutely unbending on this point—have a woman on the cover, running from a house. I hope you'll be there to lend me a hand.

# awake

Open.

Open the door.

There are flowers on the wall, and there's a man on my couch. Pictures line the shelves, but the faces are off. A man pets a dog; a woman plucks a grape. A man wraps a slice of prosciutto around a wedge of provolone. Not the same man. The dog licks his chops.

So many people. So many plates. So many semi-hard cheeses.

But no Albert.

Albert will complain about the antipasto. He is not a good eater, is Albert.

My Albert.

There are flowers on the couch, and there's a man on the wall. The TV's on the stand, but the picture is off. So many faces speaking, talking, blah blah blah-ing. Blah blah blah near the kitchen, blah blah blah near the doors.

So many doors. So many. One, two, three doors. No, four.

And no Albert.

Albert is not here. He might be behind one of the doors, might Albert.

My Albert.

The bathroom is the third door. No, fourth. The fennel mixed with roses is cloying, and everywhere are plates of half-eaten food. And glasses. Plates and glasses. The dog watches the prosciutto while the man on the wall watches everyone talk. The can is number three. No. Four.

No one goes away. No one goes home. No one comes to bed.

Not Albert.

Albert would be out there, talking. He always was a good talker, that Albert.

My Albert.

Shut.

Shut the door.

Shutting will make things easier, but then a face. It takes up space, everything. The face speaks. It says: "Sharagodeemomma. Nemoom?" It does it again. "Momma. Do yumaneebadadee?" That face—it means something is going to happen. It says: "Mommareedoo."

But ... *did* something happen? The face goes back with the others, to the flowers, to the dogs on their couches, to the plates of half-eaten meats and semi-hard cheeses, to the man licking his chops.

Shutting.

Shutting the door.

The room pulls away, and the faces go with it.

A shut door is easy. All the faces gone.

There are coats on the bed and hats on the nightstand. Bags, shriveled and deflated, line the floor; others stand tall. A memory, clear and distinct. Plate glass windows looking out over a concrete airfield, the perfumed crowds filing through a door to Hawaii. When we got there, we smelled like the inside of a can.

So many coats. So many bags. So much travel.

But not Albert.

Albert would always tire from it. He never was a good traveler, was Albert. My Albert.

Inside is here; outside, the doors. Too many. Bathroom is three. Plates of food? Inside is the lamp. And bags on the floor. And travel. And the TV. Not the TV out there. Not their TV. Our TV. The TV in here.

And this door.

Not the same door. A closet door. He keeps many things, does Albert. My Albert.

There's no one on the bed, but someone's on TV. It is not Walter Cronkite; not Peter Jennings. Nevertheless, the man blah blah blahs. He blah blah blahs to the closet door, blah blah blahs to the bags smelling of air travel, there on the floor. In here is the closet and the man who blah blah blahs to the closet door. To ... someone behind the door?

It is Albert.

Albert is here. He is behind the closet door, is Albert.

My Albert.

Open.

Open the door.

Opening a door can be confusing. So much inside.

There's a box up on the shelf. GEORGIA PEACHES. ALWAYS FRESH. ALWAYS SWEET. Heavy. It makes a squeak when it goes on the bed. There's no lid, and the box is full. Full to the top.

First thing out is a blanket, all folded up neat. It goes on the bed.

It had covered everything.

Here's a plastic airplane! And a San Francisco Giants pennant and a pair of bent Coca Cola bottle caps and a balsa glider and two ticket stubs stapled to a poster advertising the 1946 Alameda County Fair! Onto the bed.

A jigsaw puzzle. Yes, of course, that one with the pinup girl on the box cover. Brunette, busting out all over from her open camouflage-green World War II GI jacket. Black gartered stockings. Always loved a puzzle, did Albert. Give 'em Hell, Boys! 500 Pieces. Brunette goes on the bed.

The last is wrapped in white linen. It unwinds stiffly, giving out with each turn a smaller, harder bundle. Finally, the linen comes free. It goes on the bed, leaving behind only that which remains.

Inside that is Albert. Inside that is us.

Inside that is me.

When last I held the doll, my breath was sweeter than it is now, the skin of my hands not so thin and bruised, the strength of my hands not quite so spent. Yet there is strength enough.

I twist and pull. The doll comes apart in halves. Inside is another doll—like the first but smaller, harder to open. Over and over the halves peel away. Onto the bed.

With each pull there is less doll and more me.

Almost I am there. Almost I have found myself.

The churning within the layers—it is me. It is I—turning, twisting, seeking, coming.

The last doll opens. Carefully (for the skin of my mind, too, is thin and bruised) I pull out what is inside. I hold on to what remains.

Lance Corporal Albert Rosato is tall, handsome, and home. I see him perfectly.

Perfectly, I see you. Your eyes, clear as the California sky.

That summer of '46, all of America was taking sanctuary, released from the raging in Europe, looking in hope to the Pacific. You packed your uniform—so fine—and we flew in a great, silver airliner to the west coast, seeking our own separate asylum among the redwoods and the valleys of grapes and the carnival with its glittering lights and sugary air and greasy, black-mustachioed men who barked from behind their rickety wooden stands.

I hear you, Albert. I hear you singing. Ol' Blue Eyes himself had nothing on you, baby. Nothing.

The carnival had a Frank Sinatra soundalike competition. I see you winning; them letting you pick out your prize from the trunk of carnival junk.

You picked a Russian stacking doll. Such an odd pick, everyone must have thought. Sly devil! You had it all worked out beforehand. Somehow, with the carnival people, you had it all worked out. You gave that doll to me right there at the carnival, and I twisted it and turned it until, finally, the last doll opened.

What was inside, I have held on to.

Carefully now, for the skin of my hands—have I mentioned this?—is thin and bruised, I pull out what once was inside and which still is inside, and I hold in my hand the silver ring that you gave me on that long-ago day under an unadorned California sky, when you asked me to be forever with you.

For a moment, all is clear. Not just here—inside—but out there, too. Outside. The flowers. The pictures, the antipasto. What it all means. Vaguely I understand that I have done all of this already today. Vaguely I understand that soon—too soon—I will do it all over again.

Already it is going.

Quickly, before I might know too much and stop myself, I slide everything back into the doll.

Inside is Albert.

Inside is me.

Close.

Close the doors.

Closing is a comforting thing. With each twist and click there is more of the stacking doll and less of me. The halves snap together until all that remains is a bundle shrouded in a cocoon of white linen.

There's a box here. GEORGIA PEACHES. ALWAYS FRESH. ALWAYS SWEET. It makes a slight indentation on the bed. The box has no lid, and it's empty.

First thing that goes in is something wrapped in white linen. Then a poster advertising the fair, with two ticket stubs stapled to it. Also a pair of bent-up bottle caps, a San Francisco Giants pennant, a wooden plane, and then a plastic one.

Next comes a jigsaw puzzle. The cover shows a pinup girl, a brunette, busting out from behind an open camouflage-green jacket. She wears black gartered stockings. *Give 'em Hell, Boys!* she's saying. 500 Pieces. It goes in the box.

Last thing in is a blanket. Fold it up neat. Then the box goes in the closet. The top shelf will do.

There are coats on the bed and some keys on the nightstand. Bags line the floor, and the TV is on. Some bags sit there, shriveled and deflated, while others stand tall. They evoke perfumed crowds and the canned smell of flight and plate glass windows that look out onto airfields. So many bags. So much travel.

And there's a door. Not the same door.


Open.

Open the door.

Opening a door can be confusing. So much is outside.

There are flowers on the walls and a man on the couch. Pictures line the shelves, but the faces are off. A woman plucks a grape while a man pets a dog. The man wraps the prosciutto around a wedge of provolone. The dog licks his chops.

So many people. So many meats. So many semi-hard cheeses.

But no Albert.

Albert would've complained about the antipasto. He was not a good eater, was Albert.

My Albert.

There are flowers on the couch and a man on the wall. The TV's on its stand, but the picture is off. So many faces: speaking, talking, blah blah blah-ing. Blah blah blah near the kitchen. Blah blah blah near the doors.

So many doors. One. Two. Three doors. No, four.

And no Albert.

Albert is not here. He might be behind one of the doors, might Albert.

My Albert.

The bathroom is the fourth door. No, third. Plates of half-eaten food are everywhere, and the fennel mixed with the smell of roses is cloying. The dog is watching the prosciutto. The man on the wall is watching everyone talk.

No one goes away. No one goes home. No one comes to bed.

Not Albert.

Albert will be out there, talking. He's a good talker, is Albert.

My Albert.


Shut.

Shut the door.

Shutting will make things easier, but then comes a face. The face takes up space, everything. It says: "Barbadee. Mommageerooma?" It does it again: "Momma. Do shoomaneebad?" That face—it means something is going to happen. The face speaks. It says: "Mommareedoo."

But ... *did* something happen?

# for Taylor

Like "Incident on Pier 38," here is another exception to my rule of not listening to (my own) music while I write. With a steady supply of rose-scented incense helping to create the proper funereal atmosphere, I wrote most of "Awake" with Luigi Cherubini's *Requiem* playing softly in the background.

Alzheimer's is a horrible, dehumanizing disease. This story (*depiction* is a more accurate term) of a woman suffering from it while at the same time trying to process the loss of her husband is sadly personal. When my mother-in-law contracted Alzheimer's, all we siblings-in-law tacitly assumed that she would pass before her husband. But when our father/father-in-law suddenly declined, then passed away, we found ourselves in an odd position. We didn't know what she was capable of understanding. We didn't want to break her. All the flowers, all the cards, all the well-wishers and sympathizers who passed through the house—I really didn't know what my mother-in-law was making of it all.

"Awake" was my attempt at taking a guess.

Some authors write at a YA reading level, others at a college level, and still others everywhere in between. Taylor Batts, author of the Selfish Fate series, writes on a PhD level of emotional intelligence. This is necessary for an author whose characters have a tendency to reside in each other's heads. I'm dedicating this story to Taylor, whose ability to mind-meld gave me the courage I needed to pretend that I could go inside the head of a woman with Alzheimer's.

Check out Taylor's work at TaylorBatts.com.

# aporia

**aporia** (*n*)
1. A perplexity or impasse. Literally, "no passage."

**Aporia** (*geographical name*)
1. A planned community near the Allegheny National Forest in rural Pennsylvania, area contested, population indeterminate.

Soon, after the train had passed, Jo would look out the windshield of her sister Diane's tidy silver Mercedes S-Class sedan and say, Well dip me in chocolate and have me for dessert, what in hell is all this? Diane, behind the wheel and looking up from the copy of the *New Yorker* she'd been studying ever since they'd been forced to stop at the tracks, would utter her own statement of astonishment: less severe, sans profanity, and no doubt referring to something entirely separate from what Jo was talking about.

For the time being, however, there was the train.

From east to west, the seemingly endless chain of freight cars lumbered by. Jo, making use of what the fellas back at the advertising agency called (to Jo's perpetual annoyance) her "boyish" sense of wonder (and don't even *think* of getting her started on the word *tomboy*), imagined all sorts of things inside: coal in the hoppers; nuclear waste or (more probable but far too pedestrian) gasoline in the tankers; manufactured crap in the boxcars, doubtless imported from China and ready for display on Wal-Mart and Target shelves across America. And even, Jo thought, still wondering about the contents of those boxcars, maybe a hobo or two? That is, if they still even *made* hobos? Best of all, and requiring no imagination, were the flatbeds on which rode—right out in the open—heavy construction equipment, concrete pipes so wide you could stand in them, and (how-*dee!*) three M1 Abrams tanks and at least a dozen military Humvees.

The train clunked along, its shinier parts from time to time reflecting a shard of white April sun.

Jo said, At least we're off the freeway; that jam-up wasn't moving at all.

Diane sighed, but whether in reaction to this statement or to the article she'd apparently just finished reading, Jo couldn't tell. Diane flipped a few pages of her holy canon, found something more to consider, and dug in. Eventually she said, still not looking up, Maybe the jam-up was *because* of the train, did you think of that?

Jo thought about it. She concluded that it was a non sequitur and also that it wasn't right. Freeways always went over and under and *around* things like railroad tracks. She was about to say this, then spared a glance at her sister, buried in that rag of hers, and decided to hold back.

That rag. At sixteen, Diane DeLucca (*DeLucca!* Jo involuntarily pointed out to herself, brushing aside the more old-fashioned connotations of the sentiment in favor of the main point, which was Diane's perennial loneliness. Thirty-eight years old and *still DeLucca!*) had asked Dad for a subscription to the *New Yorker* as a birthday present. To the best of Jo's knowledge, Diane had never in all the intervening time failed to read a copy from cover to cover. Well, dammit, thought Jo, that's commitment for you.

The train kept chugging by.

Still not looking up from her magazine, Diane said, I just wish we'd gotten lunch before we headed off into the sticks. I mean, what are we going to find out here?

Jo looked out the windows and considered the Out Here. Someone had once cleverly described Pennsylvania as Philadelphia on one side and Pittsburgh on the other with Alabama in between. A politician had made the quip, Jo figured, but whoever it was really ought to have been in advertising. Truth is whatever sells mediocre widgets; truth is whatever sells mediocre candidates. For a while now, Jo and Diane had been driving through this In-between: past liquor stores, churches, and fireworks stands; under billboards that, in turn, reminded them that ABORTION stops a BEATING HEART, informed them that HELL was REAL, and invited them to places like PLEAZURE PALACE, EYE KANDYS, and BOBBIE'S BOOBIES BARN, where, apparently, twelve-foot-tall platinum blondes in garter belts, earrings, and either cowboy boots or high heels (But never, Jo noticed, one of each: Now *there* would be something worth stopping for!) would be so pleased to see you that they wouldn't be able to resist stripping off what little they wore while serving you your Keystone Light.

Well, Jo said, I suppose even out here there's gotta be a Mickey Dee—

Diane said, No fast food! And certainly not a drive-through! she added, disregarding the fact that Jo, who knew very well the rules about having no food in the Mercedes, hadn't suggested anything of the sort. I don't want crumbs all over me, Diane continued, looking down at her blouse as if expecting to find that some nefarious crumb had sneaked in through the ventilation system and identified her as a desirable target of contamination.

Jo sighed. Again, she considered her sister. Diane was pretty, she was rich, and she was smart. Wham bam thank you ma'am, smart as a glass of sauvignon blanc with whole-grain crackers and a smear of goat cheese. And truth was, when Diane wanted to be, she was funny, sometimes even slightly profane—a fact that caught many people off guard the first time they encountered it. Say, at a committee meeting of the local Rotary Club in its third hour, with everyone, including Jo, starting to lose their patience, when out of the blue, here comes Diane with a quip comparing a particularly underwhelming line item on the budget with the treasurer's chances of getting laid that night when he gets home.

Diane worked hard. They both did. But for Jo, the *world* worked. *There* was the difference. And although Jo wanted to help, she had no idea what she could do for her sister.

You didn't have to get all dressed up like that, Jo said, casting a sidelong glance at her sister's crisp black blazer and the pearly sheen of her pink blouse. Thing looked like a damn seashell. Up at the neck, some kind of knotted scarf contraption? Pointless. The stuff that marketing departments got women to wear! It's Dad, Jo continued, not the president of the United States. He's in a nursing home, where everybody's going to smell like pee and have drool running down their—

Diane cut her sister off with a brisk, Some people don't want to look like they've never left their freshman dorm.

Jo sighed. Her sister was referring, of course, to Jo's Stanford sweatshirt and coordinating cardinal-red-on-gray sweatpants tucked into her Converse high-tops. Her legs were splayed out, knees separated by nearly two feet, and she was sucking through a paper straw at a grudgingly allowed 16-ounce glass bottle of Coke that she'd plucked from her fridge before hitting the road. She'd packed eight of them for the trip, keeping them inside a cooler that she was resting one of her feet on. Fair enough, Jo thought. Fair enough.

Diane said, And anyway, you shouldn't be eating that fast food crap. You know better. It's loaded with bad carbs and trans fats. She shook her head at the invisible carbs and fats that surely floated just outside the windshield of her Mercedes—which continued to sit there, glinting in the late morning sun, waiting for the train to pass.

Yeah okay whatever, Jo said, and she took another swig of Coke.

Diane went back to the *New Yorker* that she had never truly left, Jo to the windows and to that which lay beyond the glass—to the Out There, the In-between, the Alabama; to the ramshackle houses and sad sheds squatting on scrap-metal-littered yards; to a girl on her swing, the screeching of its chains buried by those rumbling freight cars; to a woman framed within the rectangle of an open window, her heavy arms crossed atop the sill as she snacked from a bag of potato chips and, chewing, leaned her head out to watch the train chug along.


Reading—real reading—was proving impossible for Diane. Had been impossible, actually, ever since last night. Since the phone call. Dad.

It had been a white winter's day, and the whole school smelled of furnace. Honors Orchestra, normally fifth period, would today also be the last. The snowfall that had sprinkled a few harmless inches on the ground earlier that morning had resumed much more heavily. The PA system had announced an early dismissal.

Alicia Brown and Diane were reading off the same sheet of music as the orchestra labored its way through a rehearsal of "Dream of a Witches' Sabbath" from Berlioz's *Symphonie Fantastique*. Earlier that school year, at fall auditions, Diane had beaten out Alicia, a senior, for first chair clarinet. Alicia had been real sweet about it, though.

For the last quarter hour, Mr. Feldman had been making the orchestra grind out the same damn twenty or so bars, beginning at 127, the Dies Irae. The Day of Wrath: a reference to the so-called Last Judgment, when so-called God will pour out his righteous indignation on all the so-called sinners of the earth.

Poor sinners. As for the music, the heavy brass were making it sound more like the Day of Indigestion. Poor God.

Fed up and bored—the daily double at Freemont High—Diane and Alicia entered into a dangerous match of trying to make the other laugh.

Diane shot the first salvo by using her right hand to point with her middle finger at the notes they were playing, bobbing it along under the notes like the bouncing ball projected onto the words at a karaoke sing-along.

Alicia returned fire by bouncing the sheet music right to left, over and over, as if the page's bottom corners were its feet, and the music was dancing along to God's wrath: first slow and ponderous during the brass sections, then rapidly when the woodwinds and strings took over.

Finally, Diane reached out, tenderly shooed Alicia's hand away, and flipped the music upside down.

Judas *Priest*! yelled Mr. Feldman, killing the orchestra and throwing his baton on the floor. Do you want to do this, Ms. DeLucca? Would *you* like to conduct?

The orchestra fidgeted, traded smirks, rolled eyes. Then, as Diane didn't respond right away, people started to stare at her. Her brother David, in the trumpet section, pushed his glasses higher up the bridge of his stately nose, blanched, and hid his face in his hands.

Actually, Diane said, transferring her gaze from her embarrassed brother back to the conductor, yeah.

Mr. Feldman stared at her. The bald circle atop his head shone like a demented halo.

I mean, she added, if you wouldn't mind? Terribly?

Mr. Feldman paused, clearly confounded by the acceptance of an offer that wasn't truly meant. Then he mock-curtsied, stepped off the podium, and made a sweeping gesture toward it.

Holy shit, Alisha tremoloed as Diane laid her clarinet on her seat and climbed down off the riser.

Diane took the podium. She gave herself a minute to gain her bearings on the conductor's score. She found bar 127, ran a finger down the page, paused at certain instruments.

Okay, she said, here we go. She looked up at the orchestra, ready to begin. She was missing the baton. She held out a hand. Baton? she said to the room at large.

Alicia scrambled off her chair, grabbed the conductor's stick from off the floor, handed it up to Diane, and returned to her seat. If Alicia's crystal blue eyes had gotten any wider, they'd have fallen out of her pretty head.

Here we go, Diane repeated. Brass! she said, testing the authority in her voice. The entire brass section—nay, everyone—looked at her expectantly. Damned if she didn't have the whole orchestra in her grasp. This was going to be the best rehearsal ever. Heck, this was going to be one of the best days of her life!

She said, I know the music tells you to accent those dotted halves. But you're killing it. Like, not in a good way. The orchestra chuckled. I want less tongue on the attack, she continued. Let your breath and your embouchure do the work. And strings! Assuming we someday get to the *col legno*, I want that done *tratto*, not *battuto*.

You say po-tay-to, I say po-tah-to, giggled someone to her right. It was that kid in the flute section they called Tugboat.

Was that a question? said Diane.

Tugboat shook his head.

But ... someone else said.

Diane skimmed the orchestra. She found David. His hand was lifted halfway up, and the glare on his glasses from the overhead light made his eyes inscrutable.

Yes, David?

But, Diane, he said, unless the music explicitly states *tratto*, *col legno* is always played *battuto*.

Sitting off to the side of the room with his legs crossed, Mr. Feldman snickered.

Diane sighed. First violin, she said, holding out a hand to the concertmaster. Your music, please?

First violin flipped a couple pages into the score and handed Diane the sheet.

Diane took a pen out of her pocket. *Tra ... tto*, she wrote on the sheet as she spoke. She handed the edited score back to first violin. Mr. Feldman, she was pleased to see out of the corner of her eye, sat forward in his chair, flummoxed.

Ready? Diane said. Bar 127. She lifted her hands, and sixty-seven instruments were brought to position.

God, in his wrath, sounded greatly relieved and mercifully unbloated. The strings, when they arrived at the *col legno* section, sounded perfectly eerie and mystical, but without all the wailing banshees. And at the end of the quarter, when report cards came home, instead of her usual A in Honors Orchestra, Diane landed an A+.

She lay that evening, as was her habit, prone on the luxurious gold shag carpet of her father's study. Before her on the floor was her open chem textbook. Her father sat at his desk, looking at home among the framed portraits of Tchaikovsky, Bartok, and Brahms that hung on the wall behind him. His fountain pen scratched away at a piece of music. A capriccio, Diane had inferred from the occasional hums and whistles that had escaped her father's lips over the past several weeks. It was only a guess, though. Dad never shared an original composition until he had it perfect.

It was incredible, Diane thought, that her father—that anyone—could write music while *listening* to music. Yet, Beethoven's *Ode to Joy* processed triumphantly forward on her father's turntable, and she knew that if she asked to turn it off, even for just a moment so she could think, her father would remind her that she had her own room and that he needed that music playing if he was going to get anything written.

With her legs bent at the knees so that her feet dangled above her butt, Diane stared pointlessly at a series of reduction-oxidation reactions in her chem book. With the toes of her bare right foot, she flicked a Keds sneaker on and off the heel of her left foot—a show of impatience she'd developed years ago at summer camp while waiting for campfire stories to be done and over so she could retreat to her bed in her cabin and get back to the *real* stories. The ones with murderers and jewel thieves and Miss Marple, Kate Delafield, and Kinsey Millhone.

She'd been waiting for just the right moment to share with Dad what she'd done that day at orchestra rehearsal. She figured that now was as good a time as any.

She got up and approached her father's desk. Dad?

He raised a finger, requesting a moment. He scratched out a few more notes, completing a bar of music.

Yes, my dear? Trouble with your chemistry?

No, not really, Dad. Listen. Guess what I did today in orchestra!

Dad capped his pen, laid it down on the leather desk pad, and sat back in his chair. Diane loved this about her father. Anyone else would've simply said, What? and waited to hear what the other person had to say. But Diane had told her father to guess at something, and that was precisely what he was going to do.

Hmm, he said. Did you play through the entire *Symphonie Fantastique* from memory?

No.

Did you start in on a new piece?

No.

Did you ask Mr. Feldman if you could try picking up the bassoon? I know you've been interested in that bassoon part in the Dies Irae.

No. Not yet. But you're getting warm! Sort of. Um ... Dad? I don't think you're going to guess.

Very well. What did you do?

I got to conduct!

Dad raised an eyebrow and leaned forward in his seat. Oh? Do tell. How did this happen?

I ... well, Mr. Feldman asked me.

Dad shifted his eyes off to his right, then up, then to Diane for a moment, then in a few more directions. Oh, I see. He came to you beforehand—

No, not exactly. It was more like in the middle.

In the *middle*? Diane could almost hear her father's brows furrow. Oh, I see, he said again, this time with less assurance. Mr. Feldman is giving a handful of select students the opportunity to—

Diane *tsk*ed. Look, she said. I got in trouble goofing around while everyone was screwing up the Dies Irae, okay? Alicia and I were getting bored. Mr. Feldman asked me, sorta, if I wanted to conduct. And I did it! I conducted the Dies Irae!

A shadow passed over Dad's face, and Diane winced. Then he burst out laughing. Well, I'll be! That's terrific! How'd it go?

Diane exhaled in relief. Better than ever! And when we got to the *col legno*, I had the strings play it *tratto*—

Diane! Dad's brow furrowed again. Unless the music explicitly states—

Yeah yeah, I know. *Battuto*. Potato, potahto. But listen, that's what pens are for.

That's what—*what*?

I asked the concertmaster for her score, and I wrote *tratto* under *col legno*. It really sounded much better, Dad. I think you'd have agreed if you could've heard it.

You ... re-wrote the wrath of God? There was a pause. You edited God, he said. Dad shook his head a little. I don't know. This sounds like something your sister would do. He took a deep breath. Or your mother. Where, by the way, is your mother this evening? I expected her home some while ago.

Jo excels at everything and understands nothing. And I think Mom said she was going to a PTA meeting.

Fantastic, Dad muttered in a tone that left Diane wondering how he'd meant it. Then he looked up sharply. David! David was there, wasn't he? What did he say about it?

The exact same thing you were going to say about it. Word for word.

But in the end? Did he approve?

Actually, yes, Dad. He told me afterward that the piece had never sounded better.

Fantastic, Dad muttered again.

It was the last thing he ever said as a truly happy man.


All at once the train cleared, and Jo pointed through the windshield and blurted out the aforementioned statement of astonishment: Well dip me in chocolate and have me for dessert, what in hell is all this?

She was pointing at what she thought must surely be a mirage. An anomaly. To risk stretching a previous metaphor beyond its breaking point, an oasis of half-decent dining in a food desert of bad carbs.

She consulted her phone. According to the GPS, they were on the outskirts of a dot named Aporia. Not a sizable black circle that would indicate a major town, but rather the kind of light gray dot where you'd expect to find a population in the low four digits and where you'd be justified (but nevertheless relieved) to find a gas station. (And of course a liquor store, a church, and a BOB-BIE'S BOOBIES BARN.)

But just exactly what in hell was all *this*?

The first thing Jo noticed was an outdoor strip mall with an office supply store, a nail salon, and a pizza joint. Across the street from that strip mall was another, this one with a burger joint, a second nail salon, and a coffee shop. As Jo's gaze went farther afield, she took in a retail sprawl that made it seem like the last three hours of driving had been an illusion and that she and Diane had never left the exurbs that surrounded their Northern Virginia homes.

That was what Jo saw. What Diane saw, Jo discovered when her sister persisted in not responding to her and she was forced to look out Diane's window, was a fellow opposite the now-cleared tracks, shoveling chunks of deer onto the bed of a PennDOT pickup truck. About twenty feet to his right was a sign. It read:

## WELCOME TO APORIA

*"Where You Can't Visit Too Often Or Stay Too Long"*

The impatient honk of a horn came from behind the sisters. Jo turned around in her seat. Horny hot dogs, she said, just look at all those cars!

Clearly, the traffic behind them had been building up for quite some time. About an hour ago, she and Diane had exited the interstate, hoping to escape the jam-up. Their detour had begun well. More importantly, their conversation had finally touched (however briefly) on their father. The previous night, Diane had gone into a funk on the phone, stating that Dad would be out of sorts and unwilling to see anyone. Jo had rejected Diane's attitude. Then, today, bare moments after some useless speculation regarding the cause of the jam-up had petered out into predictable zilch, Diane had suggested it again—whereupon Jo had once again been forced to explain that *of course Dad would want to see them*, adding that if only Diane had had children of her own, she would understand. Immediately—yet still too late—Jo realized the error of her statement. Diane submerged into her present state of reticence. The traffic, along with the air, began to thicken, to the point where a couple dozen cars followed behind them. And that was before they'd come to the railroad tracks.

Now, looking behind her, Jo saw a trail of vehicles that seemed as endless as the just-cleared train.

Diane, only now seeming to notice the massive retail Elysium that lay in front of her, asked, What do you want me to do?

What do you mean? said Jo. Go. Drive.

Closing the *New Yorker* and reaching behind her to slide the magazine into the pouch on the back of her seat, Diane shifted the Mercedes into drive and crossed the railroad tracks.

She was coming even with a parking lot on the outskirts of the sprawl when Jo said, Wait! Pull in. I've gotta get my head around this.

Diane pulled into the lot. She found a spot between a pickup and a Jeep, and she squeezed in. Putting the Mercedes into park, Diane said, Where did all these fracking *people* come from?

Right? said Jo. I mean, where's the tax base that would support such a population? For one thing, you'd need a nearby economic engine. A manufacturing plant, for example, or a source of natural resources. Then—

But Diane was already out of the car, and Jo was talking to nobody. She got out as well and caught up to her sister.

Where are we going? Jo asked.

You said you wanted to see the place.

You're walking very deliberately.

Diane pointed to the store they were aimed at—a T.J.Maxx —and said, Did you pack *anything* in your overnight bag to wear besides those sweats?

So. They were back to that again.

Jo sighed. It was early spring, and what could be nicer than sweats on a chilly spring morning? They would stay one night at whatever lodging Diane had found for them, and then it would be home the next day. No need for lots of extra clothes.

Still, Jo figured, her sister did have a point. It would be well to surround their father with what dignity the two of them could muster. No, she corrected herself—*five*. What dignity the *five* of them could muster. After Diane and Jo had hung up last night, Jo made a few calls of her own. Their brother Lou would be coming, God bless them everyone. And if that wasn't enough to contend with, David would also be there. David himself was easy-peasy. But of course he'd have his husband Bishara in tow, and that meant everyone could look forward to hearing Dad pontificate about the whole gay thing. Best to keep the points of friction to a theoretical minimum. She would get something to wear.

But T.J.Maxx? They could do better. If she was going to buy clothes, she may as well get something hot, or at least semi-hot. Something she could take Jed out with when she got back home. Make it up to him for staying back with the kids. *This* was fashion with a purpose: Wow your man.

She said, Hey, how about we look around a little first?

Holding out for Saks Fifth Avenue? her sister retorted.

God, she could be like that sometimes. Jo said, I just want to look around a bit, okay?

Yeah, sure, it's just Dad, after all. No rush. I get it.

God, she could be like that sometimes.

For the next fifteen minutes, Jo and Diane strode up and down in front of various chain discount stores until Diane finally said, See anything?

They agreed to go back to T.J.Maxx. Jo picked out a pair of chinos and a button-up. At checkout, she tried asking the clerk about the town but got nothing out of him.

The clerk was about to ring everything up when he said, Seen the outlets?

Outlets? asked Jo.

The clerk pointed in a random direction and said, North, past the plaza with the Home Depot, then turn left just past the Cinemark.

What have they got? asked Diane.

You know, the clerk said.

Diane looked at Jo, then to the clerk. What? she said. Like, Ann Taylor Loft, that kind of thing?

That kind of thing, agreed the clerk.

With a wink to Diane that went unseen, Jo said, Saks Off 5th?

Maybe, said the clerk. Still want me to ring this up?

Jo said to Diane, Forget this shit, let's go to the outlets.

Diane said to Jo, Don't be a dick. Then to the clerk, Ring it up, please.

They got back to their car and took the exit out of the lot that was the closest to north they could find. They made their way past the Cinemark, turned left into the outlet mall. The plaza did indeed have a Saks Off 5th, where Jo found a snazzy leather jacket and matching red belt that went with a white skirt. At checkout, after everything was rung up, she spotted a pair of sunglasses with super-swanky red lenses and white frames. Diane announced she was getting hungry. Jo was hungry as well. So she took a pass on the sunglasses, and the two of them started talking lunch.

Jo mentioned a Panera she'd seen somewhere along the way between T.J. Maxx and the outlets.

Diane said she'd rather find something here, so as not to have to hunt for another parking spot.

Jo said she was sure there'd be something around.

Diane said it needn't be anything too fancy and then reminded Jo that fast food was out.

Jo said she was good with anything and then took the extra step of mentioning that she already knew about the no-fast-food thing, so there had been no point in Diane's bringing it up just now.

Diane reminded Jo that they needed to move along because they were to meet Dad at six o'clock that evening at the nursing home and that neither of them had been there before and that this represented an unknown with the driving situation, all of which was to say that a sit-down, waiter-type restaurant was out of the question.

Jo was about to agree and ask Diane for a suggestion but then decided instead to observe that, by the time they were finished with this discussion, they could've opened their own damned restaurant already.

Diane declared that a directory was needed. Also that they needed to figure out what to do with Dad.

They found a directory next to a koi pond with a fountain in the middle and a walking bridge that made a gentle wooden arch across the water. The two of them each silently read the dozen or so restaurant choices the directory had to offer, agreed out loud that they didn't want any of them, and in another ten minutes were back in the Mercedes on their way to the Panera.

Finding the Panera resembled the decision to go there: A direct route didn't exist. A backtracking of roads previously taken didn't work. They found the Cinemark, but instead of its being on their left, as they had expected, it appeared on their right. Diane started to make a U-turn at the next intersection, but then began wending her way around the streets, taking turns as seemed best. Just as she said they ought to be getting close, Jo spotted the Cinemark again—on their left this time and separated from them by yet another shopping plaza.

After more turns and the unnerving discovery that the GPS was no longer working due to lack of signal, they found themselves at a red light. The Panera, Jo said, should be ahead of them on the left. On their right was a turn-off lane with a sign that read TO PA-948 N/S.

That's the road we came in on, Diane said, pointing to the sign. Maybe it's time we ditch this idiot place.

Oh come *on*, said Jo, pointing through the windshield. You see that Best Buy? The Panera's gonna be right in there behind it. Somewhere.

And if you're wrong?

Then lunch is on me, said Jo.

*What* lunch? retorted Diane.

But Jo was right—the Panera was there—and parking was easy. Diane made the guy who took their order repeat it all back to her; then, after he'd finished that task, *she* said it all back to *him*, and when the food came, everything was blessedly correct. The sandwiches even came with a free danish each. When Jo's suggestion that they eat them was met with a predictable quip from Diane about carbs, they went back to the car, and Jo put the danishes in the cooler beside her remaining Cokes.

They left the parking lot and arrived back at the spot on the road where a sign read TO PA-948 N/S. Diane signaled, they drifted into the turn-off lane for the throughway, and they exited. Over the next few minutes, the exurbanite sprawl thinned, then disappeared, and they found themselves back in the hilly, wooded terrain that had characterized the bulk of their passage through central Pennsylvania.

Jo breathed out a long and low sigh. The nightmare town was behind them. Now, perhaps, she and Diane could finally discuss what to do with Dad. But first, she needed to see her purchases again. She hardly ever bought clothes. She reached behind her, grabbed the bag from Saks, opened it up, and ran a hand over the awesome leather jacket. She was going to look super hot in this ensemble. Jed was going to go crazy over it. But those red and white sunglasses! They really would've been the cat's ass. She tossed the bag behind her onto the back seat.

The road had been twisting this way and that for about three miles when they came to a fork. Ahead, a run-down dirty-white clapboard shack offered guns, live bait, and homemade BBQ. A road sign said DOWNTOWN SHOP-PING, a single arrow pointing off to the right.

Diane checked her rear view mirror, slowed to a stop at the divide in the road.

Downtown!? she said. Is my sense of direction off? I would've sworn the whole scene we just escaped would've been to our left, not the right.

Jo pointed ahead to the shack. It had a gravelly lot half weeded over with witch grass. Pull into there, so we're off the road, she said. I'll get out my phone and check the GPS.

But there was still no signal.

Shocked, Diane said.

It is at this point that the narrative, as told for all time afterward and even as promptly as later that evening to an oddly receptive Lou over a round at the hotel bar, becomes muddled. Whether there had been four distinct instances of road construction, or if two of them had counted as the same, thereby tallying only three instances; whether the accident that had cost them an hour (as favored by Jo; an hour and a half according to Diane) had involved a single motorcycle, a shiny red Farmall tractor pulling a trailer full of hay, and a gasoline tanker (Sunoco according to Jo; Sheetz if you hear it from Diane), or if there had been two motorcycles, with the Farmall merely playing spectator to the collision; and, finally (as well as, at least to Lou's way of thinking, most fascinatingly), whether the police chase that had forced them off the road happened *before* the detour that took them around the west side of Aporia or happened *after* it, or—as in some recitations of the story, initially belonging to Jo's reckoning but slowly adopted into Diane's account, Jo then taking the opposite view previously held by her sister—*never happened at all*, the two items that are universally and adamantly agreed upon by both women are (a) the proximal cause of the flat tire and (b) the infuriatingly inescapable fact that every time they emerged from a setback, they would get themselves all twisted around, come to a fork in whatever road they happened to be on, and end up back in town.

Just like they were now.

They were sitting at a red light. The light turned green. Instead of going forward, Diane jerked the car into the turnoff lane for the shopping plaza to their right. In doing this, she cut off a car, which blared its horn, prompting another car, coming out of the lot, to voice its agreement with a few honks of its own.

Diane let a curse fly, and it was a good one.

This all happened so fast that Jo was still craning her head, checking that their way was clear, when Diane pulled into a spot.

The Mercedes went from 20 to 0 in the time it took Jo to say What the fuck.

We can't go on like this, said Diane.

Jo started to speak, then paused. Being with Diane for any sustained length of time was never simple, and the circumstances of the past couple hours had been particularly trying, bordering on malevolent—as if the universe had woken up that morning determined to shit on them. But had she, Jo, said something particular? In the past minute or two? She thought about it. She didn't think she had.

Go on like what? she asked.

Diane pointed to an indicator on the dash. Damn that— that— *parking* lot! she said.

Parking lot? Jo said. What parking lot? Diane, what's wrong?

The parking lot of that— that— stupid *barbeque* and *guns* shack. There was all metal and *rocks* and stuff lying around!

Do we have a flat? Jo asked.

Yes, said Diane. Well, no, she corrected. Sort of, she said. Mercedes come with run-flats, okay? You can drive for a while on a flat.

Jo considered this. She said, Are you saying we've been driving this whole time on a flat tire?

Diane turned to look directly at Jo. She said, It shouldn't have been a problem! We should've been able to drive straight through and then taken care of it up there. What the heck *is* it with this goddamn place?

How much longer can we go?

It's hard to say, Diane said. The dashboard tells you the air is gone and which tire. At that point you're supposed to have fifty miles. If you don't drive too fast, and you take it easy with turns and potholes, and, well ... She *ts*ked. We could've made it up there on time! But now, after all this driving around and backtracking, no way.

Jo said, Let's go have a look.

The sisters got out of the car and made for the rear passenger's side. They came to the tire. The tire was flat.

Know how to change one of these things? Jo asked.

No, said Diane, that's the point. There's nothing to change. There's no spare. You're supposed to finish your trip and then push the button for roadside assistance. They come and repair the tire.

I see, said Jo. You figured we'd drive the rest of the way to see Dad, then take care of this at the hotel?

Yes.

Looks like you girls could use a helpin' hand, said a voice behind them.

Jo and Diane turned to see a woman peering at them through wire-framed bifocals. The woman said, You wamme t' call Freddy on my radio? I don't have my tools with me, or I could fix it myself. She unzipped a fanny pack strapped around her waist and pulled out, of all things, a clamshell cell phone. While Jo marveled at the woman and her "radio," the woman said, My Freddy can fix that tire right up for you girls.

No, thank you, Diane said. We have a button. Roadside assistance.

Roadside assistance! said the woman. Well, that's nice, then. You've got a button. She turned and walked away.

Diane? said Jo. Maybe we—

Come on, said Diane. Let's get back in the car. I'll make the call.

Jo turned to thank the woman for her offer, but she was already a surprising distance away.

Back inside the car, Diane pushed the button for help.

Jo sat there, bored, exasperated, and, she realized to her surprise, a little sad. Sad and scared. Not scared because of the flat—Diane had that under control, although why she hadn't just taken the old woman up on her offer, well, that was Diane for you. No, it was this whole day. This town. It felt like they'd never get out.

And, of course, it was Dad. Dad would be fine, physically. Probably. Mechanics fix flat tires; doctors fix broken hips and things. No, that wasn't the real problem. The problem was everything else. Dad's life. And by the way, what *had* she said to Diane to upset her so much? That quip about her not having kids—well, she shouldn't have said that, granted. But it didn't account for all of it. Diane wasn't happy, that was the thing it all kept coming back to. And Dad wasn't happy, either. And … and …

Well? Diane said.

Well what? asked Jo, jerking her head up, surprised to discover that her chin had been resting on her chest.

You were drifting off. In another minute you'd have been drooling on your sweatshirt. We need to talk about Dad. What to do with him. You've been putting it off.

*I've* been!?—

God, Diane could be like that!

Jo gathered a few polemic points together, preparing her retort … then stopped. They'd been driving in circles all day.

You're right, Jo said. We need to talk about Dad. I want to find a place for him.

A home, you mean, said Diane.

If you want to put it that way, yes. She paused. I know you don't want that for him.

Dad deserves to be at his own home and happy, said Diane.

Dad hasn't been happy ever since Mom died, said Jo, resisting the urge to add *And neither have you*.

I know that, said Diane.

And she *did* know that. Both sisters did.

Jo reached into her cooler and pulled out two Cokes, a pair of straws, and a bottle opener. She opened up one of the Cokes for herself, dropped a straw into it, then held the other out to Diane. Diane shook her head. Jo put the bottle, the extra straw, and the opener back into the cooler. She started to bring out the two danishes from Panera, then remembered she was in Diane's immaculate car. She was lowering the danishes back into the bag when Diane said, Oh, go ahead. Jo smiled and took them out. One was cheese, the other cherry. She held them out to Diane. Diane started to shake her head, then grabbed the cheese.

In the time it took Jo to dig into her cherry danish, Diane had already wolfed down half of her own.

Jo? she said. You know the perfect thing to go with this would be a coffee?

No coffee, her sister said. Sorry about that.

Diane sighed, paused. I'll take the Coke.

Jo gave her sister a Coke.

Diane held out a hand. Bottle opener?

Jo reached into her cooler and brought out the opener.

After a couple sips straight from the bottle, Diane held her hand out again and said, Str—

This time, Jo was ready for her.

The sisters drank their Cokes. It took almost an hour for roadside assistance to show up, and Jo and Diane talked the whole while. Mostly they spoke about their father. They each gave their reasons for what they wanted for him. They started to talk a little about Lou (What was it Mom used to say? Raising Louis was like watering a plastic plant?), shared a good laugh over that, then switched to David and what they should expect from Dad when their eldest sibling showed up with his husband, Bishara, in tow. Eight years ago, their father's love for his children had extended—barely—to attending a wedding he was deeply opposed to. Jo even brought up something that had been bothering her for almost twenty years; namely, why Diane hadn't picked up a musical instrument since the night their mother had died in a car accident.

Diane was doing her best to answer this when a pickup truck pulled up behind them. Someone—a mechanic, presumably—got out and walked up to Diane's window, motioning for Diane to roll it down.

Need some help with your tire? the mechanic said, lowering her head down to the open window to peer at them through her bifocals. My Freddy wasn't available.


They were back on the road. Aporia, Pennsylvania, was twenty minutes behind them.

Dammit, said Jo.

What is it? asked Diane.

I really wish I'd bought those sunglasses.

Ones with the red lenses and white frames?

Yeah.

They were pretty swanky, I have to say. Well, don't worry about it too much. We can pick 'em up on our way back.

Jo smiled.

They continued in companionable silence.

By the way, Diane said, I think I'm gay.

Yeah, said Jo, taking a swig of Coke. No shit.

# for Magda

Aporia, aporia. Oh, dear. My problem child.

First, matters of form. I had read a couple books that had dispensed with quotation marks around the dialog. I wanted to try my hand at doing this—another instance of writing as self-flagellation. (I'm sorry, did I say *flagellation*? I meant *assignment*.) It was fun! I had to be careful to position the dialog so that it was not just implied, but obvious.

The first person to convince me that I had succeeded was Magda Caro, to whom I'm dedicating this story. Magda unwittingly accomplished this by exclaiming, halfway through the second page during a read-through of my manuscript, "Oh my! There's no quotation marks!" Thanks, Magda.

She also commented on the single instance in my story where I'd intentionally introduced ambiguity around the dialog. I'm talking about the part that reads:

> *What do you want me to do? asked Diane.*
> *What do you mean? said Jo. Go. Drive.*

When I wrote this, I realized that Jo's line could be interpreted in two ways: She could've spoken the words *go* and *drive* out loud, but it's also not hard to imagine that these words simply reflect her thoughts and attitude.

It is written: "Unless you are certain of success, obey the rules." Or, something like that. What I take Messrs. Strunk and White to mean by these words from *The Elements of Style* is that, if you're thinking about bending the rules, think again, because you're probably not doing yourself any favors. This line above, with Jo, is the one instance in this book—and possibly in any of the books I've written so far—where I have *knowingly* strayed from clarity. Did Jo say *go* and *drive*, or didn't she?

Magda seemed confused by the implied question, but pleasantly so, and I decided that the ambiguity had value in itself. However *you* interpreted this line when you read it, you have my agreement. Yes, dear reader! That is indeed what I meant!

Now about that content. Content, in my opinion, always has to warrant form. Outrageous or unusual form must convey outrageous or unusual content. If I'm going to spew forth a run-on sentence more than a thousand words in length ("Vomiting Somewhere South of Worcester, Mass"), it will help if that sentence involves something like vomit.

What I needed, in the case of a story with no quotation marks around dialog, was the kind of story that pushed the envelope in some way. In the present case, I at some point—I don't remember, now, whether it was before or after I decided I wanted to try to write sans quotation marks—thought it would be interesting to write about a couple of people in a car who couldn't make it through a town. It would feel like something out of *The Twilight Zone*. They'd encounter one misdirection after another. The key, I thought, was to make the story itself feel like the town. Form following content, the writing needed to be dense and impassable. If you found the writing to indeed be this way, now you know why.

# poems

# writing in circles

The playground is little more than a field
Adjoining the wet blacktop, the tree line
Along the back obscured behind the arch
Of a pair of jeans—the boy's legs spread wide
You'd think he'd just climbed off a horse.
The kid's stance rests on a sneaker and a
Half, the rest falling off-frame to the right,
The boy himself standing on a puddle.
Those days, we all thought we walked on water.
The photo paper is thick, but the picture
Is so creased I hesitate to grasp it.
At the slightest application of force
The whole school might fall out, the boy with it.
About that boy, he doesn't end at the water,
But continues down into it, one arch
Reflecting the other, exactly how
He must have intended. I like to think
We're all like that, fallen through, wondering
How we're all going to come out, twisting
Along the way so that we don't come out
All upside down. Nobody wants to be that.
But I don't want to come out dry. I want
To emerge, the water and all of it
Still clinging to me: Mrs. Brandt's whistle,
Urging us back inside; the cedar smell
Of pencil-sharpening, the silver crankcase
Screwed into a plank nailed into the wall
Beside the blackboard; the golden shimmer
Of Judy Ladd's hair as she swaggered down
E-Hall toward music class; or, yes, even

The fade of a vomit stain—deposited
On the carpet of that same corridor,
A token of a day cut short too late—
That the janitor's bleach could never quite erase.
I guess the falling works both ways, one arch
Completing the other, the images
As purple and as pungent as words spun
From a mimeograph machine, whirring
Its circles. And so I pick up my pen,
And I set down the picture, and I wait.
For what is the past but a creased photo
Through which, at a touch from him, the boy falls?

# the tragedy of ebert

Upon a checkered field of squares
    The King lined up his men;
All white were they, and doughty, too—
    They numbered six and ten.
"Prepare!" cried he, "for fratch and fray!"
    But would not say just when.

He called up his enlisted troops
    To march off first to war:
"Albert! Bebert! Colbert! Dilbert!"
    He named his left-hand four;
"Ebert! Filbert! Gilbert! Hebert!"—
    These others made four more.

Yet still the King would not consent
    The battle to begin,
But called upon his nearest page,
    A beefy boy, though thin—
"Ebert," thought he (his nom de guerre),
    "What trouble am I in?"

"Take heart, my son," the King beseeched,
    His voice quite soft yet gruff;
"To win the day we must be made
    Of hard and sordid stuff."
"Mefears," the boy kept to himself,
    "That shan't be quite enough!"

The King knelt down upon the ground
    (The boy was short, you see)
And with his sword he pointed toward
    His constant enemy.

"Behold, across the grid from us,
    His blackened effigy!"

Then looked the boy across the way
    To see some awful sight;
But what he saw were sixteen men
    Who'd look like him, if white.
"Can someone say," he asked the King,
    "The purpose of this fight?"

His words were lost to time and space,
    The King was there no more;
He'd risen up, he'd sallied forth,
    He wallowed in the war.
"Just pawns," sighed Ebert, "in a game."
    (Forgive the metaphor.)

Then wood on wood and click on clack!
    The carnage did commence;
The dueling kings barked their commands,
    Not one sat on the fence;
And one by one the men went down,
    Each to his lord's defense.

As Ebert, too, was carried off,
    His eyes staring at death;
He looked behind, to bless his Sire:
    Some muttered shibboleth;
But what he saw did stop his heart,
    And steal his final breath.

The King stood o'er his vanquished foe,
    Who lay there in defeat.

"That trick you played three moves ago—
    It nearly had me beat!"
Then with a wink he lent a hand,
And helped him to his feet.

The black King rose and, dusting off,
    Said with a haughty air:
"Next time the castles shall be switched!
    Next time I shall not err!"
Then with a nod he sauntered off,
    Back to his starting square.

Upon a checkered field of squares
    The King lines up his men;
All white are they, and doughty, too—
    They number six and ten.
"Prepare!" cries he, "for fratch and fray!"
    And on it goes again.

# the 7 deadly sins

## 1. obfuscation: nacre

What's that, pity, there at the bottom? Should you lose
your unworthiness, I will slip off, and I suppose
you will just have to fend for yourself?

Your eyes awaken, and you see that
it is good for the eating. It is without price;
begotten, not made; of one substance with
stuff you've never heard about.

When you're finished, I've got some more
right here.

## 2. sloth: in search of

Who cares about other men, we're talking about me.
Who cares about other women, we're talking about you.
Or maybe we're still talking about me.
Are we still talking about me?
Okay, then.

## 3. hubris: visiting

It's done now, I'm awake.
I flip to my other side,
flip the pillow,
no good.
A paste covers my mouth, remnants
of last night's words.

The other room; your sister's hair
in rollers, a few crumbs on the table,
survivors of the night.
I take a seat and watch
the smear of dawn.
So.

This is what you wanted me to see.
But I still don't know what it is you wanted me to say.

# 4. abnegation: second fork

New dress, a light spray of perfume,
One last check through the clutch;
Premium imported Italian shaving cream,
Reservations confirmed, teeth re-brushed—

He'll be in a Lyft, five-star rating,
Seafoam-green Camry (who knew?);
She'll be out front, paisley overcoat,
Just double-park, it'll only be a few—

Hostess nails it, waiter's accent thick, she thinks,
For a place that swims in rhythms of red;
Easy on the cocktails, he won't miss a beat,
No à la carte, paella for two is perfect instead—

They talk about Cheez-Its, they talk about makeup,
They talk about the latest celebrity break-up—
She raises her brows so imperiously;
They talk about light bulbs, they talk about lettuce,
They talk about a cowboy with a pink leather fetish—
This one perhaps not so seriously.

Waiter comes, "Dessert tray?"
She says no; he gets Death by Chocolate,
Fine—
But what's this with the second fork?

No means no, sure, but what question were you answering?

# 5. imprecision: sith kitty

Sometimes I'll see her eyeing the gap,
sizing up the distance
to her object, calculating
how's she going to land. More important,
how much force to use
to get there.

Too much, and it's going to be
a mess. Too little, and she'll fall
short. End up falling flat, have to try
again. Tell me exactly what it is
she's trying to say.

Either way, she'll look at me like that was exactly what she meant to do.

# 6. pretense: 47 issues on

and I still can't tell you
why I love it or
what it means or even
remark on the shapes
of words, pushed into
the paper under the weight
of repetition, hours
—literal hours—
of spent caffeine, and peachy
significance. One year on

and I still can't imagine
the badass who first caught on
to the lilies and the rolled cigars,
and who first kept time with
the rhythmed cats, who, together,
peeking under the mask of God,
decided to call whatever it was
they found there good. What she
had looked like? What he had eaten
that morning for breakfast? The make
of their car? Like the Lady Catherine,
had I written, I would have been
a great proficient. Maybe next year. But for now,

I still can't tell you what it meant,
what I said, when I said
any of that.

# 7. closure: long ride home

The promise of forgotten beads, plucked
from a drawer and strained
across the palms. An affirmation of life, rendered
in something like Latin and delivered
across air made of roses and Chanel No. 5 and sanctified
with breath mints. The tingle of a joke, whispered
in the back of God's classroom, that, like a kiss, lingered
on the skin long after the mood was spent.

Each must mourn his own way, for love
is a wound that never heals.

Behind the wheel he says, "I don't get it. Everyone had
the nicest things to say about her. I always thought
she was an idiot." Behind her magazine she says,
"Those two things, my dear, are not mutually exclusive."

# swamp

The man would see the swamp sometimes in dreams
Or better yet in movies or in books.
Best was when he'd stand right in the thing
And see the cypress and the Spanish moss
For how it all appeared. Then the man
Would want to cross the swamp, and for this task
He used a magic wand.

That's what all the people called it, magic,
For the way it shot its bridges out in front
Of itself, dull yellow sparks that fell mere inches
In front of the man's muddy boots, seeming
To build for him, ex nihilo, as he
Walked across the swamp, step by step by step,
A narrow wooden bridge.

But the man knew the wand was really just
A stick. And as he shot his bridges (the people
Were right about those), he would now and then
Like to play a game, guessing where the bridge
Would take him. Sometimes he guessed right, and then
Sometimes the swamp and trees and Spanish moss
Would all say differently.

Then came the pylon builders, whom the man
Didn't trust, not so much because they didn't have
A magic wand like his, which really was
Just an old stick, but because they laid their pylons
Before they laid their bridges. And so they
Never did play games as he did, guessing where
Their bridges might take them.

Nor did they trust the man, particularly,
Because his wand (I had forgotten
To mention this fact) would sometimes not work—
And there he'd go, stepping into the marsh,
Sinking, his foot making brown gurgling noises
As it went down, into the mud, and more noises
As it came back out, and long before he finished,
The man would smell of swamp.

So now I've told you about the wand and
Its secret, and why the man's boots were always
Muddy, and also about the builders
Of pylons, and how they never did smell
Of anything, even after they got
To the ends of their bridges.

Given everything, I think that when I
Find a swamp, I'll get myself a pair
Of boots and an old stick.

## the refuge

You had a book, it looked good there on your coffee table,
But I took it just the same, pushing aside the Merton
And the Dillard and so on and so forth, and may I say,
The architecture of its prose rather mirrored that of
Its photogenic subject matter, its houses being
Divided roughly into three: jail, matchbox, asylum;
For what screams "Nature!" more than concrete, corners, and plate glass?—
Yet it wasn't until the following morning, as I
Sat in that same chair, before your Mondrian-esque windows,
Looking out over your ocean, that I fully grokked hate:
My indebtedness to it, how it felt good on the skin;
A luxurious old glove, missing only an object.

# my body is lithe and young

Deep breath or two. Go ahead, make it ten.
In and out.
That's better.

*Better ...*

My body is lithe and young. And light. So light,
it barely indents the quilt pulled taut beneath me.
Grandma's quilt.

The air that tickles the bottoms of my bare feet—
it's coming through the window, the one looking out
over the lake, propped open with a stick.

Through my closed eyelids, the sunlight is pink.
Across space, off the water in diamonds, mixing it up with the cabin:
The light has come a long way to be here.

See the cabin now:
Wood plank walls, a fresh coat of sky-blue paint doing no harm;
Antique refrigerator, doilies on painted furniture, shelf of paperbacks.

*The Key to Rebecca*, Ken Follett.
*The Mystery of the Blue Train*, Agatha Christie.
*Bloodline*. (Remember *that* one?) Sidney Sheldon.

Keep going.
Grandpa's ashtray. Grandpa's rocker. His pocket "calculator"
that, by the time you figured out how to use it, you could've just done the math.

More.
The metal cupboards. Inside, the drinking glass with Betty Boop on it.
Screwed to the outside, the ancient Coca-Cola bottle opener.

Drawers: A full set of silverware. (Why?)

Those spring-connected pairs of plastic disc-thingies meant to hold a hand of
    playing cards.
Playing cards. Also, cribbage set, not that you knew then how to use it.

The porch: Charcoal grill.
Rubbermaid folding chairs.
...

The alarm goes off.
No double dipping on the snooze.
That's the rule.

Heave my body into a sitting position; the bed groans.
Belch, pass gas, every vertebra in my lower back cracks.
That's better.

Stand. "I am the one who groans."
Turn off the floor fan,
shield my still-adjusting eyes against the window's glare.

Go downstairs.
She's cooking eggs, and she's already got bread in the toaster.
I flick the rocker switch on the Mr. Coffee. Green light, waker's delight.

I plop myself down into the swivel chair.
On the coffee table is a copy of *Pigeon Feathers*. John Updike.
I pick it up.

"I could read you a story," I say.
"Actually," she says, "you can butter your toast."

There are fewer things now than when I was a kid.

# ye olde rank and file
(in the spirit and rhythm of "Desolation Row" by Bob Dylan)

The generals are breaking out the tables,
They've brought the war to town;
The King in Yellow shouts in a megaphone,
"Won't you all sit down.
Don't you miss the numbers on the wall,
Don't you wear my patience thin;
We won't shoot any losers yet, and
May everybody win.
After forty moves and forty jots,
You must all reset your dial;
Now thank you all for coming down
To Ye Olde Rank and File."

The devil, he's looking rather nervous,
He winds a black hand to the flag;
Then in a cloud of sweat and onions,
He dumps his world out from a bag.
Across from him sits Shirley Temple,
She commands a pretty view;
"Sir," she says, "can you write your name for me?
I've never heard of you."
Now they hold their breaths, and they hold their heads,
And they both think for a while;
And then the fun and shots begin
At Ye Olde Rank and File.

The footmen stand gloriously uniformed,
In livery and in chains;
The drinks they serve taste somehow different,
Their heads are all the same.
Quips Philidor to Augustine in passing,

"I think we're being played."
Retorts his friend, "To save your soul,
Eat nuts and drink lemonade."
Says Hans to Fritz, "Concerning hostilities,
Don't you find it all quite vile?"
Says Fritz to Hans, "It depends on how one thinks
About Ye Olde Rank and File."

Now St. Michael's hair flies out in all directions,
He hurls himself upon a horse;
And he rides that thing just like his hair:
A regular tour de force.
And they'll ask him how he does that,
What is the secret to his speed?
He tells them wherever two and two make five,
My friend, you'll find just what you need.
To achieve your goal, avoid defeat—
Perfection knows no style;
Now take a dime with that and call collect
From Ye Olde Rank and File.

The revelers bring out their baskets,
They want a blessing for the feast;
The village idiot is occupied,
So they settle on the Priest.
With charity toward all, and malice too,
And prejudice toward one,
The Priest wipes that grin from off his face,
And reaches for his gun.
Then he stands an egg atop his head,
Yells, "Bless all those who defile!"

Thank God he's too far out of range
To bless Ye Olde Rank and File.

Old Henry lives with young Katherine
In a castle made from bones;
All her cooking looks like chicken,
Her washing tastes like scones.
"Dear Katherine, come look at this,
What's this underneath our bed?"
But nothing's there but dust and letters,
And now another head.
Then he grabs a fish and with a nod,
He fools the crocodile;
And swims the moat to make his escape
To Ye Olde Rank and File.

Queen the Second, she stands so coolly
On the corner of Main and Eighth;
Her hair is short, her breath is long—
She's waiting on her date.
Here comes the pear-shaped transvestite,
Floating down the promenade;
She thinks he's looking rather squat—
He knows that she's been made.
And in the end, they're both the same—
They maneuver to beguile;
And that is how sweet love is made
At Ye Olde Rank and File.

Now the devil, he's looking rather pale,
Shirley's got him in a fix;
But she did her dance a bit too soon,

And he played his dirty tricks.
"Don't let your youth and inexperience
Be a factor in your game,"
Opined the devil, and his hand was cold,
But she shook it just the same.
And in the end, they're all the same—
They maneuver to beguile;
It's just another sordid tale
From Ye Old Rank and File.

# for bill

I have a love/hate relationship with poetry. I like whimsy (Shel Silverstein, Lewis Carroll, Dr. Seuss) and epic grandeur (Tolkien, Dante). I hate—too strong a word—hoity-toity condescension (most of what I find in the *New Yorker*, but just keep those cartoons coming, Condé Nast, and I'll keep the sub-scription active).

Nevertheless, when it comes to writing, I'm willing to try my hand at just about anything. I would probably have scoffed at some of the poetry you just read, had I read it myself in the *New Yorker*. I'm not going to tell you what any of it means, because that would ruin the point. I rarely try to remember, myself, what I meant by any of my poetry. I will, however, put your suspicions to rest about "Ye Olde Rank and File." It's a portrayal of a chess tournament.

I'm dedicating all this poetry to Bill Kent, the man who made this book—and all the other books I've written and will ever write—possible.

They say that only God can create *ex nihilo*—a fancy way of saying it's im-possible. Bill, you proved them wrong. Out of nothing, you created the circle. Be it unbroken, by and by.

Ernest Hemingway once quipped that writing was easy: One simply had to sit at a typewriter and bleed. I think that writing is anything but easy, but I in-tend to keep bleeding until I'm all bled out.

*Those are all of sixteen reasons ...*

# author's note

They say that a circle has neither a beginning nor an end, although I've never understood why this should be the case for a circle any more than for an ellipse or a square or even, in the strictest sense of the word, a line. Now, a line *segment*, on the other hand, like a story or a book—even a book about circles—has a beginning, a middle, and an end. You've made it to the end of this book, and that means you now get to read about the various people I have to thank for it.

Don't worry, there are only a few. This isn't the Oscars.

Thank you to Nicole Klungle, my editor, for constantly striving to make my writing better. There's hardly a story in this collection that I didn't send off to her, thinking it was perfect, only to get it back with suggestions for improvement. She has edited all my books so far, and I've already got more work for her. This time around, she even did the cover design and the interior.

Thank you to my wife, Laura, and our daughter, Mallory—my patient alpha readers. When a story was still not a story, they'd let me know. And when all I really needed was someone to listen, they did that, too. I can't imagine writing without them.

And that's it. See? Not bad. Not bad at all.

Now, if you enjoyed this book, you can make like a circle and start it all over again.

# about the author

Kevin Stokker is a Constant Reader, stage actor, chess coach, philosopher, and the author of several fine books. He and his wife, Laura, live in Northern Virginia, down the street from their marvelous daughter.